Love OUT Loud

MARILYN LEE

ELLORA'S CAVE
ROMANTICA PUBLISHING

What the critics are saying...

❧

4 Lips "Marilyn Lee's *Love Out Loud* is a frustrating love story. [...] Marilyn Lee does a great job with the sex scenes, which are so hot that they will scorch your socks. *Love Out Loud* is a book you should read on a rainy day when you need some hot steamy sex to keep you warm." ~ *Two Lips Reviews*

5 Angels "Marilyn Lee has written a story about love, commitment, sacrifice and family unity. The characters are charming and each has their own allure. The backdrops for *Love Out Loud* are splendidly written and draw you into the scenes. I fell in love with this family with the first book in this series, and I'm looking forward to the next installment."

~ *Fallen Angels Reviews*

An Ellora's Cave Romantica Publication

www.ellorascave.com

Love Out Loud

ISBN 9781419958472
ALL RIGHTS RESERVED.
Love Out Loud Copyright © 2008 Marilyn Lee
Edited by Helen Woodall.
Cover art by Syneca.

This book printed in the U.S.A. by Jasmine-Jade Enterprises, LLC.

Electronic book Publication April 2008
Trade paperback Publication December 2008

LOVE OUT LOUD

Chapter One
ઔ

"I hope you're not leaving, Benai," came a male voice from behind her.

Standing in the hall of the mansion where she'd watched her best friend, Tempest, marry Layton Grayhawk several hours earlier, Benai Peters paused with her hand on the entrance door. She moistened her lips before she turned.

A tall, handsome male with high cheekbones and long, dark hair that fell past his wide shoulders faced her. Weeks earlier, when they'd first met, seemingly enthralled with her dark complexion and smile, Bancroft Grayhawk had told her that she was "absolutely perfect". His sincerity had been heady medicine for the staid accountant who held no real pretensions to beauty. Yet he'd been cool almost to the point of rudeness when they'd met at the rehearsal dinner and at the reception, which was still in progress down the hall.

He'd asked her to dance twice during the reception. She'd quickly regretted her ready acceptance of his invitation to dance when he spent the first minute of the dance staring at her in silence. Then he'd stopped moving and just stared at her with a cool look in his dark gaze. She'd pulled away from him. He'd drawn her back into his arms and continued dancing with her in silence.

When the song ended, she danced with Declan Grayhawk. Then while she waited for him to bring her a drink, Bancroft had asked her to dance again. Glancing around the room in search of an excuse to refuse, she'd met Randall Grayhawk's gaze. Like Bancroft, he was tall, well built and handsome. Randall wore his almost blue-black hair very short. Although he had a similar bone structure—with high cheekbones—to his siblings, Randall and his twin, Peyton, were the only two who had blue-green eyes.

She thought she noted a brief spark in Randall's gaze. Thank God. She was certain he would intervene—until he quickly looked away. Great. He wasn't going to help. She was on her own. She'd reluctantly agreed to dance with Bancroft again.

Halfway through that dance when Bancroft had stopped dancing so he could stand staring at her again, Randall had crossed the room.

"Do you mind if I cut in, Hawk?"

To her relief, Bancroft had silently agreed.

Although Randall had danced in silence as well, it hadn't been a silence cool enough to send a chill through her. And she'd had to steel herself against linking her arms around his neck and melting against him. Unfortunately, he'd shown no inclination to linger over the dance. Moments after the music ended, he'd walked her across the room to his twin Peyton.

"I believe this is your dance, Peyton."

Peyton had smiled graciously and swept her into his arms. During their two dances, he'd surprised her by talking about the wedding. After the second dance, Peyton walked her across the room to his sister, Lelia.

After a brief visit with Tempest in an upstairs bedroom, Benai had decided to leave before Bancroft asked her to dance. It was just her luck that he'd followed her into the hallway.

Now she'd need to make it clear to Bancroft that she didn't plan to dance with him again, at least not anytime before hell froze over. Reminding herself that he was the brother of her most important client, she decided she'd better be polite.

She flashed him a brief smile. "I was about to get my coat and leave."

"Dance with me first."

Great. He was going to make it a challenge for her to be polite. Looking into Bancroft's dark eyes reminded her of all the romance novels she'd read as a teenager where women fell in love with the big, handsome native American men who had first taken them captive and then won their hearts.

Now was not the time to let her imagination run wild. Besides, if she lost her heart to one of the seven single Grayhawk brothers, it wouldn't be to Bancroft. "Thanks but I'm leaving."

He arched a brow and glanced at his watch. "It's barely four o'clock. That's far too early to leave the reception. I know our first two dances left a little to be desired but—"

That was putting it lightly and she wasn't going to dance with him again. "Thanks but it's been a long, exciting day and I'm tired." She turned and reached for the doorknob.

He placed his palm on the door panel and leaned so close she felt his breath on her ear when he spoke. "We'll make it a quick one."

Great. He was one of those men who couldn't take no for an answer, even when he wasn't interested in a woman. Wonderful. She turned to face him. "Maybe another time."

He looked down into her eyes. "Why not now?"

She parted her lips.

"Ah, Benai. There you are," said another male voice.

Bancroft removed his palm from the door and turned to face the speaker.

Benai stepped around him. Bancroft glanced at her before turning his attention to his brother. "Give us a moment, Randall."

Oh, no! She met Randall's gaze and gave a small, please-don't-leave-me-alone-with-him shake of her head.

Benai watched the two brothers stare at each other. Although Randall was the most financially successful of the siblings, he was two years younger than Bancroft. Tempest had told her the Grayhawks accorded their elder siblings a great amount of respect and deference. All the younger siblings called their older siblings by the respectful and affectionate nickname of Hawk. She had a feeling she was about to be left alone with Bancroft.

Randall looked at her again.

Please, Randall. Don't leave me alone with him.

He raked a hand through his hair before he met Bancroft's gaze. "Actually, Hawk, she looks tired and I thought I'd take her home."

Bancroft glanced at her. "I can do—"

Fearful that Randall was about to defer to Bancroft, Benai stepped closer to Randall and slipped her arm through his. Although she felt him stiffen, he didn't pull away. Relieved, she flashed Bancroft another brief smile before looking up into Randall's wary gaze. "I'm ready."

Bancroft stared at her. "You'd prefer to have Randall take you home?"

Lord, what a question. She glanced away.

"Fine." Bancroft turned and walked away.

The moment they were alone in the ornate foyer, Randall stepped away from her.

Noting his clenched jaw and narrowed gaze, she grimaced. "I'm sorry. I know that was awkward for you. It was awkward for me as well."

He looked as if he'd like to order her out of his mansion. "He's my elder brother."

"Yes. I know and I know that means a lot to you but he was making a nuisance of himself."

"A nuisance? Do you have any idea how many women would love to be in your place and have him pursuing them?"

She sighed. This was not going well. "Perhaps nuisance was a bad choice of words but he hasn't been very friendly.

You know that or you wouldn't have rescued me from him earlier and now you've done it again."

"Rescued you? You make him sound like a stalker."

He was definitely annoyed. "Not intentionally. It's just that he seemed determined not to take no for an answer. Thank you for intervening earlier and now."

"You're a guest in my house."

Or he'd have left her to her own devices? Delightful. Clearly he had no interest in charming her. She compressed her lips. "I won't impose on you any longer." She turned and reached for the doorknob.

Just as Bancroft had done, he placed a palm against the door panel.

"Okay." She swung around to face him. "What does a woman have to do to get out of this place?"

He looked down at her. At five-nine, when she wore heels she often found herself looking down on men of average height. All the Grayhawks were tall but she guessed Randall must be at least six-six. Her nostrils flared as his cologne intoxicated her senses. Lord, he was handsome with those blue-green eyes and those deliciously wide shoulders.

To her surprise, he laughed and then stepped away from her. When he spoke, he sounded amused. "I'll drive you home."

She shook her head. "Thanks but one of your staff called a cab."

"I cancelled it."

"Why?"

The question seemed to surprise him. "I had you picked up this morning. Why would I allow you to take a cab home? Besides, when I told Hawk I'd drive you home, I didn't want to lie."

"You really do think a lot of him. Don't you?"

"Of course I do. He's never given me any reason not to think highly of him. When this period is past and you get to know him, you'll think highly of him as well."

"Probably so but that doesn't mean I'd want to dance with him any more than I do now."

"You're not seeing him at his best."

Recalling the smiling, charming Bancroft who had made her feel attractive and desirable, she smiled and nodded. "I know he can be extremely charming."

He arched a brow. "As can I."

She blinked up at him. "Are you flirting with me?"

He surveyed her, allowing his gaze to roam leisurely over her.

According to Tempest he was between girlfriends but at thirty-seven, he was wealthy enough to own a mansion and a private jet. He must be used to dating women beautiful enough to grace covers of fashion magazines. Although she knew her tall, statuesque figure often turned male heads, her sole claim to beauty was the thick, long, dark brown hair that fell around her shoulders. Her dark skin, which one lover had described as "smooth as sexy brown velvet" wasn't likely to catch his eye. Yet she'd caught Bancroft's—even if for only a brief time.

He leaned against the door, his gaze locked on her. "Would you be interested if I were?"

Would she be interested in having a tall, handsome, single, wealthy hunk flirt with her? "Have you ever met a woman who wasn't interested in you?"

"Yes, on numerous occasions."

Standing there, feeling her heart racing at the mere suggestion that he might be interested in her, she found it difficult to believe any sane woman had rebuffed him. "Really? Were they legally blind?"

A slow, warm smile spread across his handsome face. "You know just what to say to boost a man's ego."

If she had such a way with men, she wouldn't have found herself worrying about her biological clock ticking furiously away with no potential husband in sight and her thirty-first birthday rapidly approaching.

"Does your ego need a boost, Randall?"

"Sometimes." He sighed. "It's not easy to find and maintain a meaningful relationship when you have seven brothers most women would kill to date." He grinned suddenly. "Make that six. Thankfully Layton's finally taken. I now have less competition."

"Forgive me if I don't get out my violin. I'm sure you're quite capable of holding the interest of the woman of your choice."

He looked at her mouth. "Would that include you?"

She moistened her lips. "You're doing it again."

"What?"

"You're staring and flirting."

"Flirting with you?" His smile vanished and he straightened. "You've misunderstood. I don't flirt with my brothers' women."

"Your brothers'…" She shook her head. "That's commendable but I'm not your brother's woman."

He shrugged. "Maybe not yet but Hawk's clearly interested."

"Which Hawk would that be? Brandon or Bancroft?"

"Croft."

She blinked. "What am I missing?"

"What do you mean?"

"Tempest insisted Bancroft was interested in me. Now you're saying the same thing even though you've now had to rescue me twice from him."

"I didn't rescue you. I merely —"

"Okay. Even if you didn't rescue me, he has a strange way of showing interest."

"He's interested."

She sighed. "That's flattering but I'm not interested in him."

He arched a brow. "He's successful, handsome and considerate. In short, he's an amazing man with a lot to offer. I have yet to meet a woman who wasn't interested in him."

He sounded so sure of Bancroft's attractiveness to the opposite sex, she felt certain contradicting him would be a waste of both their time. "I'm sure he's every bit as amazing as you say he is and you weren't flirting with me."

He locked his gaze on her lips again. "What chance would I stand of attracting you when you could have him?"

"For a man who's not flirting with me, you keep saying things that sound suspiciously like flirting and you're staring at my mouth again."

He lifted his gaze to hers but lowered his lids to conceal the expression in his eyes. "Are you ready to leave?"

He certainly knew how to end a conversation. She nodded.

"Do you mind riding in an SUV or should I have a car brought around?"

A car? How many did he have? "An SUV's fine."

He opened the middle drawer of a beautiful Queen Anne table and picked up a set of keys. He opened the front door. "After you."

She walked past him.

He followed her and closed the door. He slipped a hand under her elbow and ushered her down the stairs. There were several SUVs parked in the oval in front of the mansion. He stopped in front of a dark blue one and opened the passenger side door for her.

She slipped inside. He closed the door and walked around to the driver's side. When she was seated beside him, the interior suddenly felt much smaller, almost cramped. She busied herself with adjusting her seat and fastening the seatbelt.

He started the engine but didn't drive away.

After several moments, she glanced at him and found him looking at her. "Did you forget something?"

He shook his head. "We'll be seeing a fair amount of each other so I probably should explain so there's no misunderstanding between us."

She swallowed slowly. He was about to make his lack of interest in her as clear as Bancroft had. The way things were going, his other five single brothers would also probably feel the need to assure her of their lack of interest as well. "I'm listening."

"My brothers and I are very close. We stay that way by not competing for the same woman. Once one brother is interested, that woman is off limits to the rest."

She shook her head. "Randall, Bancroft is not interested in me. If this conversation is your way of telling me you're not interested either, message received loud and clear."

"I don't usually have so much trouble making myself understood." He sighed. "What I meant was—"

She shook her head and held up a hand. "No further explanation is necessary."

"Are you deliberately misunderstanding me?"

"I understand you perfectly."

"I doubt that."

"You shouldn't."

He released the parking brake and drove slowly down the winding driveway.

"I live in Philly," she told him. "In the Fairmount section. Do you need directions?"

"No. I know the city. I received my MBA from the Wharton Business School."

"The University of Pennsylvania, huh? I hear you did very well in that Ivy League school."

"Who told you that?"

"Layton. He's very proud of you."

"Hawk is the ideal older brother…always supportive and overly generous."

"That's what Lelia said of you," she told him.

He cast a brief glance at her. "You've discussed me with Lelia?"

She didn't want him thinking she'd been discussing him with anyone, least of all with the younger sister of whom they were all so proud. "Before you make me sound like a stalker, I should say I wasn't fishing for information about you. They're just all so proud of you that they gush about your accomplishments at every opportunity."

"So you didn't ask her about me?"

"No."

"I see." He was silent for moment. "My siblings are all overly generous. I'm no more accomplished than any of them." His right hand left the steering wheel to hover over the dashboard. "Would you like to listen to music?"

"What kind?"

"Country. Do you mind?"

She'd never heard a country song she liked but he'd been very gallant. "No," she said, making an effort to sound sincere.

"If you'd rather not, I have some jazz CDs. Do you—"

"Country's fine," she insisted.

He turned his head and their gazes briefly met. "You know how to stroke a man's ego and you don't mind country music." He turned his attention back to the road. "How is it you're still single at…"

"Thirty."

He murmured something.

"What?"

"I said perfect."

"What's perfect?"

"You are."

She caught her breath and turned to stare at his profile. "What?"

As if conscious of her gaze, he shrugged. "Or so Croft tells me."

He certainly knew how to burst a woman's bubble. "Does he?"

"Yes. He told us that you were the most perfect woman he'd ever met. So naturally we were all eager to meet you."

"And when you had?"

He shrugged again.

"Randall?"

She watched his lips curve into a smile before he turned to look at her. "We—"

"We?"

"Okay. *I* naturally agreed with him."

"Really? If memory serves, you weren't overly impressed when we met."

"What makes you say that?"

"When I walked into the restaurant where the rehearsal dinner was held, you were talking to Lelia. You looked up and—"

"Met your gaze."

"I saw a shocked looked in your eyes before you looked away. You didn't look in my direction again."

"How would you know I never looked at you again?"

"Because I was looking at you, Randall."

"Were you?"

"Yes, I was. When Layton called you over to introduce us, you avoided looking in my eyes, barely touched my hand, gave me a very cool hello and rushed away as if you couldn't put enough distance between us to suit you."

"And from that you deduced I wasn't impressed?"

"Yes."

"And if I tell you your deduction skills need some work?"

"You're flirting again."

He sighed and pulled the vehicle over just inside the gated entrance to his property. "I apologize."

"What makes you think I want an apology?"

"Flirting with you is unacceptable."

"Says who?"

"Hawk's already staked his claim."

She cast her gaze toward the roof of the SUV as if seeking divine intervention. "Randall, if you tell me how interested Bancroft is in me one more time, I'm going to scream. Even if it were true, which I'm sure it's not, I'm not interested in him."

"Are you interested in me, Benai?"

She'd learned early that if non-supermodel women wanted to attract the male of their choice, they'd need to be willing to take a few chances. Still, she moistened her lips twice before she spoke. "Would I be wasting my time if I were?"

When he remained silent, she glanced at the steering wheel. He gripped it so tightly he'd probably leave fingerprint impressions in the expensive leather. She raised her gaze to his profile. "Randall?"

"Can I buy you dinner?"

"We ate before we danced," she reminded him.

He glanced at the dashboard clock. "I know but by the time I drive you home and you shower and change dinner will have worn off."

That appeared as close as he was prepared to come to admitting he wasn't indifferent to her. "I'd like that."

He flashed her a brief smile before pushing a button on his dashboard. The gates swung open and he drove through them. He pushed the button again and the gates swung closed.

He turned on the CD player. The voice of a woman singing about how everything had fallen into place for her to fall in love with the hero, filled the interior.

She watched Randall activate his dashboard-mounted cell phone. When it rang, he lifted it to his ear. "Peyton, I'm going to be a while... Yes, I know the house is full of guests. Play host for me...yes...yes, Peyton, I do know that... I don't need to be reminded of that... I'll talk to you later." He ended the call.

She glanced at him. "Is everything okay?"

His jaw clenched. "Peyton seemed to think I needed to be reminded of..."

"Of what?"

"Of Hawk's interest in you." He sighed. "As if I could forget."

God, she wished he would. "Why didn't you just remind him of how...unacceptable forgetting would be?"

He smiled. "Are you teasing me?"

"Never!" she assured him in a mock-serious voice.

He laughed, his shoulders relaxing.

She smiled. She liked the sound of his laughter.

They settled into an easy silence as the woman on the CD sang of love starting slowly and coming fast.

She half listened to what seemed an endless succession of country songs before he spoke on the outskirts of Philadelphia.

"There's a new restaurant at the Waterworks. I hear they have dining on a terrace overlooking the river."

"I'd like to go there sometime but not tonight."

"Where would you like to go tonight?"

"We could go someplace less formal and maybe have a steak and vegetables."

"Where did you have in mind?"

"My apartment. If you think that would be acceptable, given the situation."

"What situation?"

"My being intended for the amazing Bancroft whether I like it or not."

He laughed and then sobered quickly. "You could do a lot worse but not much better, Benai. He really is amazing."

She smiled and placed a hand on his arm. "He must be to inspire such loyalty."

"He's my brother."

She nodded and removed her hand. "But not my intended. Are we having steak and vegetables?"

"I wouldn't want Hawk to misunderstand."

"Is that an admission that you are interested, Randall?"

"What would you have me say?"

"A simple yes or no will do just fine."

"Yes. We're having steak."

"That's not the question I wanted answered."

"I know."

"If the subject comes up between you two, Randall, you can tell Bancroft there was nothing to misunderstand. We're talking about sharing a simple, informal dinner, not a night of unrestrained passion."

"No? No night of unrestrained passion? Then what's the point?"

She laughed. Moments later his laughter mingled with hers.

He sobered first. "Given the situation, if we're not very careful, things could get...messy."

She touched his arm. "Then we'll be very careful."

His right hand left the steering wheel to brush hers. "We'll have to be."

Chapter Two
ℬ

At her apartment, she changed from the long, form-fitting, sleeveless mauve gown she'd worn to the wedding into a strapless, calf-length cream dress that hugged her breasts and flared around her legs. Although Randall didn't comment on her change of dress, she noted the appreciative gleam in his gaze when she returned to living room.

He'd removed his dark tuxedo jacket and opened the first few buttons of his shirt. He'd pushed the black bowtie he'd worn at the wedding and reception into his breast pocket.

"Would you like a drink?"

"I don't think having my inhibitions lowered now would be a good idea."

"I don't bite, Randall."

"I don't want a drink."

"Okay. So...will you join me in the kitchen while I cook or would you prefer to sit here or out on the bal—"

"I'll join you."

"Great. This way."

He followed her into the kitchen.

She received a thrill each time she looked up from dinner preparations to find his silent gaze trained on her. She enjoyed the warm look in his eyes when she smiled at him. Each time she passed the chair where he sat, she felt an almost palpable tension between them.

They discussed baseball while she cooked. When the meal was done, they carried the food onto her balcony.

Ignoring her desire to discuss his personal life, she asked about Lelia instead. A warm smile spread across his face.

"She's incredible," he told her and launched into a long list of Lelia's wonderful qualities and charms that stretched beyond the meal. She listened attentively, asking frequent questions, which he readily answered.

After coffee, the night grew chilly. They took the remnants of their meal to the kitchen before they settled on either end of her sofa in the living room, half facing each other. With the lights low and soothing jazz providing a soft background, they discussed politics and the upcoming local city election. They supported different candidates.

From politics they talked about travel. "I'd love to go to Egypt one day," she said.

"It's beautiful and steeped in biblical history," he told her.

"You've read the Bible?"

"Yes. My mother believed in the ancient traditions but she used to love reading passages of the Bible to us as well."

"You're an interesting man, Randall."

He smiled. "Maybe you'd like to see my pictures of Egypt sometime. I've been three times. Once alone. Once with Peyton and once with Lelia."

"I'd love to see your pictures."

"Great. We'll set up a date."

"Great. So, I hear you're a computer genius, Randall."

"Hardly a genius. I just studied very hard and was fortunate enough to be in the right place at the right time to benefit from the internet boom."

"The right time or place wouldn't have mattered if you didn't know your stuff."

He shrugged. "I studied very hard and I was fortunate enough to have a great memory."

"You're very modest."

"No one likes a braggart."

"I guess not." She kicked off her shoes and folded her legs under her body. Resting her back against the side of the sofa, she faced him. Lord, was he handsome. "What haven't we discussed? I know. Books."

He glanced at her. "Books it is."

She discovered Randall shared her love of Tony Hillerman's Navajo mysteries. "Who's your favorite Hillerman detective, Randall? Jim Chee or Joe Leaphorn?"

"I prefer Leaphorn. He's more experienced."

"He's my favorite as well, although I like Chee too. My favorite books feature them both."

"Have you read Hillerman's latest, Benai?"

"Not yet."

"It's a great read." He turned to face her. "How long has it been since you and Croft have been out?"

"We've never been out."

"Never? You've always refused when he asked you out?"

"He's never asked me out, Randall."

He frowned. "I don't understand. I thought the two of you..."

"What did you think?"

"I thought you were dating, Benai."

"It's difficult to date a man who's never asked you out."

"Did you want him to?"

"I would have been flattered if he had asked me out when we first met months ago."

"But not now?"

"No, Randall. Not now."

He hesitated before he spoke again. "If you gave yourself time to know him—"

"I know how charming he can be but I have no romantic interest in him, Randall."

"Are you sure?"

"I'm positive."

He sighed. "I wish you'd consider giving him another chance, Benai. Once he's himself again, I'm sure you'll be suitably impressed."

"I've already admitted I know he can be charming, Randall, but frankly, he's not the Grayhawk I'm interested in."

"I see." He turned to stare ahead of him.

"Aren't you going to ask which Grayhawk I'd like to get to know better?"

He sat back against the sofa, his long, dark lashes sweeping down to conceal his expression. "No."

"Why not?"

"Because we're being careful."

"Careful? Right. Okay. Let's talk about Bancroft."

His shoulders relaxed and he turned to face her again. "What would you like to know?"

"He's not the same man he was when we first met. Tempest tried to explain but I'm not sure what happened to change him."

He sighed. "He's lost his spiritual center."

"His spiritual center?"

He shrugged. "We're Native American, Benai."

"Yes. I noticed, Randall."

He smiled. "We have beliefs some might find quaint or even impossible to believe."

She shook her head. "That's not what I meant."

"Good because some of us believe that the spiritual center or balance is very important. It helps govern who we are and how we behave, how we interact with others and even how or if we recognize when we've met our *sheenea*."

"I've heard Layton call Tempest that."

"I'm sure you have. It's a term of endearment that means…well it means different things to some of us. Layton, Brandon and Bancroft believe it means the one person who completes them."

"What do you believe it means, Randall?"

"I'm not sure I believe in one person who completes me but I do believe in a life mate."

"What's the difference between the two?"

"I suppose I believe that one day I'll meet a woman I want to spend the rest of my life with. That's not necessarily the same as believing she would be the only person in the world who could complete me. If she died before I did, I wouldn't necessarily think my life was over and that I could never want another woman again. I just wouldn't want another one while she was alive."

"So you don't have a *sheenea*?"

"No. I don't."

Good. "They're both sweet, romantic concepts, Randall."

He shrugged. "My family believes in a long line of love concept. We don't always fall in love quickly or easily but when we do fall in love, we don't stray."

"What more could a woman ask from a man?"

"Some prefer money to love," he said coolly.

"You have that as well."

"I wasn't always wealthy."

She reacted to the bitterness in his voice. "That mattered to someone you cared about?"

His jaw clenched. "We were discussing Bancroft."

So his personal life was off limits. "Yes. You were going to tell me how he lost his spiritual center."

"It started when Rissa, Brandon's *sheenea*, was murdered. We all hurt with Brandon and tried to help him work through his grief. After two years, Layton decided we needed to do something more to help him dissipate some of his grief."

"Couldn't he see a therapist?"

"It's not always easy to find a therapist who understands and respects our beliefs. Besides, Tempest might have mentioned that Declan has a healing touch."

"A healing touch? You mean he can heal people like a doctor?"

"He can't heal physical ailments but often he can help with emotional ones. Layton and Bancroft decided Brandon's emotional pain was too much for Declan to handle alone. Between the three of them, they helped Brandon rid himself of enough of his grief to help him regain his spiritual center. In the process, the three of them absorbed most of the dark, negative energy, which had been consuming him.

"As a healer, Declan was used to absorbing others' dark pain. Tempest's love and support provided an outlet for Layton's because she is Layton's *sheenea*. That left Bancroft. He has neither a *sheenea* nor a woman with whom he had a close enough emotional tie who can help him as Tempest did Layton. He's been left to struggle alone."

He raised his lids and looked at her. "Could you..."

She sighed at the pain she saw in his gaze. "I feel bad for Bancroft, Randall, but Tempest was able to help Layton and bear with the darkness in him because of her vested emotional interest in him. She loves him. I don't have any such vested interest in Bancroft. I never have."

He raked a hand through his hair. "Forgive me. I had no right to ask. It's just that he's in such pain and there's nothing we can do to help him."

"Declan can't help?"

"Croft has abilities of his own and each time Declan has tried, Croft rebuffs him. He erects mental barriers Declan can't penetrate."

She unfolded her legs and scooted across the sofa cushion to stroke a finger down his clenched right hand. "I'm not his *sheenea*, Randall. I can't help him. The darkness in him is a little…frightening."

"You'd be perfectly safe with him."

"Then why did you feel the need to rescue me?"

He pulled his hand away from her. "You weren't in any danger from him. I didn't *rescue* you."

"Okay, why did you…intervene when we were dancing?"

"Although you weren't in any danger, I could see you weren't comfortable dancing with him. You were a guest in my home so I needed to make sure you were as comfortable as possible."

"Why did you follow us into the hall?"

"I suspected you didn't want to be alone with him."

"Thanks for explaining why he's so different now."

"He won't always be so dark, Benai. When he's not—"

"I'll be very happy for him but I think I've made it clear that he's not the brother I'm interested in, Randall." She placed her hand over his.

He shook his head and withdrew it. "This was a mistake."

She felt as if he'd slashed ice water on her. "No, it wasn't."

"I shouldn't be here with you like this."

"Like what? We're talking, Randall, not making out."

"The conversation is going in directions it shouldn't."

"Why not if we both want it?" She placed a hand on his arm. "Or are you implying I'm flattering myself to think you share my interest?"

"I'm not implying anything." He glanced at his watch. "Damn. It's after eleven."

"Do you turn into a pumpkin at twelve?"

"Not tonight."

"Good. You haven't answered my question."

He rose. "I can't afford to get personal or intimate with you."

"Why not?"

"I have to go."

She stared up at him. "Randall—"

"I'd better go now, Benai before…"

She placed a hand on his thigh. "Before what?"

He stepped away from her touch. "Please don't make this any harder for me."

"It's not as if there was ever anything between Bancroft and me, Randall—"

"He thinks there is so I can't do this."

"Okay. I'll see you out." She rose. She reached for the bowtie hanging from his breast pocket.

When he reached for it, she shook her head. "I think I'll keep it as a souvenir."

He shrugged. "Fine. Keep it if you like."

"I'd rather keep you here."

"That's not going to happen." He turned and walked away.

She lightly tied the bowtie around her neck before she followed him to the apartment door.

He sighed and turned to stare down at her. "Good night."

She moistened her lips and placed a hand on his arm. "What about our date to see your pictures?"

"Give me your email address and I'll send them to you."

She placed her other hand on his chest and leaned close to him, staring up at him with her lips parted. "That wasn't the deal, Randall."

He stared at her mouth for several moments. He touched the bowtie around her neck before he sucked in a breath. "That's the way it has to be."

She slipped her hands across his chest. "So I shouldn't expect anymore cozy dinners alone with you?"

"You have no idea how hard this is for me." He closed his hands around her wrists and held her hands away from his body. "Please don't touch me like that."

"It's not nearly as intimately as I'd like to touch you, Randall."

Still holding her wrists, he leaned close, his lips parting and his head bending.

She closed her eyes and waited to feel his lips against hers.

He swore softly instead and released her. "I can't."

She sighed and opened her eyes. "Randall—"

"I'm sorry." He opened the door and left.

After locking the door, she leaned against it. She removed the bowtie from her neck and inhaled, savoring the traces of his cologne. She closed her eyes and smiled. Once he realized he wasn't betraying Bancroft, he'd be back. And she'd be waiting.

* * * * *

When Randall returned home just before twelve a.m. he was surprised to find Peyton pacing in front of the house. He got out of his SUV. "What's wrong?"

Peyton cast a quick glance over his shoulder before speaking. "Do you know what time it is?"

He glanced at his watch. "About ten of twelve. Why? Are you waiting for someone?"

"I've been waiting for you."

He arched a brow. "Why?"

"Why?" Peyton practically roared the question at him. "You left here with Benai nearly eight hours ago. Where the hell have you been?"

He frowned. "Since when do I owe you a blow by blow account of my whereabouts?"

"Please tell me you haven't been with Benai all this time."

He slipped his hands into his pockets. "And if I have?"

"You've been with her all damned night?"

"I'm not in the mood for a third degree." He walked away.

Peyton grabbed his arm and swung him around. "What the hell were you thinking?"

He jerked away. "I don't owe you any explanations, Peyton."

"What the hell is that supposed to mean, Randy? Since when have we had any secrets or anything off limits from each other?"

He sighed and shook his head. "You're right. I'm sorry."

"I don't want to hear you're sorry. I want to hear that you didn't sleep with her."

He clenched his jaw. "What the hell makes you think she's the kind of woman who'd sleep with a man on a first date?"

"A first date? So you're dating her now?"

"That was a slip of the tongue. Of course I'm not dating her."

"So nothing happened between you two?"

"No."

Peyton sighed in relief. "Thank God. I tried to cover for you but Croft's waiting for you inside and he's in a foul mood."

"There was nothing to cover for."

"Try telling that to Hawk after you've been with her for so long."

He raked his hand through his hair. "Surely he doesn't think I'd betray him?"

"I don't know what he thinks." Peyton sighed and shook his head. "I've never seen him so angry. Damn, I wish Brandon was here."

"That bad?"

Peyton nodded. "Lelia tried to get Croft to drive her home but he was determined to remain here and confront you."

"Where's Brandon?"

"He drove Lelia home an hour ago but I'm sure he'd come back if we called him."

He doubted Brandon had recovered sufficiently for an emotional face down with Bancroft. "Nothing happened between me and Benai so there's not going to be a problem between me and Croft."

"Why did you stay with her so long?"

He swallowed and looked away from Peyton's probing gaze. "We had dinner and talked."

"For nearly eight hours?"

"It wasn't eight hours."

"Fine. If we allow an hour each way for traveling that still leaves six hours. That's a long time to spend with her."

He shrugged. "I lost track of time."

"No shit? What were you two doing that you lost track of so many hours?"

"Do you doubt my word, Peyton?"

"Of course not."

"Good." He glanced at the door. "I'd better go reassure Hawk."

Peyton touched his arm. "I don't know if that's going to be possible."

He met Peyton's gaze. "I didn't touch her so there's no reason for there to be a problem between me and Hawk on her account."

"I hope you're right. Do us all a favor the next time, Randy, and remember Hawk's already claimed her."

He moved passed Peyton and ran up the steps. He opened the front door to find Bancroft waiting in the foyer for him. He inclined his head slightly. "Hawk."

Bancroft gave him a long, cool stare. "I was beginning to think you were going to spend the night with her, Randall."

Oh, hell! "There was never any question of that. I took her home and we had dinner."

"Dinner? After she was too tired to remain at the reception? Did you rock her to sleep while you were at it?"

Randall's nostrils flared. "I didn't touch her."

Bancroft studied him in silence.

Randall met his searching gaze.

"Do you like her, Randall?"

"Like her?" Hell, he wasn't sure what he felt-except... "She's..." He swallowed and glanced down at his nails before meeting Bancroft's gaze. "She's very...likable but I didn't touch her."

"So you've said."

"It's the truth."

"Are you telling me you spent all those hours alone without so much as a good night kiss or two?"

He recalled that torturous good night at her apartment door. She'd given every indication she wanted him to kiss her and he'd wanted to kiss her. "Yes, Hawk, that's what I'm telling you."

Bancroft's eyes narrowed. "Did you want to?"

He maintained Bancroft's cold gaze. "I didn't kiss her."

Bancroft nodded. "If you say you didn't, I suppose I'll have to take your word for that. Now answer my damned question, Randall. Did you want to?"

"She's...she's everything you said she was."

"Then you must have wanted to kiss her."

"What difference does it make what I might have wanted to do, Hawk? I didn't kiss her. I didn't hold her." He moved passed Bancroft, toward the right staircase.

"Randall?"

He reluctantly turned back to face Bancroft. He kept his voice level with difficulty. "Yes?"

"If you feel more than you think you should, now's the time to tell me. I can't afford to have you sneaking around with her behind my back."

He sucked in an angry breath and clenched his right hand into a fist at his side. "I didn't sneak around with her. You knew I was taking her home."

"But I didn't know you were planning to romance her."

Recalling just how much he'd wanted to do that, he felt the blood rushing up the back of his neck. "I've never betrayed you, Hawk."

"Don't let this be the first time, Randall."

For the first time in his life, he felt an almost overwhelming urge to hit one of his older brothers. "I've never given you any reason to doubt my word, Hawk."

Bancroft softened. "No, you haven't but she's absolutely perfect and you wouldn't be male if you weren't attracted to her. Why else would you have spent so much time with her?"

He swallowed slowly and forced himself to maintain Bancroft's gaze. "I...I admit I had a weak moment but I got past it."

"Meaning?"

The front door opened and Peyton entered. Peyton closed the door and gave him a quick, encouraging smile.

He turned back to face Bancroft. "I didn't touch her."

"I believe you."

He sighed in relief.

"Are you planning to see her again, Randall?"

"I…" He paused, feeling his heart racing.

"Do I have to worry about your seeing her again, Randall?"

"I…no. I don't plan on seeing her again."

Bancroft nodded slowly. "I knew I could count on you, Randall."

A picture of Benai gazing up at him with her lovely dark eyes trained on his face, her lush, full lips parted, wearing his bowtie flashed in his head. "Hawk, I'm not so sure—"

Bancroft shook his head. "I'll expect you to keep your word." He turned and ran down the staircase.

At the bottom, he and Peyton exchanged a silent look before Bancroft left.

Peyton set the alarm before walking up the stairs to place a hand on his shoulder. "Are you all right?"

He shook Peyton's hand off and mounted the remaining stairs.

Peyton followed and on the landing tossed an arm across his shoulders. "Don't shut me out, Randy."

He sighed. "I think there's a slight problem."

"You want her."

It wasn't a question. "I…I…yes."

"Does she want Hawk?"

"She says she's not interested in him."

"Because she's interested in you?"

"That's what she implied."

"What are you going to do about it?"

"What can I do about it?"

"If she wanted Hawk that would be one thing. But if she wants you, why can't you want her?"

"Because she belongs to him!"

"Not if she doesn't want him." Peyton narrowed his gaze. "Where the hell is it written you have to turn your back on what you feel if she shares your interest?"

"What would you have me do, Peyton?"

"I'd have you realize Croft's a big boy. If he really wanted her, he'd have gone after her. He's had plenty of time to do that. If he hasn't, there's no reason in hell why you shouldn't have her."

He closed his hand around Peyton's arm. "I'm having enough problems with this without you encouraging me to do something we both know is wrong."

"It's not wrong if—"

"It's wrong according to our family code of conduct!" He walked down the hall to his bedroom.

"Randy!"

He shook his head. "I know where you're coming from Peyton but please leave it alone."

Peyton swung him around. "The hell I will! I'm not going to stand by and allow him to ruin this for you."

He stared at Peyton. "Ruin what? Today was only the second time I've seen her. What do you think I'm feeling?"

"I don't *think* anything. I *know* what you're feeling even if you're not prepared to admit it yet. And hell will ice over big time before I let him hurt you."

"You're making too much out of a few hours."

"Are you going to see her again?"

"How can I?"

"How can you not?"

"You're not making this any easier for me, Peyton."

Peyton sighed. "Fine. Why don't you...place hold her—for Hawk?"

Randall swallowed several times. "That's something you'd be better suited to do."

Peyton shrugged. "Fine. I'll place hold her but not for him. For you."

"Damn it, Peyton! Will you leave me the hell alone? I'm not going to... I can't betray him."

"And I won't allow him to betray you!" Peyton narrowed his gaze. "You either place hold for him or I'll place hold for you. The choice is yours."

He watched Peyton walk down the hall before he went to his own bedroom. Once inside, he leaned against the door. The words of the first song he and Benai had listened to in his SUV danced through his memory. *The right body...the right face...Timber.*

He closed his eyes. Oh, hell, this was a bad time to wish he had one fewer brothers—namely Bancroft. Repulsed by the selfishness of the thought, he gave an angry shake of his head. Hell would freeze over before he allowed any woman to come between him and Bancroft.

To ensure Peyton didn't do anything they would both regret, he would place hold for Bancroft—if the opportunity arose—but no more than that. Place hold. Just taking her out to ensure no one else won her heart while Bancroft healed. He wouldn't touch or hold her. He wouldn't kiss her lush lips. He pushed himself away from the door and stalked across the room to the big brass bed. He sat on the side and picked up the cordless phone. After a brief hesitation, he dialed.

A low, sultry voice sounded in his ear. "Randall! Darling. I was hoping you'd call."

"Hi, Juliet. I'm feeling a little lonely. Are you alone?"

"Yes. If you can make it here in twenty minutes, we can spend the rest of the night getting reacquainted."

Juliet was a gorgeous blonde with lovely green eyes who never made the mistake of equating a man's hunger for her soft, beautiful body as an indicator that he wanted anything more permanent than a night of pleasure. He could touch, hold and kiss her all night without fear of injuring his relationship with Bancroft.

He rose. "I'm on my way."

He was annoyed to find Peyton in the foyer. "What the hell, Peyton. Are you stalking me?"

"Where are you going?"

"Out."

"Where?"

"Not that's it's any of your damned business, Peyton but I'm going to spend what's left of the night with Juliet."

Peyton frowned. "Are you sure you want to start things up with her again?"

He leaned forward and glared into the blue-green eyes so like his own. "I'm sure I want you out of my damned face."

He saw a flash of hurt in his twin's gaze and swore softly. As Peyton would have turned away, he clasped a hand on his shoulder. "I'm sorry," he said quickly. "I know you have my best interests at heart."

"Always. I'd walk through the hottest hellfire for you and gladly surrender my life to save yours, Hawk."

He nodded, humbled both by the affectionate term and the heartfelt sentiment of Peyton's words. He was the older twin by ten minutes but he hadn't behaved in a manner deserving of having Peyton accord him the respect of calling him Hawk. "I know and I'd gladly do the same for you, Peyton."

"I'm only trying to keep you from making mistakes you'll regret after the heat of the moment has passed."

"I know that too, Peyton. And maybe sleeping with Juliet is a bad idea but I need to work off some of this... I need a fuck right now before I explode."

Peyton nodded. "I understand."

"Are you staying?"

"Yes."

"Then I'll see you sometime tomorrow."

"I'll be here."

He embraced Peyton quickly before he left the house.

Chapter Three

An hour later, Randall sat naked in a chair in Juliet's bedroom. Holding the nude Juliet by her tiny waist, each time he pulled her down onto his lap, he thrust his cock as deep up into her wet pussy as he could get it.

Groaning and shuddering, she shoved against his shoulders. "This isn't a damn race, Randall, where you have to rush to the finish line."

He felt a desperate need to come. He wrapped his arms around her waist and drove his cock into her again.

"Damn it! We've fucked often enough for you to know my pussy can't take a brutal pounding like this. Your cock is too big and thick not to handle it with care."

Struggling to come and release some of his sexual tension and frustration, he found it difficult to slow his strokes.

She punched his shoulder. "You're hurting me. Slow down and stop pounding me like this is your last fuck!"

He groaned and released her waist. He leaned back against the chair. "I'm sorry."

"So am I—that you seem to have forgotten a woman likes a little tenderness. If I'd known you intended to brutalized me, I wouldn't have invited you over, Randall." She sucked in a breath and climbed off his cock.

As she stalked across the room to the big bed, he noted a trickle of pussy juice sliding down one pale, slender thigh.

She sprawled on her back and spread her legs, exposing her pussy. Slipping one hand between her legs, she stroked a finger inside herself. Smiling, she pinched her nipples. "If you're ready to play nice, bring that big weapon over here and come get some of this pussy. It's nice and juicy and wet just for you and your cock."

He rose and quickly crossed the room. Climbing onto the bed, he turned her on her side. Then he slid behind her, gripped his cock and pushed into her pussy.

She moaned and reached back a hand to push against his stomach. "We have all night, Randall. There's no hurry. I want to be fucked but not ravished."

Gritting his teeth, he forced himself to ease slowly inside her. When he was balls deep in her tight pussy, he cupped one hand over her small breasts and closed his eyes. He opened them quickly when a picture of Benai danced on his lids.

Juliet settled her ass against his groin. "Fuck me, Randall, but gently. It's been a long time since we've been together and I want it to last."

He wanted it over with so he could come but he kept his movements slow and measured with difficulty. He kept thoughts of Benai at bay with even greater effort. Juliet didn't seem to notice his struggles. Within minutes she exploded around him, finally allowing him to release the tight grip he had on himself and to come.

His climax brought none of the release he had expected. Thoughts of Benai still filled his head and he was still full of frustrations—both emotional and sexual. Damn. He eased out of Juliet and rolled onto his back, staring up at the ceiling.

"That was almost like old times, sweetie." Juliet sat up and reached for his cock. Holding the base, she began to remove the condom.

"Thanks but I'll do that." He rolled quickly away from her and discarded the condom in the wastebasket beside the bed before he lay back on the bed.

She climbed on top of him and kissed him.

He closed his eyes.

"Hey, have you forgotten how to kiss?"

He parted his lips. When she swept her tongue in his mouth, he sucked it.

"That's better," she whispered and pressed her lips against his with a series of biting kisses that did little to arouse him again. After several moments she lifted her head. "So nothing's changed. Has it?"

He opened his eyes and met her gaze. "What do you mean?"

"I mean you're still a cold, emotionless bastard." She rolled off of him and sat up. "This was just a meaningless fuck. Wasn't it?"

He sat up. "That's all we've ever shared."

"Really? If all you wanted was a fuck, you're damn well going to pay for the privilege." She slipped off the bed and left the bedroom.

Peyton had been right. Coming here had been a major mistake. He sighed and got up to dress. He sat on the side of the bed putting on his shoes when she returned to the room. She tossed an opened jewelry magazine next to him.

He looked down at a ten-carat, four-row, diamond tennis bracelet.

"Your meaningless fuck is going to cost you five thousand dollars, Randall."

He looked up at her.

She looked in his eyes and softened. She stroked her fingers through his hair. "Unless you want to discuss a real relationship that isn't just all about your getting your kicks."

That's the last thing he wanted. He rose. "I'll buy the bracelet."

She balled her hands into fists. "You are such an ass, Randall."

He sighed. "Look, Juliet, I'm sorry if you feel I used you."

"Didn't you?"

He raked a hand through his hair. "We met each other's needs."

"Fucking you no longer meets mine. I want more than that oversized cock of yours. I want to touch your emotions."

"If you'll recall on our first night together, I told you I had no interest in love or emotional attachments. You didn't object."

"That's all I wanted at the time. Now I want more."

He touched her cheek. "I'm sorry, Juliet, but I don't have any more to give."

She pushed his hand away. "You remember that the next time you get horny and want a fuck."

"There's not going to be a next time, Juliet." He crossed the room to the door. "I won't be back."

"Oh, yes you will. You always come back."

"Not this time."

"Selfish bastard!"

On the drive home, he called his executive assistant Bali's voicemail and told her to order the bracelet for Juliet. "And pick out a matching trinket and send that as well. Just have the card signed with my initials." He ended the call and drove home.

* * * * *

Two weeks later, Benai returned from lunch to find a tall, handsome man with short dark hair and blue-green eyes waiting to see her. Her heart raced and she had difficulty resisting the urge to rush across the office and toss herself into his arms. It was only when she met his gaze and saw none of the interest she'd seen in Randall's eyes that she realized the man in front of her was Peyton. She swallowed a wave of disappointment.

He smiled and extended her hand. "I know it's presumptuous of me to arrive without an appointment but I'd appreciate it if you'd give me a few minutes of your time, Ms. Peters."

She glanced at the beautiful bouquet he carried before she gave him her hand. When he released it, she led him to her office. Once she'd closed the door, she leaned against it. "Peyton. At the risk of being rude, I should warn you that if you've come to tell me I'm intended for Bancroft, you're going to get tossed out of here with no pretense of politeness."

She watched a slow, satisfied smile spread across his handsome. "You're not interested in Croft?"

"I wish him well but I have absolutely no romantic interest in him."

"Thank God."

She blinked. "Thank… I don't understand. Randall said you'd reminded him of… I got the impression you didn't approve of our having dinner together."

"That was when I thought there was something between you and Croft."

"There's never been anything between us."

"I'm very glad to hear it."

"How is Bancroft?"

He shrugged. "The same." He extended the bouquet. "These are for you."

"Thank you." She accepted them and gestured toward the chair in front of her desk. "Have a seat."

He glanced around her office before he sat on the sofa along one wall. He patted the cushion beside him. "Join me?"

After a brief hesitation, she placed the flowers on her desk. She crossed the room to sit beside him. The moment she had, she felt her cheeks burning as she recalled how just sharing her sofa with Randall had roused her passions.

"What can I do for you?"

"Have you heard from Croft?"

"No, I haven't."

He sighed and nodded. "Has Randall called you?"

She lowered her gaze to the knot in Peyton's silk tie. "No."

"Did you expect or want him to?"

She lifted her chin. "I'm not sure why you think I should answer your questions."

He brushed the back of his hand against her cheek. "Believe it or not, we're on the same side. There's no need to be defensive with me. I'm not here to extol Croft's virtues, although he has many."

She leaned away from his hand. "I'm not in the mood to hear yet again how amazing Bancroft is."

"He is amazing but that's not why I'm here."

"Why are you here if not to talk about Bancroft?"

"I'm here to ask you to bear with Randall."

"Bear with him? I haven't seen or heard from him since he drove me home from the reception."

"Unless I don't know him as well as I think I do, you will. He's loyal to a fault and is having difficulty trying to reconcile wanting to see you after Croft has staked a claim."

She exploded to her feet. "Staked a claim? What am I? Some property Bancroft or any other man can own? No one has a right to stake a claim on me unless I grant them that right and I haven't granted it to Bancroft."

He rose, spreading his hands. "I didn't mean to offend you. I was just attempting to explain why you haven't heard from Randall yet." He paused. "If you can bear with him when he does contact you, I can promise you that he's worth more than a little aggravation."

She arched a brow. "Let me guess. He's amazing man with a lot to offer?"

His lips twitched. "Yes. He is."

"Well, maybe I'll still be interested when he finally decides to make a move and maybe I won't." She glanced at her desk. "Now if you'll excuse me…"

He nodded and moved across her office. At the door he turned and crossed the office to look at her. "Let me show you what you'll be passing up if you don't wait for him."

"And how do you plan to do that?"

He arched a brow, a slow smile spreading across his face. "Like so." He swept her into his arms and tipped up her chin.

She stiffened. "What do you think you're doing?"

"This." He bent his head and pressed a series of slow, demanding kisses against her lips.

She pulled away, staring at him with her lips parted.

He curled his fingers in her hair and bent to kiss her again with a heat that left her gasping and trembling in his arms within seconds of his mouth touching hers again.

She felt his tongue probing her lips. She balled her hands into fists in an effort to resist. Nibbling at her mouth, he slid one hand down her body to cup her ass. She gasped. He slipped his tongue between her lips. The tip of his tongue touched hers, sending an electric charge through her so strong, her knees buckled.

He responded by sweeping her off her feet. Still kissing her, he carried her to the sofa. When he settled her across his lap, she felt the unmistakable bulge of his cock under her. She shuddered and dragged her mouth away from him.

To her relief, he lifted his head.

She wiped a hand across her lips and stared at him. What had he called her? Something that sounded like sovereign.

He arched a brow but remained silent.

She realized he wasn't even aware he'd called her by another woman's name. Feeling her face flaming, knees trembling, she rose.

When he stood up, she shook her head and rushed around her desk to stand behind her chair. "Don't."

He followed her but leaned across the desk to look at her. "If that aroused you, just imagine how it'll feel when Randall kisses you and means it."

She sucked in several, gasping breaths.

His eyes softened and he walked around the desk to look at her.

She shook her head. "Please don't touch me again, Peyton."

Ignoring her pleas, he cupped her face between his palms and bent his head. "You don't ever need to be afraid of me, Benai." He brushed his lips against hers in a gentle caress totally devoid of passion. He lifted his head and stepped away her. "I hope you won't hold this against me when we meet again."

"Would you please just leave?"

He lifted her hand and brushed his lips against her knuckles. "If you'll forgive me, I promise that the next time we meet, I'll be a perfect gentleman and keep my hands and lips to myself. We'll pretend this never happened."

He'd kissed her breathless, thrust his tongue, uninvited into her mouth and allowed her to feel his cock hardening under her butt. And he expected her to pretend none of that had happened when they met again? "Are you still here?"

He crossed the floor and quietly left her office. She sank down into her chair. She closed her eyes. After spending several minutes taking slow deep breaths, she opened her eyes. She reached for the card nestled between the flowers.

It read — *Native Americans make the best lovers. Give Randall a chance to prove it.*

"I'd love to do just that," she said softly and flipped the card on her desk.

* * * * *

"We need to talk, Randy."

Randall looked up as Peyton strolled into his office. He frowned. He was going to have to have his executive assistant Bali remind Karen—who was filling in for his vacationing secretary—that no one was allowed to just open his office door and walk in unannounced. He'd tell her himself except that her face always flamed red at the mildest rebuke from him.

Once his regular secretary returned from vacation, his office would run as smoothly as normal. He sat back in his chair. "What's wrong?"

Peyton sank into one of the two leather chairs in front of his desk. "Hear me out completely before you before you say anything."

"I'm listening."

"I've just been to see Benai."

"How is she?"

"Don't you know?"

"How could I? I haven't seen her since the reception."

"Haven't you?"

He'd driven by her apartment several times in the last two weeks but he'd never stopped nor had he given in to the temptation to call her. "No. Why did you go to see her?"

"I wanted to see if Hawk had called her."

He tensed. Bancroft had called him several times but each time had refused to discuss Benai. "And had he?"

"No and neither have you but you already knew that."

"What's your point?"

"Things got out of hand."

"Meaning what, Peyton?"

"One thing led to another…"

"And?"

Peyton shrugged. "The next thing I kne
on my lap."

He sat forward, feeling a rush of blood
of his neck. "What? You touched her?"

Peyton sighed. "It was just a few kisses."

He bolted to his feet. "A few kisses? You kissed her? On her lips?"

"That's where I generally kiss women."

He stalked around his desk and stared down at Peyton, who remained seated. "How the hell could you betray—"

"Betray?" Peyton's gaze narrowed and he rose, forcing Randall to step back. "Who have I betrayed? Certainly not Croft, who's made no effort to contact her. Not that calling her would help his cause any. She has no romantic interest in him as you well know. If you're implying I've betrayed you, you know damn well hell would freeze over before I'd intentionally do anything to hurt you."

The thought of Peyton tasting the lips he'd denied himself infuriated him. Afraid he'd succumb to the urge to deck Peyton, he went to stare out his office window. "Get out of my office, Peyton."

He felt Peyton's hand descending on his shoulder. "Nothing happened beyond a few kisses. I admit they got a little out of hand but she wasn't any more interested in me than she is in Croft."

He shook Peyton's hand off and turned around to stare at him. "And what makes you think she's interested in me if she rebuffed you?"

"I saw the delighted look in her eyes when she first saw me and the disappointment that followed when she realized I wasn't you. I lost my head because of that look." Peyton sighed and looked beyond him. Though he looked in the direction of the window, Randall knew he looked far beyond, into the distant past. A past life where Peyton believed he'd lost the only woman he was capable of loving. "That first look delight reminded me of her and the expression in her eyes whenever she saw me."

The *her* being Peyton's lost but not forgotten love.

Even though he wasn't sure he believed Peyton's memories of a past life were real, Randall knew the ache and pain Peyton carried was very real. He'd felt it on more than one occasion and hurt with him.

In the face of Peyton's pain, Randall's anger vanished. Peyton's eyes didn't fill with tears, as they sometimes did when he spoke of his past life. Nevertheless, Randall felt the wave of despair engulfing his twin. He embraced Peyton, who put his head on his shoulder and clung to him. "Don't risk losing her, Randy. Sometimes you only love once, no matter how many times you live. Don't let misguided loyalty to Croft blind you to what your heart tells you feels right with Benai."

At times like this, when Peyton was so filled with anguish, Randall didn't know what to say to comfort him. So he just held him until Peyton pulled away from him and crossed the office to the door.

"Peyton."

He paused but didn't turn to face him. "What?"

"Are you all right?"

He watched Peyton's shoulders rise and fall several times. "No but I'm in no danger of descending into the darkness that made Brandon so miserable and that now grips Croft."

"If you were—"

"If I were, you'd know even before I told you." Peyton turned to face him. "I'm okay, Randy."

"Good. Will you do me a favor?"

"Yes."

"In future, stay far away from her."

Peyton leaned against his office door. "Why should I?"

"Because I'll knock you on your ass if you don't."

Peyton laughed. "You might try but if you don't want her, maybe she can chase my demons away."

He clenched his jaw, shaking his head. "Stay away from her."

"If you don't want her, it's really none of your business if I seek solace in her arms."

"If you go near her again, Peyton, I swear I'll..."

"You'll what? We both know you're not going to hit me, Randy."

"Don't take advantage of that fact, Peyton. Please."

"Would you really deny me the chance to find comfort from countless lifetimes of pain with a woman for whom you care nothing?"

"If there was anything I could do to ease your pain, I'd do it and you know that, Peyton."

"Then if you don't ask her out, don't try to stand in my way, Hawk." He pulled the office door open and left.

Randall picked up his phone and called Bancroft. To his surprise, a woman answered in a sleep-slurred voice. "Hello?"

"Hello. This is Randall Grayhawk. Is Bancroft there?"

"He's asleep. Is it an emergency? Do you want me to wake him?"

"It's not an emergency but I do need to talk to him."

"Hold on."

Several minutes passed before Bancroft answered. "Randall?"

"Hi, Hawk. How are you?"

"I'm okay. How are you?"

"I've been better."

"What's wrong?"

"I need to talk to you about Benai, Hawk."

"There's nothing to discuss, Randall."

"I think there is. If you want her, why are you with another woman?"

"You want her but that didn't stop you from sleeping with your little blonde trollop again. Did it?"

He didn't bother to ask how Bancroft knew he'd been with Juliet again. As a young child, he'd learned that Bancroft and Brandon often knew things they had no rational way of knowing. "It was a mistake I won't make again and it didn't mean anything."

"Neither does this. So where does that leave us, Randall?"

"I'd really like to see her, Hawk."

"So your promise is worthless?"

"No but you haven't called her. And you're sleeping with other women. If she were important to you—"

"Since your promise is worthless, do whatever the hell you like, Randall."

He sighed. "I'm not asking this lightly, Hawk. I wouldn't ask you to absolve me of my promise if I could stop thinking about her. I can't. I fall asleep thinking about her and wake the same way. I—"

"And you think it's any different for me, Randall?"

"Frankly, yes, I do."

"What?"

"You haven't made any effort to win her, Hawk. None."

"I wouldn't need to win her if you hadn't been undercutting me with her."

He swallowed the urge to swear with great difficulty. "I never did any such thing. If you ask her, she'll tell you I've never said anything that wasn't complimentary to you."

"I don't have time for this conversation, Randall."

"I wish you'd make time because I'm having a hard time keeping my word."

"Why bother when it's clearly so worthless?"

Bancroft slammed the phone down before Randall could respond.

He sighed and sat back in his chair, raking a hand through his hair. He reached for the phone and dialed Benai's office number. He hung up before the phone rang. Just because Bancroft wasn't behaving rationally didn't give Randall the right to go back on his word. Yet he ached to see her.

* * * * *

"Any plans for tonight, Benai?"

Benai stopped picking at her salad and put down her fork. Her co-worker and friend, Jill Willers was seated across from her at a table for two in the food court of the mall.

Seven weeks after the wedding, she'd heard nothing from either Grayhawk brother. She hadn't expected or wanted Bancroft to call. But after all the long, lingering looks they'd shared over dinner, she'd expected Randall to call.

She shook her head. "I'm still trying to wind down from the wedding."

Jill sipped her milkshake. "You're trying to wind down from the wedding or the reception?"

"What do you mean?"

"Oh, come on, Nai. Remember, I was at the reception too. I saw how uncomfortable those handsome Grayhawk brothers made you." She paused for a moment before speaking again. "Has he called you?"

"No." She shrugged, "But then I didn't expect him to."

"I thought he might have called."

"He hasn't and I'm all right with that." Randall's silence was another matter. Him she'd expected to call but she'd have to learn to be all right with that as well.

"Oh. Well, some of us are going out to a new club tonight. Why don't you come?"

"Thanks but I'm really not in the mood to do anything much tonight. I think I'll just lie in a bubble bath and read until I'm sleepy."

"Why sit home waiting for a call that may not come when you could be out dancing the night away?"

About to shake her head, she nodded instead. Randall sure as hell wasn't sitting at home. Why should she? "Why not? I have this slinky black outfit I haven't had a chance to wear yet. Count me in."

Jill grinned. "We'll have a great time."

"Yes. I'm sure we will."

Her office phone rang an hour after she returned to work. She pushed the button to activate the speakerphone. "Good afternoon. Crandle and Howard, LLC, Benai Peters speaking."

"Hi."

At the sound of the deep, warm voice, Benai's heart raced. Finally. "Hi."

"This is Rand—"

"Yes. I know. This is a surprise."

"Hopefully, not an unpleasant one."

"Well…"

She smiled at the sound of his laughter.

"I'll let you tell me later if it's an unpleasant surprise."

"That's very generous of you."

He laughed again. "Yes. Isn't it?" He paused and his voice had deepened when he spoke again. "I can be very generous, Benai."

She moistened her lips. "You keep that up and I'll think you're either trying to bribe me or that you're flirting with me—again. Which is it?"

"I'll let you discover that for yourself. In the meantime, I know it's short notice but will you have dinner with me?"

"When?"

"Tonight."

"You're right. It is short notice. I already have plans."

"You do?"

She smiled at his surprise. "Yes. I do."

"You told me you weren't seeing anyone."

"Did you expect me to just sit by my phone for seven weeks hoping you'd call, Randall?"

"I...ah...I didn't expect you to start dating someone else."

"It's been seven weeks, Randall."

"I know exactly how long it's been since we saw each other but...I hope your plans aren't with Peyton."

She moistened her lips. "I suppose he told you he came to see me."

"He told me he did a lot more than see you, Benai."

She couldn't decide if she heard annoyance or anger in his voice. She shrugged. "If what happened between us bothered you, Randall, why has it taken you five weeks to call?"

"Why would you allow him to kiss you?"

She sighed. "I didn't allow anything. He was trying to convince me that you were worth waiting for."

"By kissing you?"

"He's your twin. If you don't understand his motivation, I can't see how you expect me to."

"Benai—"

"Don't get bent out of shape, Randall. Those few kisses meant so little to him he whispered another woman's name."

He laughed. "I guess that defused the moment."

"There was no moment to defuse. The kisses meant nothing to him and less to me, Randall. I have no interest in any of your brothers. Even though you tell me they're all so very amazing."

"Speaking of amazing, have you heard from Croft?"

"No."

"So you don't have a date with him?"

"Oh, Randall, do the math. How can I have a date with a man I haven't talked to in seven weeks? And how many ways can I say I'm not interested in him?"

"I'm very glad to hear that. Now about this date of yours."

"What about it?"

"I'm hoping you'll want to see me enough to cancel it."

"Why would you hope that?"

"Because I'm vainer than I should be?"

She smiled. "Vain? You have a surprising lack of vanity for a man with your looks and means."

"And you still have a charming knack for saying just the right thing. What time can I pick you up?"

A more astute woman might have played hard to get and made him jump through a few hoops before she went out with him. But she was too relieved to hear from him to play games. "Seven o'clock."

"I'm looking forward to seeing see you, Benai."

Even as she cautioned herself not to get too hopeful, a slow, satisfied smile curved her lips upward. "I'll see you at seven."

After she hung up, she called Jill.

"Randall. Wow. You've reeled him in? Way to go!"

"He asked me out. That's a long way from reeling him in."

"Hmmm. I'm sure you two will have a great time and this will be the first of many dates."

"We'll see."

"Are you going to wear that black slinky outfit?"

"I don't know. I want to impress him but—"

"I think he's already impressed, Nai."

"Hopefully. Listen, I'd better go."

"Have a great time, Nai."

"You too."

* * * * *

Randall arrived just before seven o'clock with a single white rose. As she accepted it, he kissed her cheek. She placed a hand on his chest and brushed her cheek against his.

He whispered something soft and sweet sounding against her cheek.

She lifted her head and met his gaze. "Hi."

He lifted her hand to his lips and kissed her fingertips before he breathed her name against her palm. He released her hand and stepped away from her. His gaze lingered on the bodice of the sleeveless, scoop-neck dress she wore. "You look charming."

She smiled. "Thank you."

He glanced at his watch. "We have reservations. Are you ready?"

She slipped her arm through his. "Yes."

His gaze locked on her lips and for one delicious moment, she thought he was going to kiss her. He squeezed her arm against his body instead. "We'd better go."

Oh well. The night was young.

On the drive to the restaurant, she was content to remain silent, conscious that as often as safety allowed, he glanced her way. She didn't even mind the country music. She turned to glance at his profile as a song she'd heard before began. *The right time...the right place.* "What's the name of this song?"

"Timber." He cast a quick look at her. "I'm Falling in Love".

Her heart raced. "You are?"

"That's the name of the song, Benai."

"Oh. Oh." She bit her lip, then laughed. "For a moment I thought you were about to declare your undying love."

He turned to look at her again. He murmured something indistinct.

"Which language is that?"

He turned his attention back to the road. "Cherokee."

"What did you say?"

"Nothing of importance."

"Then why not repeat it in English?"

"Let's take this slowly, Benai."

"Isn't that usually the woman's line in response to a male who wants to go too fast?"

He laughed. "So it is."

She settled in her seat. The evening should be interesting.

It was as they sat over coffee that she realized she'd been talking practically nonstop while he'd told her nothing about himself that she didn't already know. She put down her coffee cup. "Why are we here?"

"What do you mean?"

"I mean what's changed since the last time we saw each other?"

"Nothing."

"Then why are we here? Why did you ask me out?"

"I'm place holding."

"What?"

His lids lowered. "When one of us is interested in a woman who requires a little convincing of our charms, one of the others will place hold—take her out and keep her busy and the competition at bay."

One step forward and three back. "And just who are you place holding for?" She leveled a finger at him. "If you say Bancroft, I'll scream."

"Then I won't say Bancroft."

She shook her head. "Oh, Randall, surely you're not fixated on my belonging to Peyton now."

His eyes narrowed and his lips compressed. "You said what happened didn't mean anything to either of you."

"Nothing happened. It was a few kisses and they meant nothing."

"Then why does his name come so easily to your lips?"

"You two are identical. When I first saw him, I thought he was you." She shrugged. "Besides he's very charming."

"So am I."

"I'm prepared to be convinced, Randall. Now please tell me why you can't place hold for yourself."

"What makes you think I'm not?"

She moistened her lips. "Are you?"

"When I returned home after leaving you, Croft was waiting for me. He was furious that I'd spent so much time with you."

"Is that why you took so long to call?"

"Yes. He told me he was still interested in you and...I promised him I wouldn't betray him."

Damn them both. "Then what are you doing here?"

"Calling you and coming here wasn't easy for me, Benai." He reached across the table and took her hand in his. "I know you want answers. I know you deserve them but do you have to rip them from me on our second date?"

While she took issue with his choice of words, she noted the implication that he expected to share other dates with her. She shook her head. "I can wait. For a little while."

He replied in Cherokee.

"What?"

He lifted her hand to his lips. "I said you're perfect."

"In what way?"

"In every way that matters." He glanced toward the dance floor. "Let's dance."

"Okay."

At the reception, he'd held her with an arm linked loosely around her waist while he held her hand in his. Now he held her with both hands pressing against the bare skin of her back. Resisting the urge to link her arms around his neck, she placed her palms on his chest.

They shared several intimate dances in silence before he brushed his lips against her forehead. "Will you ride me tomorrow?"

She lifted her head to look at him. "What? Will I what you tomorrow?"

"Will you ride with me tomorrow?" He frowned. "What did you think I'd asked?"

"That might have been what you intended to ask. What you actually asked was if I'd ride *you,* not *with* you."

"Did I?"

"Yes, Randall, you did."

He laughed. "A Freudian slip."

"Really?"

He drew her closer.

"If you hold me any closer you're going to leave fingerprints on my back," she teased.

"Don't tempt me to tell you where I'd like to leave fingerprints." He brushed his lips against her forehead. "Do you ride?"

She spread her hands along his chest. "Do I ride what? Horses...or men?"

She watched his Adam's apple bob. "Both."

"No. I don't."

"Which one don't you ride?"

She leaned closer, so her breasts pressed against his body. "Horses."

"But you do ride men?"

"Why do you ask?"

He brushed his lips against her cheek, very close but not quite touching the corner of her mouth. "Because I'd love to be ridden."

She closed her eyes. "Given the right incentive, I might be persuaded to ride you."

He swept the tip of his tongue against the corner of her mouth.

She shivered, longing to press against his groin.

"Have you ever heard a song called "Longfellow Serenade", Benai?"

"Yes."

"Do you remember the chorus?

She recalled the male singer crooning about him and a lady being lonely before the start of the ambiguous chorus. She nodded and met his gaze. They spoke one word together, "Ride."

Come on, baby, ride.

She slid her hands up his shoulders and linked her arms around his neck. "Are you planning to make my dreams come true, Randall?"

"I'd like to."

She sucked in a breath. "Are you finally admitting that you want me?"

"I'm here after Croft asked me to stay away from you."

"And?"

"And can we leave it at that for now?"

She heard the tension in his voice. She knew how much he valued his brother's good opinion. There was no need to make things more difficult for him. "Okay."

He reached behind his neck to take her right hand in his, placing it flat against his chest, over his heart. "Will you ride with me tomorrow?"

"I'd like to say yes but I've never been on a horse. I don't think I'm brave enough to climb up on one of those creatures."

He lifted her hand to his mouth, kissing her fingertips, sending shockwaves of delight surging through her. "We'll share a horse and take a short ride."

"I don't know, Randall."

"You can trust me to ensure your safety."

Although fearful of mounting a horse, she liked the idea of his sitting close behind her with his arms around her. "Okay."

He trailed his fingers over her breasts while brushing his lips against the corners of her mouth. "I think we'd better go now before I…"

"Before what?"

"Before I forget that I promised myself I'd behave like a gentleman tonight." He released her and stepped back.

She compressed her lips on the urge to tell him she didn't want him to be a gentleman.

Back at their table, he took care of the bill and they left the restaurant. He didn't touch her on the walk to his car but she was very aware of him.

"So tell me, Randall, what kind of women do you like?" she asked when he slipped into the driver's seat.

"I like you."

"Charmingly put but somehow I don't think I'm your usual type."

He started the engine before he replied. "In the past I've preferred lithe, green-eyed blondes."

She liked that he didn't pretend she was his type. "Small blondes?"

"Yes," he admitted. "And you?"

"I like the Denzel Washington types...tall, dark, expressive brown eyes and an amazing smile. I remember when I first saw him in a uniform in a movie called *Crimson Tide*. He looked so sexy."

"So you don't have a thing for Native American men?"

"No more than you have one for tall, black women with no pretensions to beauty."

"No pretensions to..." He shrugged. "Beauty is in the eye of the beholder."

"And?"

He turned to meet her gaze. "I've already told you the moment I saw you, I agreed with Croft that you were perfect just as you are."

"Randall Grayhawk, you are an amazing man."

He guided the car out of the parking lot. "Am I?"

"Yes. You could have any woman you want." She lightly brushed her hand along his right thigh. "That you want to be with me, even if it's only for one night, makes me feel very lucky."

"*You* feel lucky? How do you think I feel knowing you prefer me to all my brothers?"

She decided not to admit she preferred him to any man she'd ever met.

He glanced at her. "And who says I only want you for one night?"

She settled into her seat, smiling. Things were definitely getting interesting. She frowned. Well, not that night since he was determined to be a gentleman. But there would be other nights when she would refuse to allow him to be a gentleman.

At her apartment door, he refused her offer of coffee. "I'd better go."

Noting the wary look in his eyes, she brushed her hand against his. "Are you having second thoughts?"

"About seeing you tonight? No but I do need to talk to Croft. I should have done that before I asked you out."

He sounded as if he'd rather be run over by an eighteen wheeler. "I'll come talk to him with you."

He smiled and squeezed her hand. "Thanks but this is something I have to do alone."

"Why?"

"He'll view this as a betrayal. As I would in his place."

She pulled her hand away from his. "Then you'd be as wrong as he is. He's never once called me or asked me out. There's never been anything between us. How can our seeing each other be a betrayal to him?"

He sighed. "Benai…"

She leaned against him. "I'm trying to understand his situation, Randall, I don't care what he says. We have a date and I expect to see you tomorrow. Don't stand me up."

"Benai—"

"We have a date tomorrow." She whispered the words against his lips.

He stared at her in silently.

She sighed and went inside. She leaned against her closed door. Would he keep their date?

Chapter Four
ཙ

On the drive home, Randall called Bancroft. Brandon answered. "Is Hawk there?"

"No."

"Do you know where he is?"

"No. He's not answering my calls so I'm hanging out here until he returns."

Damn. Where the hell did that leave him with Benai? "I need to talk to him, Brandon."

"Is there something I can help you with, Randall?"

He sighed. It would be a relief to unburden himself with Brandon, who, at four years his senior, was second eldest after Layton. Brandon might have been willing to intercede with Bancroft on his behalf, had Randall asked him to before he'd asked Benai out. In his selfish haste to see her again, he'd behaved badly, again. This time he had betrayed Bancroft or come so close that the difference no longer mattered.

"This is something I need to discuss with him."

"If it's about Benai, I think you should remember that Croft isn't himself."

"I understand that but—"

"If he were himself, he wouldn't want you to do anything to endanger what might be your one chance for real happiness."

"Croft told me she was his."

"I know what he told you, Randall. I'm telling you he's not himself. Peyton and I have intimate knowledge of the unmitigated pain losing your one love can cause. There's no reason you should join us. I know this is your decision but I'm begging you to remember that if he were himself, he'd want you to be happy instead of putting roadblocks in your way."

"If I see her again before he and I—"

"He's dating other women."

"I know, Brandon but—"

"Are you seeing anyone else?"

"No."

"Do you plan to?"

"No."

"Then I'd say you're far more interested in her than he is."

"Maybe so but—"

"When he's regained his spiritual balance, he'll be upset that you allowed yourself to be bound by unreasonable promises. For now, see her if that's what you need to do. Things with Croft will work themselves out."

"I don't want him to think I betrayed him, Hawk."

"You haven't and when he's himself again, I know he'll tell you so. Do you love her?"

"Love her? I know you and the others believe in romantic love but I'm not sure I do, Hawk. At least not for me. Not anymore. I tried it and didn't like it."

"Once was enough for you?"

"Yes."

"Then why are we having this conversation, Randall?"

"I like her a lot and I really want to see her but I'm not in love with her."

"Are you likely to fall in love with her?"

He'd spent seven long weeks aching to see her. He wanted her with a passion he hadn't felt with anyone else—not even with Pam. But that wasn't love and he'd do his best to ensure he didn't fall in love with her or anyone else ever again. "No."

"No? And yet you'd risk what you view as a betrayal to see a woman you don't love?"

He sighed. "Okay, I know I'm not making much sense but—"

"Could that be because you're in love or so close to it the difference doesn't really matter?"

After watching their father's countless infidelities wither away their mother's spirit and being hurt himself, he'd vowed never to surrender his heart again. That determination had only been strengthened when he witnessed the drastic change in Brandon after the death of the woman he'd called his one true love. After he recovered from Pam's desertion, Randall had worked hard to safeguard his heart from the perils and pains of romantic love. "I'm not in love with her."

"Not surprising considering she's not your usual type."

"I know which type I prefer," he said coolly.

"So do we all. So what's the attraction?"

He shrugged. "I'm not sure," he admitted. "The moment I saw her at the rehearsal dinner, I... She's honest, funny and outspoken." Reluctant to say anything that might lead Brandon to think she was easy, he didn't mention her failure to play hard to get.

"Those are all admirable traits in a woman but she's not exactly cover girl material."

"She suits me fine, just as she is, Brandon!" Brandon's implication that Benai wasn't attractive annoyed the hell out of him.

"I can see that. But why?"

"What?"

"She seems like a sweet woman who deserves a relationship with a man who's at least open to the possibility of falling for her."

"So now you think she's too good for me?"

Brandon laughed. "All I'm saying is that if you're only interested in a casual fling, you should choose a woman who's used to meaningless affairs and won't end up hurt when you're ready to move on."

He tightened his hands on the steering wheel. "You think I'll hurt her?"

"I know you wouldn't deliberately hurt her but if she wants a real relationship and you don't, she's probably going to get hurt."

"She's an adult and I've been honest about my intentions."

Brandon sighed. "I've never known you to be otherwise, Randall, but remember just because you don't believe in romantic love doesn't mean she can't fall in love with you and get hurt."

"Look, Hawk—"

"Just do your best not to hurt her. End of big brother lecture. Go see her. I'll try to track Croft down and make him understand."

"Thanks, Hawk." He ended the call and drove home. To his relief he had the house to himself. After undressing, he lay in bed, his thoughts on Benai. As he'd told her, he preferred petite blondes. Yet he'd felt an undeniable and immediate attraction from the moment he looked into her dark gaze.

If Bancroft had taken off, as he sometimes did, that might give Randall time to get what felt like an addiction for Benai out of his system. Hopefully, by the time Bancroft returned, Randall would be over Benai and Bancroft would be in a forgiving mood.

* * * * *

Benai looked up at the huge, dark stallion standing quietly in front of her before she turned to look at Randall. He wore jeans, a leather bomber jacket over a plaid shirt, boots and a black cowboy hat. Whether Randall wore a tailor-made business suit or jeans, he was so handsome just looking at him left her breathless.

Her own jean suit and silk-blend blouse was new but because she feared excessive sweating, she wore only foundation and lipstick. She'd pulled her long, dark hair into a ponytail and placed a baseball cap on her head.

Staring at her reflection in her bedroom mirror, she'd worried she looked frumpy. The gleam of appreciation in his gaze when he'd arrived with a dozen roses had reassured her.

Now that she stood in front of the horse he expected her to ride, she bit her lip.

He stepped close to her and touched her hand. "Ready?"

"He's ginormous."

"He needs to be to carry us both but he's well behaved and responsive to my commands."

"I'm sure he is." She glanced back at the Wissahickon Inn behind them. "I've come up with a new idea. I'll sit on the terrace and have a cup of coffee while you have a ride. When you're finished, I'll be waiting here for you."

He shook his head. "You're coming with me."

"Actually, I'm—"

"You are coming with me, Benai." He mounted the horse then reached a hand down to her. "Place your foot over mine in the stirrup and I'll pull you up."

She stared up at him. "What if he moves and—"

"He won't move. You'll be perfectly safe." He smiled at her. "Give me your hand, Benai."

"Randall—"

"Trust me."

"I...I do."

"Then?"

Taking a deep breath, she placed her foot over his and gave him her hand. He pulled her onto the horse, settling her in front of him. He brushed his lips against her ear. "I promise you'll be safe with me."

She caught her breath, leaning back against him. Seated as she was between his legs with his arms around her, her thoughts turned to pleasure rather than safety. "I'm not sure what I'm supposed to do with my hands."

"Aren't you?"

She hesitated before placing them on his thighs. His muscles felt hard and tense. "Do you need to unwind?"

He made a small sound and then laughed.

She tightened her hands on his thighs as the horse began to move.

"It's all right," he told her. "He won't canter."

She nodded, loosened her grip on his thighs and settled against his body. After several minutes, some of her fear subsided. She looked around. They were on a wooded trail surrounded by trees. She could hear birds and the sound of the nearby creek. Glimpses of sunlight filtered down through the tall trees.

The smooth motion of the horse and the tranquility of their surroundings soothed away her remaining fears. Desire took over. She longed to rub herself against his chest, reach between their bodies and cup her hand over his groin.

She closed her eyes and imagined herself holding and massaging him until his balls tightened and his cock hardened against her ass. She licked her lips, leaning back against him.

Almost as if he sensed her desire for him, he removed one hand from the reins and slipped an arm around her waist.

She tilted her head.

He responded by sliding his lips and tongue against the side of her neck.

She shivered, grinding her behind against his groin.

As he traced her earlobe with his tongue against her ear, he slid his hand from her waist up her body, resting it just under her breasts.

She practically purred in response,"Hmmm."

He flicked his thumb against her right nipple.

Heat spread through her. "Randall," she whispered.

In response, he cupped a hand over her breasts and licked the side of her neck.

She sucked in a breath and leaned away from his lips. "Randall, this is very nice but shouldn't you be watching where we're going instead of what you're doing?"

"Gray knows the way," he murmured, sucking the side of her neck.

She moaned, moisture pooling between her legs. "Oh…"

He whispered to her in Cherokee.

Her hands tightened on his thighs. "Randall."

Trailing his hand down her body, he cupped his palm between her legs. "Yes?"

She arched her back, feeling as if every bone in her body had turned to liquid need. If she didn't stop him immediately, she wouldn't stop him at all. She didn't want their first time together to happen on a horse.

She lifted his hand from between her legs. "If you keep this up, we're going to end up falling off him and it's a long way to the ground."

He laughed but to her relief, lifted his head from her neck. "Is that your charming way of telling me you want me to stop?"

"Yes."

"Killjoy!"

She half turned to look at him. "What did you have for breakfast?"

He took her hand and lifted to his lips. "Instead of worrying about what I had for breakfast, you might want to worry about what I'll want for dessert."

The intimate look in his eyes left her in no doubt as to his meaning. Feeling her cheeks burn, she turned away.

He tightened his arm around her waist and kissed her cheek. "What? No snappy comeback?"

She shrugged. "If you keep flirting with me, I'll begin to take you seriously. Where will that leave you, Randall?"

He nipped her earlobe. "What makes you think I'm not already serious?"

The chance of his wanting to share anything beyond meaningless sex with her was slim to none. A large part of his attraction was probably rooted in his belief that she was off limits. The forbidden was always more attractive than that which was easily attainable.

Nevertheless, she would surrender to him. Sooner rather than later. Once they'd satisfied their shared desire, he'd return to his tiny blondes and she'd have the experience of having slept with the most attractive man she'd ever met. As long as she kept sight of the level of his interest, there was no reason they shouldn't have a brief fling.

Of course that didn't mean she shouldn't make him work a little for it. "You're a placeholder. Remember?" She pulled her hand from his. "Placeholders should keep their lips to themselves, Randall, unless they want to be taken very seriously."

He recaptured her hand, again holding it against his heart. "I'll remember that."

He lifted her hand and brushed his lips against her fingertips. Their gazes met and locked. Oh, yeah. She would definitely be surrendering sooner rather than later. She had no doubt it would be the sweetest surrender of her life.

"Are you ready to head back to the inn for lunch or would you like to ride a little longer?"

She nodded. "I think Gray and I have spent enough quality time together. Let's go eat lunch."

He turned Gray around and an hour later, they returned to the inn. He dismounted and reached up to lift her down. He kept his hands on her waist for longer than necessary before he released her and stepped away from her.

One of his employees waited at the inn. Randall handed Gray over to him to be rubbed down and put in his trailer to be taken back to his mansion before he escorted her to his SUV where she retrieved her purse.

"I'll be in the dining room," he told her.

She nodded and made her way to the ladies' room. She washed her face, applied fresh make-up and removed the band and cap from hair. It fell around her shoulders in an unruly dark cloud. Too bad she'd forgotten to bring her travel curlers.

Grimacing, she combed and brushed her hair before putting the band back on her hair. She gave her reflection a last look and went to the dining room.

Randall smiled and rose when she joined him at the table for two by a window that overlooked the creek below. Over lunch, she noted several women casting frequent glances at him. One in particular was a beautiful blonde who looked as if she'd catwalked off the cover of a fashion magazine. He endeared himself to Benai by not allowing his gaze or attention to stray from her.

"Do you have any plans for the rest of the day, Benai?"

"No."

"I have a cook who can make anything melt in your mouth. Will you have dinner at my house?

Aware of the blonde still staring in the direction of their table, she sipped her coffee. "Is there a tiny blonde who might object?"

"I'm not seeing anyone else so there's no one, blonde, or otherwise who has any right to object."

"Then I'd love to have—"

"Randall, I thought that was you."

Benai looked up. The beautiful blonde who had been staring crossed the room to their table. She was petite with a resolute look in her eyes.

His eyes flashing with annoyance, Randall rose. When he turned to Benai to introduce her to the other woman, he'd lowered his lids. "Benai Peters, Juliet Warner."

Benai smiled. "Hello."

The woman stared at Benai with a surprised look on her face before she flashed a brief smile in her general direction. "Benai? Nice name. Well, Benai, Randall and I are old friends. Would you mind if we had a brief moment alone?"

Benai glanced at Randall.

He shook his head. "Benai and I were just leaving."

The blonde compressed her lips. "I see. Call me when you're free."

"It's over, Juliet," he said coolly.

"That's not what you said when you—"

"It's what I said the last time you called and it's what I'm saying again now."

"I didn't mean the things I said the last time we saw each other."

"I did."

"Randall—"

"Look, this doesn't need to turn unpleasant—unless that's the way you want it."

She gave him a long, cold stare before she turned to face Benai. "If I were you, honey, I wouldn't count on being anything except a booty call. In fact, I'm surprised he even wants that—"

Randall interrupted her. "If I were you, Juliet, I'd leave well enough alone. You should leave now while I'm still inclined to be polite."

"Don't call me the next time you get horny, Randall!" She turned and walked away.

He resumed his seat. "I'm sorry about that."

"Former lover?"

He nodded. "Yes."

"She didn't sound very former."

"There was never anything serious between us. What little there was has been over for a while."

"Has it?"

He met her gaze. "I made the mistake of sleeping with her again when I shouldn't."

"When?"

"Does it really matter when?"

"Oh, I don't know. If it happened last night or the night before, it might matter."

"It's been far longer than that. It was protected and she was willing to sleep with me knowing all I wanted was sex."

As Benai herself had just decided to do earlier that day. "So you got what you wanted and then tossed her out on her butt?"

He sat back in his chair. "At the risk of sounding like an ass, she knew from the start of our relationship that I had no interest in anything serious."

She stared at him in silence.

He frowned. "Haven't you ever slept with someone you shouldn't have?"

"We're discussing your relationship with her."

"She and I no longer have a relationship. She only intruded to try to ensure you and I don't develop one. Has she managed to do that?"

Since she planned to sleep with him with the full knowledge that all he wanted was sex, she shook her head. "No."

She saw the relief in his eyes. "I promise you that I am not sleeping with or seeing anyone else."

She believed him. "Neither am I."

"You're not? Who did you have a date with last night?"

She shrugged. "A friend."

"How good a friend?"

"Not the sleeping with kind."

"Good. Now you were about to agree to have dinner with me before she interrupted us."

She nodded. "Yes. I was."

"Would you like anything else?"

"No. Thanks."

He glanced at his watch. "Are you ready to leave?"

She nodded.

Forty minutes later, they stood outside her apartment door. "I'll be back to pick you up at six o'clock."

"And then drive me to your house and back here again? That's a lot of driving for one day. I'll save you some time and effort by driving myself to your house."

"Thanks but if I didn't think you were worth the effort, I'd send my driver instead of coming myself."

She smiled. "You sound as if you really mean that."

"I nearly always say what I mean, Benai."

"That makes it all the sweeter."

"Really? Well, if you're worried about me, bring an overnight bag. You can stay in one of the guestrooms...or if you can't trust yourself alone with me in the same house, you can have your choice of two guesthouses on the grounds."

She laughed. "Don't you wish."

He nodded. "Yes, actually, I do."

She smiled. "You're flirting again."

He shrugged. "I can't seem to help myself."

The admission pleased her. "You're hopeless."

"I hope you like hopeless males. If you do, you might want to consider spending the night with me."

Her stomach muscles clenched.

He turned her hand over and pressed a moist kiss in her open palm before he released it. "You can think about it and give me your answer later. I'll pick you up at six."

She nodded. "I'll be waiting for you."

* * * * *

They had dinner on his patio. Sitting across from her only half listening as she talked about a movie she'd seen, he had difficulty keeping his gaze from lingering alternately on her breasts and her lips. He raised his gaze to her face. Her beautiful, dark hair provided a perfect frame for her warm, dark skin, which looked as soft as velvet. Her full lips begged to be kissed. Her dark eyes sparkled with promises of endless pleasure in her arms. His gaze shifted downward. The dark pink dress she wore provided a tantalizing glimpse of the cleavage of her large breasts. How the hell could Brandon possibly have implied that this sexy woman was anything but stunning?

No longer able to contain his hunger for her, he rose and walked around the table. "Dance with me."

She looked up at him. "You haven't heard a thing I've said. Have you?"

"No," he admitted.

"Randall—"

"I need to hold you."

"Need or want?"

79

"Need. I *need* to dance with you."

She smiled up at him. "Need, huh? I think I like the idea."

He reached down to slide his palm over the back of her neck. "Then slow dance with me."

He watched her moisten her lips before she slowly rose.

She slid her hands up his chest before she linked her arms around his neck.

He placed his hands on her hips and drew her close.

She settled her hips against his.

Damn. He closed his eyes, pressing his lips against her cheek. The scent of her perfume intoxicated him. After seven weeks without sex, he could almost taste his need for her.

"Randall—"

"Let's not waste time talking, Benai. Talking now is not what I need or want." He drew her closer, allowing her to feel that he was already aroused. If she pulled away, he was going to need an extremely long, cold shower.

She trembled but made no effort to put any distance between her body and his cock.

Thank God. He slowly rotated his groin against her.

She sucked in a breath. Then she slipped a hand from his neck to push against his shoulder. "Before we get too revved up, let's not lose sight of the fact that it's going to be very embarrassing if one of your staff walks in and catches us groping at each other or worse."

"No one's going to walk in on us. All the staff is aware that a closed room means do not enter. They don't come into any room unless the door is open. The living room doors are closed. We don't be disturbed."

She brushed her lips against his chin. "You're sure?"

"Positive."

She lifted her head.

Randall looked into her dark eyes and experienced a falling sensation. Enjoying the plunge, he bent his head. He wanted to savor the first taste of her lips. He gently traced the outline of her mouth with the tip of his tongue, resisting the urge to totally plunder her mouth.

It was difficult when she parted her lush, warm lips and rubbed her breasts against him. He slipped his fingers in her hair and settled his mouth on hers. She moaned softly and flicked the tip of her tongue against the tip of his. With the loss of the rest of his self-control, he quickly abandoned his plan to woo her slowly.

Releasing her hair, he slipped his hands down her back to cup his palms over her ass. He devoured her lips, kissing her with a hunger that threatened to consume him.

She pressed closer, raking her fingers through his hair. Her nipples hardened against his chest. Her parted lips moved under his with a desire that matched his. She sucked at his tongue.

He tightened his hands on her ass and deepened the kiss.

She moaned.

When he ground his groin against her, she rotated her hips in a slow, sensual invitation that inflamed his senses. He had to have her. Dragging his mouth away from hers, he swept her off her feet.

She rubbed her cheek against his shoulder and whispered his name.

He quickly carried her across the patio and into the living room. He only made it a few feet into the room before his need to be inside her made it impossible to carry her any farther. He set her on her feet.

Gazing up at him in the moonlit room with her soft lips parted and her hair hanging around her face and shoulders in a wild, dark cloud, she was the most desirable woman he'd ever seen. Curling his fingers in her hair, he tasted her lips again. He savored the feel and texture of her mouth, feeling his cock harden. As he kissed her, he used his hips to press her against the wall.

She linked her arms around his neck, her lips flowering apart under his. She rubbed her breasts against his chest as she sucked at his tongue again. He could taste her surrender in the long, greedy kisses she accepted and encouraged…feel it in the eager hands she stroked down his back.

When she closed her fingers over his ass, he knew she was ready to be his.

He lifted his lips from hers. She made a small sound of protest, tightening her arms around his neck. He eased her away from the wall. Staring down into her eyes, he reached behind her to slide down the zipper of her dress. He rained kisses on her neck while pushing it off her shoulders. Then, impatient to have her naked, he gripped the hem of her dress and pulled it up and over her head and shoulders.

He knelt to remove her heels. Placing a hand on his shoulder, she lifted first one foot and then the other to allow him to slide her sheer stockings off. He rose and stepped back to look at her.

His desire to disrobe her rapidly was momentarily diverted. The white lace thong set she wore complimented her beautiful, dark skin. She had a voluptuous body with large but firm breasts, a flat stomach and long, shapely legs. How had he ever thought he preferred a petite blonde with pale skin to this lovely, sensual woman with a body so beautiful she made him ache to possess her in the most primal and basic way?

She shook her head. "I don't understand Cherokee, Randall. Please speak English."

Unaware that he'd spoken at all, he shook his head. "I don't want to talk."

"But you have been talking—just not in English."

He unhooked her bra, baring her breasts. She had the largest and lushest areolas he'd ever seen. Her nipples were hardened peaks that beckoned to him. He pulled her into his arms, rubbing his face against her breasts. "I want to make love to you."

She stoked her fingers through his hair. "Take me, Randall. I'm yours. All yours."

She was all his? The words were almost as sweet as her lips. The desire to slide inside her was so strong, he feared he was in danger of his first premature ejaculation in years. He'd need to make sure he satisfied her before allowing his cock anywhere near her pussy.

After tasting each of her nipples, he kissed his way down her body, over her belly, allowing his lips to come to rest just above her thong. Sitting back on his heels, he slipped a hand inside her thong.

She gasped as he palmed her. He slid his fingers around until he could part her outer folds. Eager to ensure she was ready for sex, he slipped a finger inside her. She wiggled her hips. He gently slid another finger inside her. Her internal muscles pulsed around his fingers. She felt tight and very wet…ready to receive his cock.

He withdrew his fingers from her and quickly slipped the thong down over her hips. Sitting back on his heels, he buried his face in the pretty lace, inhaling her aroma.

She stroked her fingers through his hair. "Oh. Randall."

Her voice sounded low with need—almost as if she wanted him as much as he wanted her.

He rose, pushing the thong into his pants pocket. He had to have her. Discarding his tie, jacket and shirt, he kicked off his shoes and unzipped his pants.

She caught her breath.

He met her gaze. "Touch me."

"Yes." Pushing his hand aside, she slipped her hand through the opening in his briefs to wrap her fingers around his cock. "Oh, yes," she whispered.

He closed his eyes, enjoying the feel of her warm fingers on him.

She slipped her other hand inside and cupped his balls before slowly drawing his shaft out of his briefs and pants.

Oh, damn! Gripping his cock, he rubbed it along the length of her wet slit.

Moaning softly, she parted her legs and rotated her hips in a slow, suggestive manner.

Ignoring the urge to plunge into her, he dropped to his knees, his gaze centered on the riot of dark hair between her long, luscious thighs. Slipping one hand around her body to cup her firm, round ass, he used the fingers of his other hand to part her wet folds. With her pink pussy exposed, he leaned forward to taste her.

He brushed his lips against her pubic hair. The sweet fragrant scent of her aroused pussy, intoxicated him.

Encouraged by her soft moan, he located her clit. He blew gently on it, then rubbed his thumb against it.

"Hmmm."

Slipping two fingers inside her, he slowly dragged his tongue along her slit while he gently finger fucked her. She curled her fingers in his hair, pulling his face closer.

"Oh, God, Randall, that feels so good."

Her internal muscles tightened around his fingers. He felt and smelled her pussy filling with fresh moisture. She ground herself against his face. He doubled his efforts, thrusting his fingers in deeper. He tongued her clit. She bucked her hips, moaning. When she arched her back, he knew she was close to coming.

Slipping his other hand over her ass, he sucked her clit. She gasped and then exploded. He repositioned his mouth, slipping his tongue as deeply inside her as he could get it. Her body shook. He sucked and lapped at her, eager not only to lick her climaxing pussy but to feel her coming.

While tremors still shook her body, he rose and kissed her.

She linked her arms around his neck and returned his kiss with a hunger that sent a rush of heat all through him. He reached between their bodies and gripped his cock. Now that he'd made sure she'd come, he had to thrust as deeply into her as possible.

She stiffened and pushed against his shoulders. "Randall! What are you doing?"

He muzzled her neck. "Isn't it obvious?" He rubbed his cock along her slit before pressing it against her entrance.

"No!"

He froze and stared down at her. Oh, damn if she turned out to be a tease, he was going to be hard pressed not to kiss and caress her until she changed her mind. "What the hell do you mean no?"

She stroked his shoulders. "Oh, don't look at me like that. I'm not backing out."

"Good because I'm not in any condition to allow you to say no now." He pushed her legs apart and thrust against her. The head of his cock lodged between her slippery outer lips.

"No!" She shoved at his shoulders. "Not without protection!"

"Not without…" For the first time he realized he wasn't wearing a condom. For one moment, he was tempted to thrust his hips forward and drive his bare cock deep inside the pussy he'd longed to ravish from the moment their gaze met and locked across the room. He might have actually done it if she hadn't pushed at his shoulders again.

"We have to use a condom, Randall."

Of course they had to use a condom. He took a deep breath and stepped away from her. He reached in his back pocket for his wallet with trembling hands. She took the condom from him. Instead of applying it, she knelt and ran her tongue along the underside of his cock.

He caught his breath and closed his eyes when he felt her soft lips closing around him. It would be beyond sweet to have her suck him to a climax. Maybe later. The first time she made him come, he wanted to be buried balls deep inside her.

He opened his eyes. Gripping her shoulders, he reached down and lifted her to her feet. "I need to be inside you."

She ran her tongue along her lips, a sultry smile spreading across her face. "And that's exactly where I want you to be." She tore the condom open.

He gritted his teeth, trying to conceal his impatience as she slipped the rubber over his shaft with an agonizing leisure.

Then she leaned against the wall, a smile on her soft, lush lips. "Come take what you need, my handsome Randall."

"Oh, baby, I've never needed or wanted any other woman as much as I do you now."

She smiled, cupping her breasts in her hands. "Prove it."

He lifted her right leg, moved against her and thrust his hips forward.

She gasped. "Oh. Yes. Yes. That's what I want. Give it to me. Give me every hard, wonderful inch, Randall."

He closed his eyes as his cock slid slowly into her. He kept pushing until he felt her pubic hair against his. Sweet Jesus, she was his at last.

Almost as if she had read his mind, she whispered against his lips. "At last." She slipped her arms down his body to cup his ass. "Randall. You're inside me at last."

He opened his eyes and found her gazing up at him, her lips parted. "I need to fuck you."

"Please do."

He released her leg and drew all but the head out of her. Then, sucking the tip of one breast between his lips, he slipped back inside her.

"Hmm. Yes."

Kissing his way across her beautiful, warm flesh, he nibbled at her other breast. Her vaginal muscles encased his cock in a moist, heated tunnel that sent incredible sensations through him. Sliding in and out of her felt so good he wanted it to last forever but his need to ejaculate was too powerful to resist.

Despite his efforts to prolong the joy of fucking her, he felt the build-up of heat and pressure at the base of his cock each time she tightened herself around him. "Don't," he pleaded. "You're going to make me come."

She laughed. "That's the idea, my handsome Randall." Grinding her hips around his, she squeezed her pussy around him before pressing the tip of a finger inside his ass.

A shock of delight rippled through him. He clutched her close, sucked her neck and came. The feel of her finger in his ass intensified and prolonged his orgasm until it was an exquisite pleasure. When it was over, he found himself leaning heavily against her, murmuring incoherently as he trembled in her arms.

He felt her lips moving against his hair. "It's all right," she whispered. "I have you, my handsome Randall."

Embarrassed, both by how quickly he'd come and how spent he felt after his climax, he straightened and pulled out of her arms. He eased his cock in his pants, slid up the zipper and then sank onto the floor.

Chapter Five

She sat beside him.

He could feel her looking at him.

He sighed. "I'm sorry."

"For what?"

She was going to make him spell it out. "I usually last a lot longer than that."

"Oh. That."

The clear amusement in her voice annoyed him. He clenched his jaw.

"No apology necessary. You satisfied me first. Besides, it's kind of flattering."

He glanced at her, still annoyed. "Flattering? What am I missing?"

She slipped her arm through his and smiled. "I like that you couldn't control yourself with me…as long as you don't make a habit of it."

About to assure her that it wouldn't happen again, he paused. Even after one of the most powerful climaxes he'd enjoyed in years, his craving for her had not abated. A knot of need still threatened to consume him. "I'll do my best."

"That's good enough for me." She leaned against his shoulder. "Does the use of a bed come with the invitation to spend the night with you or am I to be consigned to sleeping on the carpet now that you've had your wicked way with me?"

His remaining irritation evaporated. He turned to find her smiling at him. Damn, she looked sexy with her hair wild and that satisfied look in her eyes. "I've only had part of my wicked way with you." He caressed her cheek. "There are all manner of things I'd love to do with and to you."

She lowered her head. Her dark hair swung forward, concealing her face.

He lifted her chin, pushing her hair behind her ear. "Are you shy?"

"Not when I'm sure of the man I'm with."

He sighed at the uncertainty in her voice. "And you're not sure of me?"

"Actually, I am fairly sure of you."

He arched a brow. "Are you?"

She nodded. "I really enjoyed what we just shared and I hope you did too but—"

"I did. But?"

"But I'm not your type. I'm a realist enough to know what that means."

"Please feel free to share the wealth."

"That means what we're having is nice, brief fling."

He stifled a sigh of relief. Thank God Brandon had been wrong about her. He could sleep with her indefinitely without worrying about the possibility of her getting hurt as a result of unreasonably high expectations.

Nevertheless, while he'd never had a problem informing other lovers he had no interest in love or marriage, he was reluctant to admit the same to her. He caressed her cheek. "Is that what you want?"

"It's what's available, given your preference for petite, green-eyed, gorgeous blondes."

He decided it might not be wise to admit he wouldn't trade the coming night with her for a dozen with any other woman. He cupped a palm against her cheek. "You're the only woman I'm interested in talking about tonight."

She rubbed her cheek against his palm. "Smooth talk like that will get you everything you want."

"I meant that, Benai."

"Filthy rich, handsome, smooth and honest. How have you managed to avoid marriage?"

"It hasn't been easy. I've had to work very hard at it."

She laughed. "Take me to bed and tell me about your struggles to stay single."

He brushed his lips against hers. "I don't want to talk."

He felt her lips curve in a smile against his. "Then let's go do something else. But first I think I'm going to need a nap."

He groaned.

She laughed. "Just a short one."

He rose and lifted her to her feet. "A very short one."

She grinned. "I love a handsome, charming man who can't get enough of me."

"That about describes how I'm feeling."

Nice. Very nice.

* * * * *

Benai felt warm, insistent lips kissing hers. A big palm caressed her bare breasts. Two fingers slipped in and out of her pussy. She opened her eyes. She lay on her back in a bedroom lit only by moonlight. Randall lay on next to her on his side, naked like her.

She turned onto her side to face him. "What do you think you're doing?"

He smiled, sliding his fingers deep into her. "Waiting for you to awake up."

She shivered. "If you're waiting, what's that thrusting in and out of me?"

"Hey, don't blame me if you're so sweet my fingers have a mind of their own."

Ignoring the pleasurable sensations his fingers created, she reached down to ease his hand from between her legs. "Tell them to wait for permission."

"I did but, as I said, they have a mind of their own." He eased her on her back and settled between her legs. "So does he."

She could feel him pressed against one thigh. Her stomach muscles clenched. She wanted him between her legs and inside her. She ran her hands down his back to his taut ass. "What does he want?"

"He wants you to ride him," he whispered, rubbing his length against her thigh.

She shivered with anticipation. "Oh, he does, does he?"

He adjusted his body so he was pressed against her entrance. "Yes. He does."

She tossed her legs around his lower body and arched her back, pressing herself against him. "Tell him to put on his raincoat and maybe he'll get lucky."

He ground his groin against hers and pressed a long, moist kiss against her lips. She shifted her hips until she felt the tip of his shaft between her wet folds. She shuddered and clung to him. "Oh, Randall!"

He groaned and rolled away from her. He reached into the top drawer of the nightstand on his side of the bed before he crossed the room to sit in one of two Queen Ann chairs on either side of the balcony doors.

He sat with his legs parted, his cock, fully erect. "Come here," he ordered.

She slipped from the bed but took her time obeying. Standing by the bed, she tossed her head. As her hair cascaded around her face, she cupped her breasts and undulated her body slowly. She pinched her nipples and thrust her hips from side to side, licking her lips as she smiled at him.

He closed his hand around his shaft, pumping himself as he stared at her.

Watching him massage himself turned her on. "He's a very pretty boy, Randall."

"He's a lonely boy. Come sit on him to say hello. "

Eager to have him inside her again, she quickly crossed the room and knelt in front of him. He had a beautiful body with wide shoulders, a big chest, six-pack abs, long and muscular legs. She turned her attention to his shaft. It was deliciously thick and exquisitely hard with a big, helmeted head. Beneath it was a pair of big, heavy balls. She liked that they were separate rather than one big sac.

She sighed happily. He had the sexiest genitals she'd ever seen. But then everything about him was perfect. For the remainder of the night at least, he was hers. She cupped a hand under his nuts.

He parted his legs farther. "Taste me."

She bent to kiss his shaft. Parting her lips, she extended her tongue. She dragged her tongue along the underside of his shaft, savoring the taste and texture of him. He felt warm and smooth.

She liked the feel of his pubic hair against her face. She rubbed her cheek against it. The aroma of their juices heightened her passion. She kissed the big, moist head before turning her head and slowly drawing him between her lips. She flicked her tongue against the tiny hole at the top of his shaft.

"Yes," he encouraged.

She swirled her tongue around his length, loving how he felt against her tongue and lips.

His hands closed on her shoulders. "Honey, don't or you'll make me come too soon!"

She sat back on her heels and looked at him. "You can come whenever you like."

"No. Not again. This time I want you to come from intercourse." Taking a hand in his, he urged her to her feet. He slipped a hand down her body.

She parted her legs, giving him easy access to her pussy. He slipped a finger inside her. "You're warm and wet."

"And ready." She arched a brow. "Well…almost."

He gave her the condom.

She smiled. "Now he's ready to play."

"So what are you waiting for?"

She opened the condom and quickly slipped it over his shaft.

He took her hands in his. "Sit on me, baby, and ride me."

Eager to obey, she rose. Placing her hands on his shoulders, she tossed a leg over his. She bent her knees, preparing to sit down on him.

He gripped his hips. "Turn around," he said slowly.

"Around?"

"Sit with your back to me."

She hesitated. She wanted to face him so they could kiss.

"That'll allow me to caress your breasts and play with your clit."

She smiled and turned her back to him.

"Damn!"

With her rear half a foot or so from his lap, she froze. This was a fine time for him to decide he had a problem with her behind. "What's wrong?"

"Wrong? Nothing." He caressed her cheeks. "Oh, baby, you have a big, beautiful ass."

She glanced at him over her shoulder. "So that was a good damn?"

"Hell yes." He stroked a finger down her crack.

She bit her lip.

"An ass this big, round and beautiful was made for one purpose."

"Sitting on?"

"No. Fucking." He gently parted her cheeks before he pressed a finger against her tight hole. "Have you ever had anal sex?"

"Yes," she admitted, her breathing quickening.

"Do you enjoy it?"

"Yes."

"Really."

She shook her head at the excitement in his voice. "But I'm not interested in anal sex tonight. Tonight my pussy is greedy and wants your cock all to herself."

"Isn't she the selfish little one?"

"Are you complaining?"

"Hell no." He caressed her ass cheeks. "But sooner or later, I'm going to fuck your luscious ass."

"Sooner or later, I might let you."

"Damn you make me so hard and horny."

"Good because I like my men hard, hot and horny." Smiling, she reached between their legs to palm him. Placing him against her entrance, she lowered her hips. She eased the big head between her lips.

He sucked in a breath.

She reached her other hand down to fondle his balls before she closed her eyes and enjoyed the sweet sensation of his slick, hard length sliding up into her. Once seated on his lap with a pussy full of delicious cock, she sighed and licked her lips.

She leaned back against him. "Randall?"

He stroked her breasts. "Yes?"

"I love how having you deep inside me makes me feel so deliciously full."

He tweaked her nipples until they hardened. "Are you going to talk or are you going to give me that ride we talked about?"

She rotated her hips. Seated as she was on his lap, with her legs pressed tightly together, she felt every inch of him. Good, but now she wanted more and she wanted it immediately.

She lifted her hips until only the head of him pulsed inside her.

He kissed her neck and gripped her hips.

She smiled. "Patience, handsome."

"Maybe I'll be patient after we've done this a hundred times or so. Right now I want the ride you promised me." He jerked her hips down.

A ripple of delight washed over her as he powered his cock balls deep inside her.

She moaned, tossed her head back against him and furiously ground her ass on his lap.

He wrapped an arm around her waist and licked the side of her neck as he began to thrust in and out of her with an intensity that made her toes curl and her back arch.

Pleasure shot through her. The muscles in her stomach tightened as her vaginal muscles contracted around him. Lord, she loved his big, thick cock sliding in and out, in and out of her stuffed slit.

With his mouth open against her ear, he slid his hot palm down her breasts and belly to cup between her legs. He nipped at her ear, sliding the tip of his tongue along her lobe. "Sweet...hot...so good," he groaned and surged strongly into her—several times in rapid succession. Each time he pushed back into her, he rubbed his thumb against her clit. "You're so sweet."

A rush of bliss buffeted her body. Another and then another followed until she lost herself in a compelling sweet joy that totally encompassed all her senses. The physical pleasure meshed with an emotional one and she exploded, coming all over his cock.

Sliding his hands down to her hips, he held her still as he fucked her hard, deep and fast until he sucked on her neck and came inside her.

She collapsed against his damp chest, allowing her head to loll against his shoulder.

He cupped his palms over her breasts and kissed her ear. "God, you're so sweet."

Smiling, she took one of his hands from her breasts. She pressed it between her legs. "Feel the effect you have on me."

He withdrew his cock and slipped two fingers inside her flooded channel. "I'd rather taste it," he told her and licked his fingers. "Musky and strong, sweet, perfect. Just like you."

"Oh Randall." She rubbed her cheek against his shoulder. "You make me come with so little effort."

"Yeah?"

She smiled at the sound of masculine satisfaction in his deep voice. "Oh yeah. Believe it or not, I don't usually arouse this easily or come as hard as I did with you."

He brushed his lips against her cheek. "What do you attribute that to?"

"This big hard cock of yours and the exquisite skill with which you wield it to such wonderful effect." She reached between their legs and cupped his nuts. "Do you have a license for him?"

He laughed and squeezed her. "I've never met anyone half as exciting as you are. You're attractive, sweet, as sexy as hell and unashamed to admit you enjoy a good fuck. You really are perfect."

She suspected he was talking with his cock but she wallowed in his words anyway. She turned her head and licked his warm lips. "You know you make me feel so wanton and hungry for you."

He murmured softly in Cherokee before he slid his fingers in her hair and devoured her lips. Within minutes, she was wet and aroused again. As she returned his hot, drugging kisses, she suspected she would get little sleep that night. Hell, who wanted to sleep when a handsome hunk couldn't seem to keep his cock out of her for more than a few minutes at a time?

"Let's go back to bed," he suggested.

She nodded, eager to snuggle in his arms.

* * * * *

When Benai woke again, sunlight streamed into the room. She was alone in bed. She glanced at the bedside clock. A vase containing a dozen red roses sat behind the clock. Smiling, she sat up. There was no card nestled in the roses but she noticed a folded piece of notepaper on the adjacent pillow.

She picked it up.

I'm in the family room, which is next to the living room. Join me when you're ready. You'll find a new toothbrush and anything else you might want in the master bathroom.

Randall.

She slipped out of bed. Her overnight bag, her purse and the clothes he'd stripped off her the previous night were neatly folded on a chair by the patio doors. Thoughtful bugger.

She showered, dressed and left the bedroom, leaving the door open. As she descended the right staircase, she noted pictures of the Grayhawks adorned the adjacent wall.

At the top of the stairs, was a large watercolor of Malita Grayhawk, the family matriarch. Her shoulder-length hair was gray. Although she smiled, Benai noted a trace of sadness in her dark gaze.

Next to her was a picture of Layton with a laughing Lelia on his back. Near the bottom of the stairs was a picture of Peyton in the cockpit of a small plane. Beside it was a picture of a young Randall posing in a boxing ring with boxer's shorts and gloves on. She studied both pictures, uncertain how she knew which pictured Peyton and which pictured Randall. In the place of honor at the bottom of the staircase, was a picture of Lelia, smiling into the camera. She was astride a huge horse with her long, dark hair hanging around her shoulders under a dark cowgirl hat. She looked happy and beautiful. Why wouldn't she be with eight older, adoring brothers each eager to ensure she wanted for nothing?

"Lucky girl." She smiled. Of course after her night with Randall, she felt pretty lucky herself. Hearing the strains of guitar music, Benai walked down the hall.

Just before she reached the second open door, the housekeeper a pretty, middle-aged blonde, exited the room. She smiled at Benai. "Good morning."

Benai returned her smile. "Good morning."

She looked into the room. Randall and Peyton sat on two stools facing each other, each playing a guitar. Peyton was singing in a warm, deep baritone voice. The words sent a tingle of expectation through Benai.

"The right time. The right place…"

And then Randall sang. *"Timber. I'm—"*

As if he were suddenly aware of her presence, he stopped and looked up. Their gazes met and locked—such as they had done in the restaurant at the rehearsal dinner.

Go ahead, Randall. Finish. Sing it while you look at me. Even though you don't mean it…will probably never mean it with me.

"Falling in love," Peyton finished.

Randall put his guitar aside and rose. Smiling, he crossed the room. He bent and kissed her lips. "'Morning."

She resisted the urge to wrap her arms around him and kiss him breathless. "Good morning." She smiled and stepped around him. Rather to her surprise, she felt no shame as she faced Peyton, who rose to meet her. "Good morning, Peyton."

Peyton slipped an arm around her waist and bent to kiss her cheek. "You are a sight for sore eyes."

She grinned. "You know how to make a gal feel welcome."

He laughed and kissed her, this time on the corner of her mouth.

Randall pulled him away from her. "All right, Peyton, that's enough of that. If you're feeling lonely or needy, go find your own woman."

Peyton turned to face Randall. "Why? Is this luscious one taken?"

Benai watched closely as the two brothers stared at each other. She could almost feel Peyton trying to will Randall to say she was taken by him. There wasn't a chance in hell of Randall making any such admission.

Randall turned to look at her. "Are you interested in Peyton?"

She shrugged. "Well...he is handsome and charming and knows a good thing when he sees it. All three qualities make a man difficult, if not impossible, to resist."

Peyton grinned.

Randall frowned. "Impossible to resist?"

She nodded. "He's such a handsome devil too."

Randall turned back to Peyton. "Take your handsome, charming ass out of here and get your own woman."

Peyton's grin widened. "It seems my jealous older brother doesn't want any competition. I can't say I blame him. If you were mine, I wouldn't want any either."

He paused.

They both waited for Randall to respond. When he didn't, Peyton tipped up her chin and spoke in a pseudo whisper. "I'm going but if he doesn't come up to scratch and you want to try the more refined model, call me. Although he's far richer than I'll ever be, I'm far more charming, far more handsome, unafraid of commitment—eager, in fact, for it. I'm free of romantic entanglements and—"

"Now that you've gone out of your way to be so damned supportive, get the hell out of here, Peyton!" Randall said.

"Open your eyes and see what's before you, Randy, and you'll have all the support you've ever wanted or needed. Not just from me." He looked at Benai. "From another, far more pleasing source."

Benai's cheeks burned.

Peyton kissed her on the corner of her mouth again. "Bear with him, Benai. He'll be worth the effort."

She placed a hand on his arm. "I don't think I can wait."

"Try. Please."

Then, just as Randall clamped a hand on his arm, Peyton crossed the room, picked up his guitar and left.

The moment Peyton closed the door behind himself, Randall slipped an arm around her waist, drawing her close. He didn't kiss her. He stared down at her in silence.

She placed her hands on his chest, smiling up at him.

"Do you really prefer Peyton?"

She frowned. "What kind of question is that?"

"One I need an answer to."

"Why should I?"

"Because if you do, I'll have to kill his ass."

Realizing he was joking, she laughed. "Don't be ridiculous. He's totally devoted to you."

"That won't save him if he's trying to take you."

She knew that was as close as he was prepared to come to admitting any real interest in her. How could a man with so much to offer be so unsure of himself? She slipped the fingers of her right hand through his hair. "He doesn't want me any more than I want him."

"So you don't prefer him?"

"Of course I don't. Like you, I was teasing." She caressed his neck. "You can take a joke. Can't you?"

He rubbed his thumb against her bottom lip. "Not as well as I thought." He slipped his other arm around her and licked her lips. "You are so sweet."

"Yeah? Are you going to talk about how sweet I am or are you going to actually kiss me?"

He whispered something in Cherokee before he pressed a long, slow kiss against her lips.

She linked her other arm around his neck. Leaning into him, she moved her hips against him, parting her lips.

Cupping her ass in his hands, he swept his tongue into her mouth.

She welcomed it, loving the taste of his mouth and tongue and the feel of his cock slowly hardening against her.

He kissed her with a hunger that sent liquid heat sizzling through her. She shivered and thrust her lower body against his.

He responded by lifting her off her feet.

She leaned her cheek against his shoulder, inhaling the scent of his cologne as he carried her across the room to the loveseat. He sat with her in his arms and buried his face against her neck. He whispered to her in Cherokee.

She stroked her fingers through his hair before she cupped her hands around his face and lifted his head. "What are you saying?"

He blinked at her. "What? When?"

"Just now. You were speaking to me in Cherokee again. What were you saying?"

He brushed the back of his hand against her cheek. "Peyton had it right."

"He did?" She moistened her lips. Was he about to admit he wanted her to be his woman?

"You are luscious."

"Oh. That." She forced a smile. "I hear that all the time."

He nodded. "I'm sure you do but that doesn't make it any less true."

She smiled. "That a man as handsome as you are should think I'm luscious is quite a compliment, Randall."

He rubbed the palm of one hand over her breasts. "I'm not the only one who thinks you're luscious."

"Peyton only said it to be gallant."

"Bancroft thinks so too."

She shook her head. "The less said about him the better."

"Benai, he's—"

"I don't mean any disrespect, Randall. I just don't want to talk about him."

"Understood."

She smiled. "Any chance of getting breakfast?"

"It's on the terrace."

She rose. "Then let's eat."

He stood up and led her out onto the terrace. He seated her at a table with a sun umbrella and then walked over to a large, wheeled food warmer. "What would you like?"

"Hmm. Eggs and sausage and wheat toast if you have it." She rose. "I can get it myself."

He shook his head. "No."

"Why not?"

"You're my special guest, Benai. It's my pleasure to wait on you. Please sit."

She resumed her seat and smiled at him when he set a tray on the table. He put her plate, a glass with ice, two carafes and several containers in front of her. "It smells great. Thanks."

He sat across from her. "My pleasure."

She tasted a mouthful of the most delicious egg whites. "These practically melt in your mouth."

"I'm glad you like it." He poured her a cup of orange juice. "Can I get you anything else?"

"No. Thank you. Aren't you eating?"

"I'm used to rising and eating early. I hope you don't mind that Peyton and I shared breakfast."

"Of course not. I'm sure you two had a lot to talk about. You certainly know how to treat a guest."

He smiled. "My mother taught her sons to respect and cherish women."

"She must have been a remarkable woman."

He nodded. "She was incredible."

"So, Randall, tell me how have you managed to stay single cherishing every woman you meet?"

He shook his head and sat back in his seat. "I cherish very few of the women I meet but I do endeavor to respect each woman. As for marriage…I have no interest in it."

She paused with her coffee cup halfway to her lips. "What do you mean you have no interest in it?"

"I mean just what I said."

"You don't ever want to get married?"

"No."

She sipped from her cup. "What happens when you fall in love?"

"I don't intend to fall in love."

She set her cup down. "That doesn't mean it won't happen. What have you got against love and marriage?"

"Marriage won't work or last until the two people involved are deeply in love and wholly committed to each other. Sometimes it doesn't last even then. As for love…" He took a deep breath. "That hurts and destroys. As it did my mother. As it's almost done to Brandon. As it's done with Peyton."

She stared at him. "Yes, love can hurt but it can also bring joy and intense happiness, Randall."

"So I've heard but what I've actually seen is the destruction and endless heartache it causes. Since I have no intention of entrusting my heart and happiness to any one ever again, there would be no point in getting married."

"So you have been in love?"

He shrugged. "Once."

"Only once? That's quite a feat for a man your age."

"I told you, I've worked hard at staying single and keeping a firm grip on my heart and emotions."

And if that wasn't a very strong hint for her not to fall in love or expect anything meaningful from him, she'd never heard one. "So you did. Who was this lucky woman you were once in love with?"

She watched the muscles in his jaw clench. "I fell for a woman who taught me a bitter lesson about guarding my heart and emotions."

The resentment in his voice indicated he'd been badly hurt. "What happened?"

"I'd rather not talk about her."

"So? Is that supposed to dissuade me from asking questions?"

"Yes. It is."

"Well it doesn't. If I remember correctly, I stated a preference for not getting up on your big beast of a horse but ended up there anyway because you had a different preference. So what happened?"

"Okay." He sighed. "We had just graduated from college. She led me to believe she intended to marry me. I was so in love with her I thought my need for her would consume me."

"She didn't love you?"

"I think she did."

"Then what happened?"

"I think she just loved money more. After graduation, all I had was my degree. We both knew I had potential but she was too impatient to wait for it to be realized. She met an older man who was already where I wanted to be and left me for him." He raked a hand through his hair. "She ripped my heart into so many small pieces, I never found them all."

"You still love her. Don't you?"

He shrugged.

She sighed. "I suppose she was a tiny blonde?"

He nodded. "Very tiny, very blonde, very greedy and very impatient. Everything about her was very—except her ability to be faithful."

"And you still love her?"

"What makes you think that?"

"Why else would you still sound so bruised and injured after all this time?"

"Maybe because the little gold-digging bitch battered the hell out of my heart."

She reached across the table to touch his clenched fist. "Oh Randall."

He met her gaze. "But that doesn't mean I'm still in love with her."

She feared that's exactly what his lingering hurt meant. "Have you seen her since?"

"Yes."

"Well? Details. I want details, Randall."

"I don't want to talk about her."

"And I do. You're going to tell me everything that happened between you two, Randall. Now or later. Why not do it now and get it over with?"

"Talking about her just pisses me off. Why is this conversation necessary?"

"I have no desire to piss you off but is it so wrong for me to want to know everything that makes you who you are?"

"No," he admitted. "I actually like that you want to know but—"

"Then tell me what happened."

"Okay. Six months after she married him, she showed up at my door in the middle of the night—naked under a long mink coat."

She nodded. "It didn't take her long to discover that she loved you more than the money after all?"

He shook his head. "No. She'd just realized she wanted it all—his money and my body. Apparently he was a huge disappointment in bed."

"You mean she wanted you to be her lover?"

"Actually, she wanted to pay me to be her boy toy."

She paused and moistened her lips before she spoke again. "Were you tempted?"

"I'd like to pretend I was a much better person than her and wasn't in the least tempted." He sighed and raked a hand through his hair, his lips tightening. "The money didn't tempt me but I was tempted to become her lover again."

She stirred her coffee before she asked a question she wasn't sure she wanted an honest answer to. "How tempted?"

"Not tempted enough to forget the devastation an adulterous relationship can have on the injured spouse. It took me longer than it should but I never succumbed and I finally sent her on her way."

"And since then?"

He shrugged. "She usually turns up like a damned bad penny from time to time trying to tempt me into her bed."

"Has it ever worked?"

"No. I don't cheat."

"But are you still tempted?"

"I've never slept with her since we broke up."

So he wasn't going to admit the temptation to sleep with her was ongoing, which probably meant he still loved her. Great. "I'm surprised she didn't divorce him once she realized how well you've done."

"She is divorced."

"Since?"

He shrugged. "About five years."

"What's her name?"

"Pam."

"Did you want to rekindle your relationship after her divorce?"

He inclined his head slightly.

Oh, hell. Just great. "Then why haven't you?"

"What would have been the point? I'll never trust my heart to her or anyone else again."

"Well isn't that just dandy? She hurt you and every other woman gets to atone for her mistake?"

He narrowed his gaze. "I haven't asked anyone to atone for anything, Benai."

"You think not? Because she hurt you...what? Sixteen or seventeen years ago, I'll never have a shot at winning that battered and bruised heart of yours?" She smiled. "I'd treat it with tender, loving care, Randall."

He sucked in a breath. "I wouldn't make a very good... Despite the money, I'm not that great a bargain."

"Even if you were poor, you'd attract countless women. And who says you're not a great bargain?"

"I'm a realist, Benai. What you see is what I have to offer."

If that wasn't a take-me-as-I-am-or-leave-me-spiel, she'd never heard one. "I see."

"I hope so because I'm bored with talking about me. Let's talk about a far more interesting subject—you. Have you ever been married or in love?"

She took a forkful of eggs and sausage, chewed and swallowed before she spoke. "I've never been married."

"Why not? You must have had plenty of men who wanted to marry you."

She saw his sincerity in his gaze and smiled. "Not as many as you might think."

"But you have been in love?"

"Yes." She picked up her fork and began eating.

"Are you going to tell me about him?"

She swallowed and put down her fork. "Like you and your blonde, Bill and I were college sweethearts. We met in our sophomore year but didn't become an item until our junior year when I fell head over heels in love with him."

"How did he feel?"

"He felt the same way. We talked about marriage but decided we should wait a few years after graduation to give ourselves time to get to know other people." She grimaced. "Of course I never actually thought either of us would be tempted. A few months after graduation, he fell in love with someone else and moved to the West Coast to be near her."

Randall's eyes narrowed. "He hurt you?"

"Not intentionally, but I think I spent the first few months afterward crying every time someone spoke to me." She shrugged. "But I got over it and it didn't turn me against love or him."

He arched a brow. "He hurt you and you don't hate him?"

"There's something magical about really falling in love for the first time. How can you hate your first true love? Do you hate Pam?"

"I…well…I don't like or admire her but I'm not sure I hate her."

"And I don't hate Bill. Besides, he was always honest with me. When he knew he was falling out of love with me, he told me. He didn't start seeing her until after he'd ended our relationship. Although I was hurt, he behaved in an honorable manner. And as a matter of fact, she and I have since become friends."

"Friends? With the woman who took the man you loved from you?"

"There was no point in being angry and bitter. That was only going to hurt me. They were getting on with their lives so I made up my mind to do the same."

"What was she like?"

She smiled. "She wasn't a gold-digging bitch."

He laughed.

"Three years after their wedding when he was in town on business, he called me. We spent the day and evening together looking at pictures of his wife and twin boys. When he invited me to the west coast, I went and she and I became friends over the years. She's a warm, friendly, pretty woman.

"Bill later told me that they met at a job fair. She asked a question. He turned to look at her, their eyes met…and it was 'goodbye that's all she wrote'. He said he fell so hard for her he felt as if he couldn't breathe. It was almost as if…" She shrugged. "I'm not sure how to describe it any better."

"As if his entire world was turned upside down and nothing would ever be the same?"

The softly voiced question surprised her. "Is that how you felt the first time you met Pam?"

"No. I've only ever felt like that once in my life."

"And it wasn't with her?"

"No."

So there was another woman out there who had rocked his world? Lovely.

"Have you fallen in love with any other man besides this Bill?"

"I've lusted after a number of men." She grinned and licked her lips.

He smiled. "But no cigar?"

"Nope. I've never really fallen in love again but I'd like to."

"Why would you want to fall in love when you have first-hand knowledge of how much it can hurt?"

"Because I not only believe in love and marriage, I'm looking forward to experiencing them both."

He shook his head. "I can't imagine why."

She shrugged. Clearly they would never agree on either subject. "Speaking of charming, Peyton arrived bright and early."

"We were supposed to go riding but as you might remember, I got sidetracked with you."

She finished her coffee before she spoke. "Well, you can tell him it won't last."

He frowned. "What's that supposed to mean?"

"It means I won't be taking up all your weekends. In no time at all, you'll be chasing some tiny, gorgeous blonde and be available to go horseback riding with him whenever you like."

"Would you like to go riding with me today?"

"No. Thanks."

"You didn't enjoy it?"

"It wasn't as awful as I expected it to be but I don't know if it will ever become a favorite pastime."

"Pity. What would you like to do today?"

"I think I'll have a lazy day at home."

He reached across the table and took her hand in his. "Oh, no. We're spending the day together. If you're feeling tired, we can just spend the day out at the pool."

"Wouldn't you rather—"

"I usually say exactly what I mean."

She arched a brow and smiled. "Oh you do, do you?"

He flashed her a brief smile. "I did say usually."

"So you did."

"Yes I did and if I wanted to do anything other than spend the day with you, I'd say so."

"Very charmingly put, Randall, but—"

He rose and walked around the table. He lifted her to her feet. "Why does there need to be a but?"

She lowered her gaze to his chin. "If we spend too much time together, things could get messy between us."

He tipped up her chin. "We'll be careful not to allow that to happen."

She stepped away from him. "That might not be so easy for me after last night."

He caught her hand and held it against his chest. "I didn't defy Bancroft because I want to hurt you."

"I'm not saying that you do or even that you will."

He lifted her hand from his chest and kissed it. "Then what are you saying?"

"I'm just saying that we should quit while I'm ahead." She sighed. "I don't want to really fall for you."

He caressed her cheek. "Why not?"

She blinked. "Why not? How can you expect me to feel any other way after what you've just told me?"

"I was honest with you."

"I know and I appreciate that."

"You should also know that I don't stray when I'm in a relationship and I'm long past the stage where I'm interested in sleeping with more than one woman at a time. For here and now, I can't think of a single other woman I'd rather be with."

"Not even Pam?"

Chapter Six

Ꮽ

"Especially not Pam."

She studied his face. He didn't need to lie to get her into bed again so he was probably sincere.

"Would falling for me be such a bad thing?"

"Nothing good can come of that for me, Randall."

"I know Peyton is far more charming and Brandon is—"

She pressed her fingers against his lips. "I don't think any of your amazing brothers are capable of overshadowing you in any way."

He kissed her fingers before drawing his head back. "Then?"

"You've been running away from the very things I want and need in a relationship. I enjoyed last night but I don't want a series of one-night stands with you."

"One-night stands implies all I want is sex."

"But that is all you want."

He shook his head, his lips tightening. "You think I risked my relationship with Bancroft for a series of one-night stands?"

She held up her hands, palms out, shaking her head. "Wait a minute, Randall. There's nothing to risk. Bancroft has no claim on me."

"He thinks he does."

"I'm trying to be understanding, Randall, but I've already told you I have no romantic interest in him."

"Benai—"

"Look. I know you think a lot of him. I know he's a great guy. I don't mean to sound… It's just that I'm a little weary of your belief that he has some claim on me when he doesn't. I'm free to see whoever I like."

"I'm aware of that—"

"Are you?"

"Yes, Benai, I am but he's not himself and—"

"I know and I don't mean to sound like a bitch." She sighed. "Last night was great and I don't regret it but it's time to face reality. If you think seeing me is such a risk to your relationship with Bancroft, let's end this now and he won't have any real or imagined basis for feeling betrayed."

"That's what I should do."

"Fine. Let's do it." She turned away, hurt at how easily he'd agreed with her.

He caught her hand and turned her back to face him. "I don't want to end it."

She caressed his cheek. "I think it's time you stopped thinking with your third leg, Randall."

He stepped away from her. "You think this is all about sex?"

"Frankly, Randall, yes I do. It's about sex for both of us. You're determined not to fall in love with me, you're not interested in marriage and I sure as hell don't want to fall for you. The only thing we have in common is sex. The sex between us is great but I don't think it's worth risking your relationship with Bancroft nor is it worth risking my heart."

"It's not just sex."

"Then what is it? What's driving you, Randall?"

"What's driving you?"

"Sex."

His nostrils flared. "Then Peyton would do as well?"

She sighed. "Okay, so maybe it's a little more than just sex. And no, he won't do just as well."

He put his arms around her. "Then stay. While we're seeing each other, I won't stray or give you any reason to doubt my fidelity. I'll do my best never to hurt you. Stay with me, Benai."

"Randall—"

"Let's just take this slowly and see where it leads us. Stay, even if it's only for a few hours."

That was the last thing she should do. Rational thought didn't come easily when they were together. She closed her eyes and lifted her chin. When he kissed her, she prayed that her heart wouldn't be broken for a second time.

He whispered against her lips.

"In English, Randall."

"Trust me."

She trusted him with her body. Should she trust him with her heart?

He took her hand. "Let's spend the day by the pool."

She nodded. "Okay but when I leave, it needs to end, Randall."

Even as he nodded, the look in his eyes assured her he was only humoring her. He was no doubt used to having his way and her insistence on leaving probably only made him determined to have her stay.

They went back to his bedroom. She picked up her overnight case and moved to the bathroom.

"Where are you going?"

She turned at the door. "To change."

"You're kidding. Right?"

"Kidding?"

"Yes. Kidding. Have you got anything under your clothes I haven't seen, touched, or kissed?" He kicked off his shoes and unbuttoned his shirt. "If you have, I plan to rectify the omission as soon as possible."

He was right. It was ridiculous to leave the room to change after having spent the previous night with him. "Point taken." She leaned against the door and gestured. "Don't let me keep you so overdressed."

He grinned and unzipped his pants. He kicked them off. His briefs followed.

When he straightened, she licked her lips and stared at him. "Do you have any idea how beautiful you are?"

"Beautiful?" He laughed and walked across the room to his dresser drawer. "Hardly." He slipped on a pair of swimming trunks before he turned to face her. "Now it's your turn."

"Okay. Handsome. Do you have any idea how handsome you are?"

"I'm glad you think so. Now stop stalling and undress for me."

She kicked off her strapless sandals and quickly pulled her sweatshirt over her head, revealing her mauve bra that showcased her ample cleavage. She allowed him a brief look before she bent to remove her sweat bottoms. Her thong, little more than a mauve strip left most of her pubic hair on display.

She removed the band from her hair and shook her head. She trailed a finger along the thin strip barely covering her clit. "So?"

His nostrils flared as he quickly crossed the room. He slipped a finger inside her thong and inside her slit.

She gasped.

He bent his head and kissed her, pressing his tongue between her parted lips. As he did, he reached behind her to unhook her bra. Tossing her bra aside, he slipped his hands inside her thong and pushed it over her hips.

Dragging his lips from hers, he pushed the thong down her thighs to her ankles.

Placing a hand on his shoulder, she lifted her right leg and then her left so he could remove her thong. He rose and embraced her, rubbing his groin against her pubic hair.

She trembled in his arms. "Didn't you say something about swimming?"

"I need to fuck you," he whispered against her ear.

She slipped a hand between their bodies and into his trunks. She closed her fingers around his warm, hardening flesh. "What do you know? I need you to fuck me."

He lifted his head and stared down at her. "Need or want?"

She gently massaged him. "Need." She eased his cock out of his trunks, gripped his hips and staring up into his eyes, she slowly rotated herself against his cock. "I need this buried as deep inside me as you can thrust it."

"You make me so hard."

She drew her hips back and rubbed the head of his shaft along her slit. "Feel how wet you make me."

He shuddered and stepped away from her. "Put on your bathing suit so we can go out to the pool and fuck."

Her nipples hard and taut, her pussy slick and aching, she clumsily pulled on her cream-colored bikini.

He retrieved a beach bag from his closet.

She shivered as she watched him stuff condoms, various tubes and a medium-size butt plug inside the bag before he looked at her. "Ready?"

She nodded and followed him out of the bedroom.

Fifteen minutes later, she lay on her back on an oversize custom-made float with a retractable sunshield and recesses on both sides to hold various items. Randall, having removed her bikini and kicked off his swimming briefs lay between her legs, sucking her breasts and finger fucking her.

Minutes later, her pussy was dripping wet and she was within a breath of coming all over his fingers.

Her hips jerked upward. "I'm almost there," she moaned.

He lifted his lips from her breasts and removed his fingers from her.

"Don't stop," she protested as he rose onto his knees, still between her legs.

"Patience," he said.

She opened her eyes to see him reaching in one of the recesses for a condom.

He handed it to her.

She took it and sat up. She opened it and slowly rolled it over his stiff, long shaft. Then she lay back on her back with her legs spread in a shameless invitation. "Fuck me," she whispered.

"In a moment." He reached into the recess again. When he settled between her legs, he held a tube and the butt plug in one hand. He stroked her bare cheeks with the other hand. "You have a beautiful ass."

She bit her lips, eyeing his fully erect cock. "I don't think I'm ready to have that up my ass, Randall."

"Okay. Let's just take the first step today."

She hesitated before she finally nodded.

He gave her a quick smile.

She watched in silence as he laid the ebony-colored plug aside and poured lube onto his right index and middle fingers.

"Lift that lovely ass up for me."

She rotated her hips slowly before lifting her ass a few inches off the float.

He pressed his finger firmly against her rear until he was able to slide it into her tight hole and up into her ass.

She moaned in response.

He paused. "Are you okay?"

She nodded. "Hmmm. Yes."

Slipping the fingers of his other hand back into her slit, he gently finger fucked both openings.

"Oh...Randall..." She bit her lip. "That feels good. I like having your fingers in my ass and pussy at the same time."

He smiled at her and slipped his middle finger into her ass. "Still all right?"

It had been a long time since she'd had anything in her rear. Her ass felt stretched over his fingers but she nodded.

Rubbing his thumb over her clit, he eased his fingers in and out of her ass.

She closed her eyes and moaned with pleasure. "Oh, yes, my handsome Randall. Oh, yes."

"I think you're ready to be fucked."

"Yes."

"But first, let's insert the butt plug."

She opened her eyes and waited impatiently as he lubed up the plug. To her surprise, he handed it to her.

"I want to watch you put it inside your ass," he told her. "Then while it's in place, I'm going to thrust my cock up inside your tight, sweet pussy and then I'm going to fuck you until you forget your name." He grinned at her. "But not mine."

She licked her lips and gave him a licentious grin as she pressed the plug against her hole. It slid inside relatively easily.

He pushed her hips down onto the float and sprawled between her legs with his cock resting against her entrance. "Let's fuck."

She looked down her body. The sight of him ready to plunge into her sent a fresh surge of moisture into her. She reached down to hold his hips. "Yes. Let's." She pushed her hips off the float.

His length slid several inches inside her.

She closed her eyes, moaning softly as he quickly drove his entire shaft balls deep into her. With her ass plugged and her pussy full of hard, hot cock, she was in heaven. "Oh...yes...yes."

He settled his body against her, his lips brushing her ear. "Now you're mine again."

She slid her hands down his body to ass. "All yours, my handsome lover. Now fuck me like you own me and my pussy."

He lifted his head and drew all but the thick head of his shaft out of her. "Look at me."

She opened her eyes.

His eyes blazed down at her. "I have news for you, sweetheart." He thrust his hips down, quickly sliding back inside her. "This pussy is all mine."

"All yours," she gasped. She crossed her legs over his thighs and rubbed herself against him.

He crushed her breasts under his chest. Sliding his lips over hers, he swept his tongue between her lips and fucked her with short, hard strokes.

Each time he bottomed out in her, the plug was driven into her ass. Having both openings filled as they fucked enhanced her pleasure. She dug her fingers into his ass, greedily returning his kisses. She sucked on his tongue. A spark of pleasure built in her belly. He drove it quickly down to her pussy, where it caught fire.

Plunging his cock in and out of her with a heat and depth that pushed her to the edge of orgasm, he suddenly rolled them onto their sides. His hand brushed against her ass.

She gasped and shuddered with a delicious delight as the butt plug started to vibrate in her ass. Sliding his hand over the plug to keep it buried inside her, he sucked the side of her neck. He thrust deep and hard into her until the world around her tilted and blew apart, sending her into a powerful climax that had her sobbing as hot flames of lust incinerated her ability to think. But she felt the fire roaring in her. It consumed her when he removed the plug from her ass.

He rolled her onto her back again and plunged in and out of her climaxing pussy until he groaned and clutched her tightly. He whispered to her in Cherokee as he came.

"Oh, Randall. I wish I knew what you were saying," she whispered as her legs fell away from his body. She sank against the float.

"Are you all right?"

"I've never been better."

He buried his face against her neck, collapsing on top of her.

Though all her lovers had satisfied her physically, none had touched her emotions so deeply since Bill so many years earlier. In college, Bill had been young and inexperienced, Randall was older and knew how to make the best use of the satisfying length and girth of his cock in ways Bill had not.

His sweet, relentless fuck had conquered her body and emotions in a way that both frightened and excited her.

She drifted to sleep whispering his name with his cock still inside her.

* * * * *

When Benai woke again, she was pleased to find Randall lying on the float facing her. A large towel covered their naked bodies.

He stroked her shoulder. "Are you awake?"

She stretched. "Yes. I'm also starving."

He tipped up her chin and kissed her.

She shivered at the passion she tasted in his lips. She drew away after several kisses. "Surely you've had enough."

He pushed the towel aside. "You have such a lovely body." He caressed her breasts. "Have I told you how beautiful your breasts are?"

She lifted his hand away from her breasts. "We've made love several times in less than a day. Isn't that enough?"

He eased her on her back and stretched out on top of her. "Does this feel like I've had enough?"

She pushed against his shoulders. "Has anyone ever told you how oversexed you are?"

"You can tell me. After we make love again."

"Randall, we can't spend the whole day having sex."

"Why not?"

"Because it's getting late, I'm starving and I need to get home."

He rubbed his groin against her.

Even flaccid, the feel of his cock excited her. She turned her head so that his lips brushed against her cheek instead of her mouth. "This has been very nice, Randall, but I'm not going to spend the rest of the day having sex with you."

He nibbled at her ear. "Why not?"

She pushed against his shoulders. "I need you to stop while I can still walk away from you without getting stung."

He rolled off her to lie on his stomach with his face turned away from her.

She sat up. Thankful for the sunshield over the float, she quickly pulled on her bikini. She raked her fingers through her hair and then quickly braided it. Satisfied she'd done as much with her hair as she could without a comb and brush, she leaned over him. "Are you sulking?"

He turned on to his back. "No. I was trying to decide what I could say or do to change your mind."

Despite the inclination to allow her gaze to rest below his waist, she kept her eyes trained on his face. "Nothing. I'm not having sex with you again, Randall."

He sat up. "Okay. If I promise not to try to get you into bed again, will you spend the night with me?"

"I need to get home and prepare for work tomorrow."

"I'll drive you home tomorrow morning in plenty of time to get ready for work and I promise I won't attempt to cajole you into making love again."

"Randall—"

"I promise, Benai, I won't make any effort to change your mind about sex. I just want to spend the rest of the day and night with you."

She met his gaze and sighed. Why was she such a pushover for him? "Okay but if you don't keep your—"

He shook his head. "I will keep it."

"Okay. So after I shower and change how are we spending the rest of the day?"

He pulled on his trunks. "However you like."

"Feed me."

"Of course."

After a brief lunch he drove her around the property. She was surprised to learn the two guest houses had four bedrooms and three baths each. They were half a mile from the mansion. There was also a stable and staff bungalows on the grounds.

"As you know, I have eight siblings. I want them to feel as if they're always welcome, even when I want the house to myself." He stopped the SUV and turned to look at her. "What about you, Benai? Do you have any siblings? What about your parents? Are they alive?"

She turned a mock frown on him. "Didn't you hear anything I said about myself?"

He grinned, shaking his head. "At the time I had other things on my mind but you have my full attention now. Tell me about yourself."

"I have an older brother, Reed, who lives in Colorado with his wife of thirteen years and their two adorable sons, John and Ray. My parents retired to California five years ago. They've been married for forty-two years. What amazes me each time I visit is getting up in the morning and finding them sitting on their patio just gazing into each other's eyes. After all their years together my dad looks at my mom as if she's the most beautiful woman he's ever seen. I just know they'll love each other forever."

She sighed. "That's what I want, Randall. A love that will last forever."

"That's a tall order, Benai. I don't know of anyone who's been married for more than five or ten years."

"Well, I do. There's my parents and my brother and two uncles who've been happily married for over thirty years. There are more examples in my extended family."

"You must have an exceptional family."

"Maybe so but I know people can fall in love and stay in love. There must be someone in your family who's been married for longer than ten years."

"Married for longer than ten years? Yes. But happily married? No." He shook his head. "My parents were married for far longer than that but you couldn't call it a happy marriage by any stretch of the imagination. My father started cheating five years into the marriage and I don't think he ever stopped."

"Why didn't your mother divorce him?"

He narrowed his gaze. "Because she *loved* him. A fat lot of good that love did her. That undying love drove her into an early grave."

She heard the bitterness in his voice and saw the pain and anger in his gaze. There was definitely no future for her with him. She brushed her fingers against his cheek. "I'm sorry you don't believe in romantic love, Randall."

"I didn't say I don't believe in romantic love. I do. I know how powerful a force it can be. What I'm saying is that when it ends—and it always does—whatever so-called joy you experienced while in love isn't worth the pain and heartache when it ends."

"I happen to disagree, which is why you and I would be better served not trying to extend this fling past the weekend."

He turned and started the SUV. He drove back to the mansion in silence. In the family room, he offered her a drink.

She accepted.

He poured her a martini before sitting beside her on a loveseat. "I need to talk to you."

She sipped her drink. "Go ahead."

"I know we want different things in a relationship and I can understand why you think that's reason enough for us not to go on seeing each other."

She turned to face him. "But?"

"But where's the harm? Neither of us is seeing anyone else at the moment."

She sipped her drink again before putting it on the end table. "Knowing how you feel, I'd be a first-class fool to attempt an exclusive relationship with you."

"I didn't say it had to be exclusive—on your part."

She frowned. "What?"

"I won't see anyone else but you're free to see whoever you like."

"Are you telling me that would work for you?"

"Yes."

"You're saying yes but your eyes are shouting *no*, Randall."

He shrugged. "It's definitely not my usual style but I want to go on seeing you."

"Why?"

He shook his head. "I have no idea. I just do."

"I can see it in your eyes that arrangement wouldn't work for you. And I can see it leaving you with an even worse impression of romantic love. I wouldn't want that."

"My feelings about romantic love are already formed and I'm a big boy. I can handle your seeing other men as long as you don't flaunt it. And if things get serious with someone else, just be honest with me and I'll…"

"What? Wish me well?"

His jaw muscles clenched several times before he nodded. "Yes."

Right, when pigs flew. "I'll have to think about it, Randall."

"Fair enough."

To her surprise, he didn't mention their seeing each other beyond that weekend. They shared an intimate dinner in the small dining room, watched the end of a baseball game and went upstairs to prepare for bed.

In his bedroom, he stripped and got in bed. He laughed when she picked up her overnight bag and headed toward the bathroom.

"Oh, come on, Benai. I thought we'd already agreed it was silly for you not to change in front of me."

"We did but I want to freshen up so wipe that smirk off your face."

He laughed again.

She ignored him and went into the master bathroom. When she returned to the bedroom wearing a white lace thong set, he bolted into a sitting position.

"Damn, Benai, you look lovely in white lacy things."

The look in his eyes made her feel beautiful. She paused at the foot of the bed and smiled. "You like?"

"Oh hell, yeah!" He whistled. "Now take them off."

"You promised, Randall."

"I promised I wouldn't try to make love to you. I didn't say I wouldn't ask you to sleep nude. I'll keep my word. Take off your underwear and let me enjoy your beautiful body."

She saw desire reflected in his gaze, along with a promise she trusted. Kicking off her slippers, she slowly removed her bra. She laid it across the end of the bed before she removed her thong.

He stared at her in silence for several moments before he tossed the cover back.

To her relief, she saw that he wasn't aroused. She slipped into bed beside him. She turned onto her side, lying spoon fashion. She expected him to scoot behind her and hold her.

He turned out the lights but didn't lie behind her. After several moments, she turned onto her stomach. With him lying close but not touching her, she lay sleepless long after he fell asleep. If nothing else, he was a man of his word.

Several hours later, she woke to find herself sprawled across his chest with one of her legs between his. The feel of his flaccid penis excited her. The temptation to rub her pussy against him and kiss him awake was difficult to resist. As she started to ease herself off him, he stirred, whispering her name. Her name. Not some beautiful woman against whom she could never hope to compete.

He slipped an arm around her waist and kissed the corner of her mouth.

"Randall…"

He kissed her again, this time full on her mouth.

His lips were warm but tender rather than passionate.

She hesitated. She wanted the intimacy of a few shared kisses without his taking it as an invitation to have sex with her.

He whispered her name again.

She sighed and responded.

He caressed her back, kissing her again, still without passion.

They shared several kisses before he pulled her body completely on top of his.

She pressed her cheek against his shoulder. She drifted to sleep feeling content.

* * * * *

Randall woke her early the next morning holding a tray with coffee, eggs, bacon and toast. He'd shaved. His hair was damp and he wore a dark suit with a white shirt and a dark blue silk tie. He caressed her cheek. "Time to rise and shine."

"I feel like I've just closed my eyes." She sat up and stretched. "What time is it?"

His gaze went to her bare breasts. "Five thirty. Eat and dress, then you can sleep on the way home."

She yawned again. "Do you want to share?"

With his gaze still on her breasts, he rose. "No. I'll go bring the car around. Come downstairs when you're ready."

She nodded and picked up the fork as he left the bedroom.

She slept on the drive home. He kissed her awake. She linked her arms around his neck. "Are we there yet?"

"Yes, we are."

Just before seven o'clock she walked into her bedroom with a towel wrapped around her body. She dressed quickly, her thoughts on the weekend she'd spent with Randall. Recalling his hunger for her body, she sat at her vanity. She'd always considered the face that stared back at her, bare of makeup, plain.

Plain? Perhaps as traditional beauties went. But she had managed to attract at least two of the handsome Grayhawk brothers. Recalling the delight of Randall's thick cock sliding in and out of her pussy with a rapacious hunger, she smiled.

Maybe she wasn't nearly as plain as she'd always considered herself. Perhaps her best features—her hair and her body—compensated for a lack of classically beautiful features.

Although she definitely felt more confidence than she'd ever allowed herself to feel about her attractiveness to the opposite sex, it would take far more than a nice head of hair and a body padded in all the right places to make a man with Randall's looks and means want anything more than sex with her. "So don't go getting any ideas because he wants more than one weekend with you," she told her reflection and rose.

When she was dressed and ready to leave for work, she walked into her living room and paused in the doorway. Randall, who she'd invited in for a quick cup of decaf, stood at her living room window. "Randall. I thought you'd left."

He turned to face her. "I thought I'd hang around and follow you to work."

"That's nice but I've been there before. I know the way."

He smiled.

She glanced at her watch. Seven forty-five. "We'd better go or I'll be late."

He reached for her briefcase.

Wasn't he the gentleman?

They left her apartment and rode the elevator in silence. At her car, he held out her briefcase.

"Thanks." She took it and slipped into the driver's seat. She started her engine and made the thirty-minute drive to work. He followed in his car.

She pulled into the company parking lot. He alighted from his car as she did. She locked and set her car alarm before turning to face him. She kept her gaze on his chin. "Well, I'd better get inside. I had a… I enjoyed the weekend." She paused, moistening her lips. "I'll see you around, Randall."

"Is that your charming way of telling me you'd rather I didn't call you?"

"Yes." She lifted her gaze and met his briefly. "But Tempest is my best friend and you're Layton's brother so I'm sure we'll see each other from time to time."

"Then you're not interested in my suggestion?"

"It's tempting but I really don't think it would work. Goodbye, Randall." Ignoring the part of her treacherous heart that longed to throw herself into his arms, she turned and walked toward the building. At the entrance, she glanced over her shoulder. He stood where she'd left him, staring at her. She pulled the door open and entered the building.

She spent two hours working before she called Tempest and told her about her weekend spent with Randall. "You're very quiet, Temp. You think I made a mistake?"

"That's a decision only you can make, Nai but I don't think he needs to beg any woman to see him. If he practically begged you, I think maybe he feels more than he's ready to admit."

"Really? Well, if he won't admit it, how am I supposed to know he feels it?"

Tempest sighed. "Look, Nai, I'm the first one to admit dealing with a Grayhawk male isn't easy but I think they're all worth whatever effort a woman has to expend to land them. Because of their father's long history of infidelity that destroyed their mother, some of them have problems committing. Randall is clearly one of those commitment-shy Grayhawks. One thing I know about them all is the near reverence they have for their elder siblings. There's no way Randall would see you in defiance of Bancroft's wishes if all he wanted was sex."

"I'm inclined to believe that but he was very clear about what he doesn't want and that's love and marriage. I'm not interested in anything else."

"I know the feeling but it's a little early in the relationship to expect someone with his background to be willing to risk the heart he's been so careful to protect most of his adult life."

"Temp, you're acting like he actually wants more from me than he's willing to admit. I'd like to believe that but—"

"Why don't you?"

"Because he told me himself he prefers tiny, gorgeous blondes who weigh about ninety pounds. That kind of leaves me out in the cold. Doesn't it?"

"Does it? Haven't you ever heard that opposites attract?"

"Yes, I've heard it, but I don't see how that particular truism applies here."

Tempest nodded. "You have me there, but what will you say when he asks you out again?"

"That he's one of those men who want anything he thinks he can't have."

Tempest laughed. "Give him a chance, Nai, if you can. If you can't, just know your Mr. Right will come along soon."

"He'd better."

"He will. Just don't give up."

"Don't worry. I won't. If nothing else, the experience with Bancroft and the weekend with Randall have taught me I've been underselling my charms."

"Yes! I'm glad you finally realize that, Nai."

She laughed. "Well, it took a while but I think I have a new view of my ability to attract the opposite sex. But enough about me. How's married life?"

"Can you say wonderful? Sometimes I wake in the middle of the night and just lie watching Layton sleep...afraid that if I go back to sleep when I wake up again, I'll find it's all been a dream and we're not really married. Oh, Nai, I am so happy."

Benai smiled. "I'll bet Layton is too."

"Yes. Yes, he is and that's what I want for you."

"I'll get there. Now tell me, are you going to be able to make it to the next Girls' Night Out party?"

"Yes and I'll be dragging Layton along with me. Who are you bringing?"

"Myself."

"You could ask Randall."

"I can't see him agreeing to go to a party where he knows he'll be expected to dance with any and every female who asks him."

"I can't see that either. So if you tell him about it and he comes, you can draw your own conclusion as to what it means."

She laughed. "You are incorrigible."

"Maybe I am but Layton doesn't seem to mind."

"I'll bet he doesn't." Benai smiled. "Well, I'd better get back to work. Talk to you later."

* * * * *

"You want us to what?"

Randall turned from the window in his office to face Peyton, who sat in one of the chairs in front of his desk. "I want you and Dalton and maybe Declan and Jordan to ask her out."

"Why?"

"To keep her too busy to date other men."

Peyton sighed. "Does that seem fair to you?"

Randall narrowed his gaze. "What's unfair about it?"

"Let's see. She's been honest with you and told you she wants love and marriage."

"I've been honest with her as well."

"You don't want love or marriage."

"I know what I do and don't want. What's your point, Peyton?"

"It's unworthy of you to try to interfere with her finding a man who's at least open to giving her what she wants and needs in a relationship. If you have no real feelings for her, leave her alone before you hurt her."

"When I want a lecture, I'll ask for one, Peyton. Are you going to help?"

"No. I'm not."

He stared at Peyton. "Why the hell not?"

Peyton rose. "I'm not going to help you hurt her."

"I don't want to hurt her."

"But that's what will happen if you don't leave her alone. Don't try to spoil her chances for happiness, Randy. If you don't want to give her what she wants, leave her alone."

He sucked in a deep breath. "So that's how it is, is it?"

Peyton frowned. "I know that look, Randy. No. That's not how it is. I'm not interested in her romantically. I'm just not interested in trying to spoil her chances for happiness. I can't speak for Declan, Jordan or Dalton but I will not help you spoil her chances with other men."

He watched as Peyton walked out of his office. Damn Peyton's self-righteous attitude. He sank down into his chair. With or without Peyton's help, he'd do whatever was necessary to ensure she saved all her loving for him. He sent a dozen roses to her apartment before he turned his attention to work.

That afternoon, he invited Dalton, Declan and Jordan to have dinner at his house. All three were at the mansion when he arrived. Over dinner they discussed sports and riding. Over coffee he asked them to place hold for him with Benai.

After a slight hesitation, Dalton and Jordan agreed.

He turned his attention to Declan. "Lan?"

Declan sighed. "I'm not sure that would be wise or fair, Hawk."

He clenched his jaw. "You've been talking to Peyton."

"No. I just don't want to do anything to hurt or mislead her."

"I'm not asking you to lie to her. She knows about place holding. Tell her the truth if you like. I need you to do this for me, Lan."

"I'll do what I can but if it feels like she'll end up hurt, I–"

"I understand, Lan. The last thing I want is for her to get hurt."

Then leave her alone. Ignoring the voice of his conscience, he picked up his drink. After dinner he and Jordan played pool while Declan and Dalton watched a game in the family room.

Later he found sleep elusive. Each time he closed his eyes, pictures of Benai's beautiful brown body lying under his flashed through his memory. At twelve thirty, he got up and went out to the pool. He swam until he started to feel fatigued. He swam two more before he returned to his bedroom where he was finally drifted into a deep, dreamless sleep.

He felt restless and tired in the morning. Overcoming the temptation to call Benai, he worked out in his home gym before he showered and went to work. Once there, he refused to allow himself to indulge in thoughts of her.

That night lying in bed, thoughts of her kept him awake again. Damn. At this rate he'd be reduced to sleepwalking soon. It took several nights before he was finally able to fall asleep within a reasonable amount of time of getting into bed. Even then the moment he woke, he longed to be with Benai. Damn her. What the hell had she done to him?

He called Bancroft several times but either Brandon or a woman answered his phone. Clearly Bancroft was avoiding him. He wasn't sure why.

* * * * *

On Friday night, Benai had dinner out with Jill, who was hosting the next Girls' Night Out party. "Are you ready for next Friday, Benai?"

She nodded. "Yes. I've been window shopping and I saw the perfect dress. It's white satin and lace with satin straps and an empire waist with a pleated skirt. The neck and hem have scallop edges. It ends just below my knees and it has a sheer matching bolero."

Jill smiled. "Sounds like a knockout. You always look great in white."

She smiled. Randall had certainly liked her in white lace. "I think I'll go buy it tomorrow after I spend an hour or so at the gym."

"Are you coming alone?"

She nodded. "Looks like it. What about you?"

"Worse luck, I'll be coming alone too but I talked to Tempest today and guess what? She and Layton are coming. She's working on getting him to bring a couple of those single, handsome brothers of his. Wouldn't that be great if one of them came?"

She knew at least one of them who wouldn't make an appearance. Thank God. It would take a few months before she was prepared to face Randall without longing to spend another passionate weekend in his bed. "Maybe Peyton will come. He's charming and very single."

Jill grinned. "That's how I like them…single, handsome, rich and charming. He is rich. Isn't he?"

Benai shrugged. "I doubt if he's a pauper but I don't have any inside information on his finances."

"Then we'll have to find out. Won't we?"

"Not me. I'm not interested."

"Oh? So which brother do you have your eye on?"

Benai frowned. "What makes you think I'm interested in any of them?"

"Oh, Benai, come on. What single woman wouldn't be interested in one of those hunks? I think if you look in the dictionary under hunk, you'll find a picture of one of the Grayhawks. Which one would you like to spend a night with?"

She shrugged. "If I were into fantasizing, I'd pick Randall."

Jill blinked. "But aren't he and Peyton identical twins? Why would you want to spend a night with Randall but not Peyton?"

"He can be very charming when he wants to be." She sighed. "Very charming."

Jill leaned forward. "You've been out with him?"

She nodded. "Yes but nothing came of it."

"Why not?"

"I'm not his type. He likes petite, pretty blondes like Cindy. Is she coming?"

"Yes and she's coming alone."

Benai groaned. "Alone? At this rate, the only man there will be Layton."

They laughed together. Jill sobered first. "If you're not his type, why did he ask you out?"

"I have no idea. Maybe he wanted to see how the other half lived."

Jill shrugged. "Or maybe he liked what he saw when he looked at you."

Or maybe he just wanted an easy lay, which is exactly what she'd been for him.

"He struck me as the type of man who knew what he wanted and went after it."

She hoped not because that would mean he hadn't pursued her because he'd only wanted a casual, weekend fling after all.

Chapter Seven
ಐ

Five days later, as she was about to sit down to a lonely dinner, Randall sent a dozen roses. Her heart pounded as she reached for the accompanying card. There was no message, just his initials.

She sighed. Why was he sending her roses? She lay awake for over an hour that night before she fell asleep. Several hours later, she woke from a graphic dream of him making love to her, aroused and frustrated.

She turned to look at her beside clock. It showed three forty-four. "Damn you, Randall! Why won't you leave me alone?"

The next night she decided to take a long, warm bath before she went to bed. As she emerged from the bathroom feeling relaxed and ready to tumble into bed, the phone rang. She glanced at the caller ID. Her heart raced. She swallowed several times and sank onto the side of her bed.

Did she want to answer it? Even as she posed the question to herself, she lifted the phone from her nightstand. "Hello?"

"Hi, Benai."

She moistened her lips. "This is a surprise, Randall."

"It shouldn't be. I told you I wanted to see you again."

"And I said that wouldn't be a good idea."

"You've had nearly two weeks to change your mind. Have you?"

"I don't know," she admitted.

"Then why don't we have dinner tomorrow night and we can figure out together where we're headed?"

"I already have plans for tomorrow night."

"What are they?"

"I'm going to a party."

"Do you have a date?"

She should say yes—if only to discourage him. Too bad neither her body nor her heart wanted to dissuade him from seeing her. "No."

"Great. I'll be your date."

"I'm sure you're used to high-society catered parties only attended by people with lots of money. This is just going to be a small party with most of us coming stag."

"Why would that change my wanting to accompany you to the party?"

"You'd be expected to dance with any woman who asked you to. Not exactly your style."

"I do socialize with wealthy people from time to time but I only do the catered, exclusive party thing when it can't be avoided. I don't particularly enjoy such parties and those aren't the kinds of parties I generally give. I'd love to escort you to this party, Benai. I'll dance with anyone who asks. All I ask is that I get to dance with you at least once."

She closed her eyes and sighed. How was she supposed to resist him if he insisted on saying things like that? "Randall—"

"What time shall I pick you up, Benai?"

"Randall—"

"If you're short of men, I'm sure I can persuade at least one or two of my brothers to come."

"Really? That would be great. Peyton will be a big hit."

"Peyton won't be coming."

"Oh. Why not?"

"He's being difficult at the moment."

"Why?"

"He thinks I should leave you alone."

"I think you should too."

He sighed. "Let's not go there, Benai. Monday is your Independence Day. If you don't have any plans, we're all getting together at my house."

"Do you celebrate the fourth?"

"We don't do barbecues or fireworks but we do observe it."

"How?"

"We all make an effort to spend the day together as a family. We talk of our heritage and we generally only speak Cherokee for the day. Now that Layton is married, we'll speak less Cherokee out of respect for Tempest. I'd love to have you come as my special guest. Your being there will make the day even more special than just spending it with family."

"Thanks but I already have other plans for the fourth."

"You do? Of course you do. What plans? Who with?"

"We can discuss that later."

"All right. We can discuss it when I pick you up."

"I'll see you at seven thirty."

"Can we make it seven o'clock so we can have a drink somewhere before the party?"

"Okay. Seven o'clock tomorrow night."

"I'm looking forward to seeing you again, Benai."

"Good night," she said and hung up before she admitted that she was looking forward to seeing him as well. He'd discover for himself soon enough how eager she was to see him.

* * * * *

Benai left work half an hour early so she'd have time for a fifteen-minute soak before she dressed. Her phone rang at six forty-five. She slipped on her heels and picked up her cordless phone. "Randall?"

"I'm in the lobby. Buzz me in."

"You're early, Randall."

"I couldn't wait to see you."

"Charmer." Smiling, she punched in the code to release the lobby door lock. Giving her reflection a last quick glance, she slipped on her bolero, picked up her tiny evening bag and walked into the living room.

She took a deep breath when her apartment doorbell rang. "Yes?"

"It's Randall."

She crossed the room and opened the apartment door. He looked stunning in a dark suit with a white shirt and silk tie. She smiled. "Randall."

He smiled and bent to press a quick kiss against her cheek. "Hi." He lifted his head and offered her a single red rose.

"Thank you."

He stepped back to study her. "You look great."

Her smile widened. "I was hoping you'd feel that way."

"Why?"

"I bought it with you in mind," she admitted.

He rewarded her with another kiss on her cheek.

"Would you like to come in for a drink?"

He stepped inside and closed the door. "I'm driving. Would you like to offer me something else instead?"

"Will you settle for coffee?"

He slipped his hands in his pants pockets and stared at her. "How about a quickie?"

"Dream on, Randall."

"Okay but I really need to kiss you."

"Let's take it slowly, Randall."

"Slow? Damn. Fine. We'll take it slowly."

"Thanks. So which of your charming brothers are coming to the party?"

"Declan and Jordan."

"Great. They'll be a hit. So will you. You'd be interested in meeting Cindy."

"Why?"

"She's your type."

He shook his head and pushed himself away from the door. "Oh, give that a rest, will you? If I wanted to spend the evening with anyone but you, I wouldn't be here."

She sighed. "I always feel so attractive when I'm with you."

"I have news for you. I happen to think you are as sexy as hell."

She smiled and leaned into him. "You may be no good for my heart but I swear you're great for my self esteem."

"I mean it, Benai."

She nodded. "I know you do. Now let's get out of here before I let you do something I'll regret."

He pulled her close and slipped his hands under her skirt to cup her ass. "Maybe it'll be something neither of us will regret. We can push your thong aside, unzip my pants and I can be inside you in seconds."

Her pussy pulsed but she shook her head firmly. "I'm going to the party, Randall. Are you coming?"

He groaned but pulled open her apartment door. "After you."

* * * * *

On arrival at the party, Randall noted the ratio of women present to men. Wonderful. He feared it was going to be a long night of endless dances with women in whom he had no interest. It would be a long, unpleasant evening but worth it if it made her happy.

Benai squeezed his arm against her body. "I'm counting on you to be charming to my friends tonight, Randall."

He turned to look at her. "I'll do my best but—"

"Come meet my friends and get ready to spend the night dancing." She smiled, released his arm and started away.

He caught her hand and turned her back to face him. "I'll keep my promise but—"

"No buts. Please, Randall." She glanced around. "Oh, look, there's Temp and Layton."

Randall was surprised to see them. Layton had lately become obsessed with wanting to spend every waking moment with Tempest, who was nearly five months pregnant.

Tempest sat on a loveseat talking with a pretty blonde. A few feet away, Layton danced with an attractive brunette. Although Layton smiled, Randall suspected his oldest brother was as bored as he was about to become.

Benai slipped an arm through his and turned a smiling face up to his. "Oh, Randall, doesn't Tempest look lovely?"

He nodded but looked at Benai instead of Tempest. "Yes," he said. "Lovely."

Her smile widened. She leaned against him. "Randall, you can be so sweet. I meant *she* looked lovely."

He shrugged. "She'll do but I'd rather look at you."

"Really? Well, I'd rather look at you than any of your charming, worthy brothers."

"Including the handsome, charming and impossible to resist Peyton?"

"Including him."

He grinned and slipped an arm around her waist. "Then I'm a lucky man."

"Let me introduce you to our host before we go speak to Temp. Then it'll be time for you to begin dancing the night away."

He groaned.

She laughed, rubbing her cheek against his shoulder.

He resisted the urge to lean down and kiss her. He followed her across the room instead. Minutes later, he found himself dancing with Benai's friend Jill. He danced with a quick succession of women after her. Just as he finished one dance, another smiling woman waited to ask him to dance.

Half an hour later when Declan and Jordan arrived, a smiling blonde with dark brown eyes approached Randall. "Hi. I'm Cindy."

"I'm Randall."

"I know and I'd love to dance with you."

He hoped his smile concealed his lack of enthusiasm. "Thanks but I think it's time I danced with Benai."

"She's the one who suggested I ask you to dance while she's dancing with that tall, dark, hunk over there."

He glanced across the room. Benai danced with a tall male with dark skin. Who the hell was he? When had he arrived? And why the hell was Benai smiling up at him like that?

"Randall? Benai said I was your type. I hope she's right because your brothers are handsome and charming but they rather pale in comparison to you. Am I your type?"

He looked at her. Blonde. Petite. Pretty. She was definitely the type of woman he usually preferred. Usually. Benai wanted him to dance with her while she danced with another man? So be it.

He smiled, extending his hand. "Shall we dance?"

She pressed so close in his arms he felt her small breasts against his body. He suppressed a sigh. When this long night was over, he and Benai were going to have to have a long talk.

143

"Benai tells me you're not seeing anyone special."

Damn Benai. He looked down at Cindy. "You mean besides her?"

He watched the color rise in her cheeks. "Her? But she said you and she were just friends."

"Did she?"

"Are you more than friends?"

He arched a brow. "Do you sleep with your friends?"

"No."

"Neither do I."

"Oh. So…she's more than a friend?"

He glanced across the room. The man swung Benai around, providing Randall a brief glimpse of her smiling face.

"Randall? I asked if you two were more than friends."

He kept his gaze on Benai. "Draw your own conclusions."

"You're stepping on my feet."

He tore his gaze away from Benai and looked down at the woman in his arms. What the hell was her name? "My apologies." He smiled and swung her around so that he faced away from Benai.

"You can make it up to me by giving me a second dance," she suggested, smiling up at him.

"That's a charming offer but I think it's time I danced with Benai."

She glanced around his shoulder before looking up at him. "Now? Just when Nai looks like she's finally found her Denzel lookalike?"

The music ended. He released her. "Thanks for the dance."

"I'd love another one."

"Maybe later."

"I'll hold you to that promise, Randall."

He watched her walk away before he glanced around the room. Benai and the man sat close together on a loveseat in a corner. What the hell. He clenched his right hand into a fist and started across the crowded room.

He felt a soft hand brush against his. Impatient to reach Benai and remind her she was with him, he turned.

Tempest smiled up at him. "I think this dance belongs to me, Randall."

He smiled. "Can I have a rain check?"

She shook her head and slipped her arms around him. "We'll make it a quick one, then Layton and I are leaving. I'm feeling tired."

He cast a quick glance over his shoulder. Benai looked up at the man, smiling and nodding. The man leaned closer and Randall feared he was about to kiss her. If he did, he would get knocked on his ass.

"Randall?"

He sucked in a deep breath and turned to look down at Tempest.

She smiled at him.

He slipped his arms around her. "Who is he?"

"Who is who?"

"The man with Benai."

"He's Jerri's brother."

He didn't recall being introduced to any female called Jerri. "What's his interest in Benai? What's hers in him?"

She shook her head. "If you want to know how she feels about him, ask her."

"I'm asking you, Tempest."

"And I'm telling you to ask her."

He compressed his lips.

She rubbed a hand over his arm. "If you want her complete attention, Randall, you know what you need to do to get and keep it."

He stiffened and stared down at her. "So this party tonight and her spending half the damn night with him when she's supposed to be my date is a ploy to reel me in?"

Her eyes widened. "It's not a ploy. Neither of us knew he'd be here tonight or —"

"Never mind, Tempest. I understand now." He shook his head. "You can tell Benai that it will be a cold day in hell before I allow her or any other woman to play me."

She pulled out of his arms. "She's not trying to play you, Randall."

Layton would not appreciate his calling her liar. He arched a brow, making no effort to conceal his disbelief.

She narrowed her gaze. "Fine. Think what you like but while you're wallowing in conspiracy theories, tonight should make you realize that you are not the only male interested in Benai. She doesn't have to settle for you."

"Settle for?"

"That's right, Randall, settle for you. Good night."

He watched her stalk away before turning his attention back to Benai, who was slow dancing with her Denzel Washington type. Damn her. Two could play games. He swung around, located Cindy, smiled and asked her to dance.

"I'd love to dance with you again, Randall." She practically threw herself into his arms.

He spent most of the evening dancing with Cindy. Just after eleven o'clock, Cindy slipped him her phone number. "I hope you'll call me, Randall." She smiled at him and left.

"Did you have fun, Randall?"

He slowly turned to face Benai. Was it just his imagination or did her lipstick looked smeared? "Did you?"

She nodded. "I'm glad I came." She yawned. "It's getting late and I have an early day tomorrow so if you're ready to leave, so am I."

"What about the dance you promised me?"

She shrugged. "You were clearly charmed by Cindy so I didn't want to interrupt."

He longed to reach out and shake her. He smiled coolly instead. "I'm ready whenever you are."

She frowned. "What's wrong?"

She'd spent all night with another man and then wanted to know what was wrong? Hell would freeze over before he gave her the satisfaction of knowing how well her ploy to make him jealous had succeeded. "Nothing's wrong."

"If you really want to dance—"

"Don't do me any damned favors, Benai."

She sighed. "Fine. Let's go."

They said their goodbyes and left the party. In the car, he turned on the CD and adjusted the volume loud enough to discourage conversation.

She turned the volume down. "Why am I getting the silent treatment?"

He kept his gaze on the road ahead. "I'm not in the mood to play games with you, Benai."

She sighed. "Temp told me about your conversation. Do you really think I'm trying to reel you in?"

"Aren't you?"

"No. I know you and I have no future together. Instead of wasting time trying to reel you in, I've decided to concentrate my efforts elsewhere."

He swallowed hard. "On your Denzel Washington lookalike?"

"Temp told me you were annoyed about—"

"Tempest talks too damned much about things that are none of her concern."

"She's my best friend."

"And so that gives her the right to stick her damn nose into my personal business?"

She touched his arm. "I know the evening didn't turn out as you wanted but let's not fight. I spent the night getting reacquainted with Bill and you got to spend the evening with Cindy."

"Had I wanted to spend the evening with her, I wouldn't have asked *you* out."

"Didn't you enjoy meeting her?"

"No, Benai, I did not enjoy meeting her. This might come as a surprise to you but I don't need your help to meet women."

"I'm sorry. I thought I was doing us both a favor."

"How the hell is spending the entire night with another man doing me a favor?"

She removed her hand from his arm. "We hadn't seen each other in a long time and once we started talking, time got away from me—us."

"Is he interested in taking you out?"

"I think he might be."

She sounded surprised but pleased.

The realization of who Bill was suddenly dawned on him. "Bill? Did you say Bill?"

She nodded slowly.

"The same Bill who was your first love?"

"He used to be."

Oh shit. "What happened to his beautiful wife and charming kids?"

"He's divorced."

He narrowed his gaze. "Well that's too damned bad. He had his chance with you and he blew it. Why the hell has he come sniffing around you now that his perfect marriage has fallen apart?"

"There's no need to make him sound like a heel, Randall."

How could she be so defensive of a man who had hurt her so badly? "You think I'm being unreasonable?"

"A little. Yes."

"Really? Okay. How about if our positions were reversed and I invited you to a party, threw a Denzel Washington lookalike at you and then proceeded to spend the evening dancing with Pam? Are you telling me you wouldn't be furious?"

She sighed. "Of course I would and I see your point. You're right. I was totally inconsiderate and I'm sorry, Randall. I just didn't see it that way."

Although he felt her apology was sincere, it did little to appease him. "Are you interested in going out with him?"

She didn't answer.

"Benai? Are you going out with him?"

"I'm not sure, Randall. I might consider going out with him if he asked me."

He tightened his hands on the steering wheel. His chest felt tight. Breathing became difficult. "Where does that leave me?"

"Free to find the tiny, petite blonde of your dreams. Are you sure you're not interested in Cindy?"

"I'm positive I'm not interested in her."

"Well, the world is full of blondes just like her. You'll find one you can't live without."

He took a deep breath. "Didn't the time we spent together mean anything to you?"

She sighed, placing a hand on his arm. "I think you know it did."

"Then how the hell can you toss your friend at me and then spend the entire damned evening with the man who hurt you?"

She squeezed his arm. "I have to do what I can to safeguard my heart from you, Randall."

"Why the hell does everyone expect me to hurt you?"

"I'm certain you wouldn't do it intentionally."

"But?"

"But I don't want to be hurt again. If I continue to see you that's what's going to happen."

"I thought we'd agreed you could see who you liked, in addition to me."

"That's your plan, Randall. Not mine. I'll admit that I like you far more than I should."

"Just like?"

"No. More than like but—"

"Then spend the night with me."

"I'd like to but—"

"Why does there need to be a but?"

"Because I don't sleep with more than one man at a time."

"You're not sleeping with him so there's no reason why you shouldn't spend the night with me."

"Randall—"

He pulled the car over to the shoulder of the highway. He put the car in park before he turned to caress her cheek. "Spend the night with me."

She sighed. "I'm only a breath away from falling in love with you."

He unbuckled his seatbelt, leaned close and kissed the corner of her mouth. "So take a deep breath and let it happen. Fall in love with me."

She jerked away from him. "That's easy for you to say, Randall. Your heart isn't involved so you're not likely to be hurt."

He moved back to his seat and refastened his seatbelt. "You think knowing you want to see another man who just happens to be your first love leaves me unmoved?" He stared at the dimly lit highway before he turned to look at her. "You think knowing you might soon be sleeping with him doesn't sting like hell?"

"I want and need more than you're willing to give me, Randall."

"Can't we discuss that some other time? Can't we just spend the night together and pretend we're the only two people in the world tonight?"

"I...I..." She sighed. "I...oh Randall. Why won't you leave me alone?"

"I would if I could. I can't."

"Why can't you?"

He knew what she wanted him to say. He shrugged. "Does it matter why I can't? Isn't it enough to know that I can't?"

"No, it isn't. I want to know why."

He sighed. "Bear with me, Benai. Please. And spend the night with me."

She looked away.

He stared at her profile, waiting for her to speak.

After a minute or so, she inclined her head slightly. "Okay."

He released a sigh and brushed the back of his hand against her cheek.

She turned her head and kissed his fingers.

Their gazes met and locked. "I've missed you," he told her softly.

"Me or sex with me?"

"This isn't just about sex, Benai."

"I know it's not for me."

"It's not for me either. It's never just been about sex for me. If all I wanted was sex, there are plenty of women willing to give it to me without my having to pursue and practically beg them for it."

"It's not about love either. At least not for you."

"If you're so in love with me, Benai, why are you making me beg you to spend the night with me?"

Her soft, sweet lips curved upward in a sudden smile. "Because you do it so nicely."

He laughed but sobered quickly. "I don't usually have to beg a woman for anything."

She shrugged. "Yeah, well, Randall, there's a first time for everything."

"So they say."

"I hope they're right."

"Your place or mine?"

"Mine."

He nodded, put the car in drive and drove off the shoulder onto the highway.

They made the rest of the drive in silence. Ten minutes from the off-ramp, there was a minor fender bender that resulted in a five-car pile up. The forty-minute drive to her place took two hours.

Seated beside her, knowing they were going to spend the night making love, each passing moment felt like hours to him. By the time they reached her apartment, he felt ready to burst.

Once they were inside his patience evaporated. He locked the door and quickly stripped her.

"Hey. Be careful. Do you know how much that dress cost?"

"I'll buy another one," he said, tossing it aside. He stepped back to stare at her for several moments in silence. He'd never been particularly attracted to black women but damn if she didn't get more attractive each time he saw her. Greedy to be inside her, he pushed her against the door.

"You're doing it again, Randall."

"Doing what?"

"Speaking in Cherokee."

"You are so beautiful."

She caressed his cheek. "I'm feeling more and more like I am each time you look at me as if I'm the only woman in the world worth looking at."

"You are." Pressing his body against her, he kissed her. The feel of her warm, full lips slowly parting under his, got him hard in record time.

She linked her arms around his neck, rubbing her hips against his.

He reached between their bodies to unzip his pants. Dragging his lips from hers, he dug in his pocket for a condom. Slipping it quickly over his cock, he gripped her hips, rubbing himself against her body. "I need you so badly. Right here right now."

She pressed her hands against his shoulders. "Lustily put, but I do have a bed, Randall."

"I can't wait." He pushed his hips forward. He paused with the tip of his cock lodged just inside her. Damn. She got sweeter each time he entered her.

She sucked in a breath and stared between their bodies. "Randall...oh. Each time you slide into me I feel as if I'm only minutes away from heaven."

He stared down at her. "It's like that for me too, sweetheart."

She smiled up at him.

"I've never been with anyone sweeter. I'd walk barefoot over hot coals for just a few minutes alone like this with you."

"Oh, Randall. Please don't make verbal love to me like that."

"Why not?" He bent to brush his lips against her nipples.

"You're determined to make me fall in love in love with you. Aren't you?"

"Yes." Cupping her breasts in his hands, he eased. "I want you in love with me...only me."

She moaned. "Hmmm."

He loved the sound of her soft moan.

"Randall." She tugged at his hips. "More. Give me all of it."

"Open your eyes and look at me."

Her eyes fluttered open and she gazed up at him. "Randall?"

He slid his hands over her body to cup his hands over her ass. "You don't want to share this sweet delight with anyone but me. Do you?"

"No," she admitted. "No."

"Neither do I," he whispered in a brusque voice. "You promised me this sweet, tight pussy was all mine."

"It is," she whispered. "When you're inside me, you must know you're the only man I want."

He eased his hips forward.

She licked her lips and closed her eyes. "Oh, Randall, there's nothing sweeter than sex with you."

"This is far more special than just sex, Benai."

She wiggled her hips. "Please...do it."

Her soft plea excited him. He slid his entire shaft inside her.

"Oh...yes...yes, lover."

He shuddered and leaned against her, his lips pressed against her ear. "I'm your lover and you're mine." He stroked slowly in and out of her. "You're the only woman I want to share this with, Benai. For me there is no other woman. There's just you, sweetheart. You. Only you."

She slipped her hands inside his pants and briefs. With her bare palms over his ass, she ground her hips against his. "I couldn't bare it if I had to share you."

"There's no question of sharing me. I'm one hundred percent yours."

"And I'm yours. Take what's yours." She tightened her vaginal muscles around him. "And give me what's mine."

He shuddered. Placing his hands against the door on either side of her body, he kissed her. As he did, he pushed into her with slow, deep strokes, enjoying the exquisite heat and tightness of her body.

He whispered softly to her. Sex had never felt more natural or more emotionally rewarding with any other woman. Nor had the need for sexual and emotional intimacy with any other woman so consumed him. The certainty that he would need to tread very carefully with her or he'd be in danger of losing his head and possibly his heart with her excited rather than gave him pause. It heightened his passion and fueled his need to be ever closer to her.

She moaned his name against his lips.

The sound, the feel of her breasts against his chest, the way she tightened around him drove him wild. He dragged his mouth away from hers and thrust his hips against her rapidly, pushing in and pulling out of her with a force and depth designed to drive them both quickly over the edge.

Each time he drew his hips back, she tightened her vaginal muscles around him, making him fight to pull even an inch of his cock out of her. When he pushed back inside, she moaned with pleasure, her pussy quickly enfolding and surrounding him with a moist heat that made it difficult not to surrender to the urge to pound her until they both exploded.

Wanting deeper penetration, he lifted her left leg and drove his cock as deep into her warm, moist channel as he could get it.

She rewarded him by slowly grinding her hips in a circular motion so that he experienced a series of incredible rippling sensations along the length of his cock that pushed him to within an inch of climaxing.

Fearful of coming before he had satisfied her, he sucked her right breast into his mouth. Sliding a finger down the anal crack, he pressed a finger against her tight, puckered bottom.

As he thrust back into her, he pushed his finger into her rectum.

"Oh." Her fingers tightened on his ass, her pussy convulsed around his pumping cock. She cried out his name. "Randall…oh, God…Randall." She rubbed against his cock and then exploded.

Determined to allow her time to enjoy her climax, he clenched his jaw and held himself still inside her. Her rapid vaginal convulsions made it impossible for him to last more than a few moments. No longer able to hold his own explosion at bay, he grabbed her hips, held her still and powered into her while he expelled jets of seed.

His relief was intense and prolonged. As the last blast of cum shot out of his cock, he shuddered, groaned and pulled out of her, easing his finger from her rear. With his knees buckling, he sank down against the wall, his breathing erratic.

She sat beside him. "Randall? Are you all right? You're not having a heart attack or anything are you?"

He laughed and turned to look at her. "What the hell are you doing to me, Benai?"

She caressed his cheek and leaned forward to press a warm kiss against his lips. "I thought I'd just given you what you wanted, Randall." She reached between his legs and cupped a hand over his cock and balls. "You sure gave me what I wanted and needed."

It was hardly the first time a woman had touched his genitals after sex but something in the caressing fingers, sent a chill of fear and delight through him. He'd never felt so vulnerable or so needy with any other woman.

He leaned against the wall. "I'm not sure I know what I want anymore."

She leaned her head against his shoulder, still caressing his cock and balls. "It might be fun and exciting to discover that together, Randall."

He sighed again and slipped his arm around her. "This is new territory for me, Benai."

"What are you afraid of, Randall?"

"You and how you make me feel," he admitted.

Stilling her hands on him, she leaned up and kissed him again. "And how is that?"

"Like you're the only woman in the world."

"You must have known countless tiny, beautiful, blondes in the biblical sense." She licked his bottom lip.

He shivered. "There's not one of them I'd rather be with now."

She brushed her lips across his cheek. "You're still erect." She leaned away from him and carefully removed the condom from his cock.

She held it up. "Your cum overflowed the reservoir. Wow. You were horny."

To his dismay, he blushed.

She glanced up. "Why are you blushing? I can't be the first woman to remove your condom."

"Actually, you are."

She dropped the condom in a wastebasket by the door. She sank back to the carpet beside him. "Why?"

He shrugged. "It's not something I've ever really wanted a woman to do."

"Why not?"

"I don't know why not. I've just never... I guess I've always considered it too...personal."

"That's sweet." She nibbled at his ear and reached down to fondle him. "You're still erect. Don't you ever get enough?"

"Not with you."

A pleased smile spread across her face. "Talk like that will get you all the loving you want."

He curled his fingers in her hair. "I want as much as you'll give me."

She extended her hand. "Then let's get you ready to spend the night loving."

He rose.

She stared up at him as he quickly undressed.

"Very nice equipment," she told him, when he was nude. "Long, thick and erect. And nice, tight balls. What woman could ask for more?"

He grinned. "I aim to please."

"And you do, Randall, over and over."

Pulling a condom from his wallet, he sank down onto the carpet beside her.

She took the condom but instead of tearing it open, she leaned over him and kissed the head of his cock.

He shuddered.

Closing her fingers around the base of his shaft, she licked the underside. She dragged her tongue up from the bottom. At the top, she laved the head of his shaft before she smiled at him. "I like the taste of your cum."

"Damn, Benai."

She sucked him slowly, gently massaging his thighs and nuts as she did.

He leaned his head against the wall near the door, thrusting his hips in time with the sucking motions of her warm mouth. She whirled her tongue around him until he longed to fuck her face.

Almost as if she were aware of how close he was to losing control, she lifted her head and quickly rolled the condom over him. She straightened, meeting his gaze.

He sucked in a slow breath. "There's not a woman alive I'd rather be with."

She smiled. "How sweet. I have confession of my own."

"I'm listening."

She straddled his hips so that her slit pressed against his cock. "I wouldn't trade tonight with you for a lifetime with anyone else."

He stared at her. "No shit?"

"No shit, lover," she whispered and slowly pushed her hips forward.

When he would have surged forward and quickly filled her, she pressed her hands against his hips. "Take your time, darling. I like it best when you go in slowly so I can enjoy each wonderful inch surging into me."

"I just want to plunge in and fuck like there's no tomorrow."

She linked her arms around his neck. "I know the feeling but getting to watch myself being impaled on your cock is too delicious for words."

"Oh, damn, baby, if you keep talking like that, you'll ruin me for any other woman."

She grinned, linking her arms around him. "I thought I'd already done that, Randall."

"You have."

She tightened herself around him. "I want you and this…" She reached between their bodies to stroke his pubic hair. "All for myself."

He wrapped his arms around her and thrust forward, sending the last few inches of his shaft as deep as possible. "I'm all yours, baby," he groaned and began to fuck her.

The position was awful and limited his penetration. He eased out of her, drew her up to her hands and knees. Positioning himself behind her on his knees, he stroked slowly into her.

When his balls brushed against her body, he leaned over her back to cup his hands over her breasts. Raining kisses over her neck and shoulders, he fucked her slowly.

She glanced over her shoulder at him. "Oh yes. I can feel you sliding in so deeply."

He whispered in Cherokee as he leisurely fucked her to a sweet, delicious climax. With his cock still imbedded in her, he rolled them onto their sides. Lifting her top leg, he drilled her from the rear.

Although sated, she reached between their bodies to massage and caress his genitals, squeezing his balls. She enjoyed holding him and feeling him pulse.

She turned her head to kiss him. She rocked her ass against his groin, tightening herself around him until he bit her lip and exploded.

They remained on their sides for several minutes after he'd come. When he finally eased out of her, he rolled onto his back, removed the condom and spread his legs. She kissed and licked his nuts, sticking her tongue out to catch cum that trickled down to his balls and the base of his cock.

"Oh, hell, Benai."

Smiling, she removed his cock and then stretched out on top of him.

He wrapped his arms around her and kissed her.

"We're good together, Randall."

"We're so good together, I'm never going to do this with any one else…only you. "

"Because you're mine."

"Yes, I m yours."'

They dozed briefly before they got up and went into her bedroom. They tumbled into her bed and fell asleep in each other's arms.

They woke several hours later. He lubed the butt plug and watched her insert it up her ass. This time he started the vibrating function. Holding it in her ass, he bent to kiss and eat her pussy.

He made sure she came from having her pussy eaten and her rear digitally fucked. They fell asleep just after she'd come.

Chapter Eight
ဆၣ

Randall kissed her awake the next morning. She opened her eyes to find him lying between her thighs with his bare cock pressed against her pussy. She sucked in a breath and overcame the urge to thrust her hips upward, which would force his hard length between her slit and deep inside her.

She pressed her hands against his shoulders. "He can't play without his raincoat."

He bent his head, brushing his lips against hers. "He doesn't want to wear one. He wants to slide into you just as he is and be inside you with nothing between your hot pussy and him."

"Really? Well, you tell that sex-crazy maniac that no one but my husband gets to play without protection." She shoved against his shoulders.

He rolled off her.

She sat up and pulled the sheet up to cover her breasts.

He sat up and turned to look at her. "Are you afraid of getting pregnant?"

"No, I'm not because I don't engage in stupid behavior — such as having unprotected sex."

"I don't either."

"Then what did you think you were doing?"

"Losing what's left of my common sense." He sighed. "I haven't had unprotected sex since my senior year of high school."

"And you're not having any with me."

He yanked at the sheet over her breasts. After a moment, she allowed him to pull the cover away. He caressed her breasts. "Don't you want kids?"

"Yes but I'm old-fashioned. I want them *after* I'm married."

He slipped an arm around her shoulders. "We could make beautiful babies together, Benai." He cupped a hand over her breasts.

She shivered and eased away from him. She got out of bed, giving him a cool, determined look. "If you want to get someone pregnant after unprotected sex, you'd better find yourself a willing tiny blonde because it's not going to happen with me, Randall."

He narrowed his gaze and got out of bed. When she would have walked away, he caught her hand, turning her back to face him. "Isn't it clear to you by now that I'm not interested in anyone but you?"

She saw the truthfulness of the statement in the intense gaze he turned on her face. "Okay, so I believe that. It doesn't do either of us any good."

He drew her close, slipping his arms around her. "I'd take very good care of you and any child we had together, Benai. I wouldn't stray. I'd never give you reason to doubt me and I'd give you anything you wanted."

"Anything but what I want and need most—your love and your name."

"I can't help how I feel about love and marriage."

She sighed. "I know but neither can I."

"What I feel for you is probably as close to romantic love as I'm capable of."

She longed to link her arms around his neck and give him everything he wanted. She caressed his cheek. "When it comes to love and marriage, Randall, close is not good enough."

He tightened his arms around her. "I need you."

"We're no good for each other." She stepped away from him. "Now it's getting late and I have a plane to catch."

He followed her into the bathroom. "Where are you going?"

At the shower door, she turned. "I'm flying to California tonight. My brother and his family are flying in from Colorado and we're going to spend the fourth with our parents."

"When are you returning?"

"In a few weeks."

"A few weeks?" He raked a hand through his hair. "When were you going to tell me?"

She shrugged. "I don't know that I was going to tell you." She opened the shower stall and stepped in.

He followed her inside, placing a hand over hers to stop her from turning on the water. "Did you tell him?"

"If you're going to start asking me about Bill all the time, let me remind you that I spent last night with you. Not him."

That little fact didn't seem to impress him. He eased her against the wall and stared down at her. "I've changed my mind."

"About what?"

"He can't have you."

"That's my decision, Randall."

"Really? Well, hell will freeze over before I allow him or anyone else to take you from me."

She stared at him. "No one but me decides who I'll sleep with, Randall."

"Really? Are you aware that I can make things very difficult for him?"

She frowned. "Is that a threat, Randall?"

"I'd never threaten you."

"But you would threaten him?"

"I have no problem with him as long as he gets his own damned woman and leaves mine alone."

Leaves his alone? The beginnings of hope stirred. Would he be so jealous if his interest didn't extend beyond sex? "I need to shower, Randall. Please close the door on your way out."

To her surprise, he obeyed, stepping out of the shower and leaving the bathroom without a word.

She turned on the water and stood under the warm spray. Did she dare allow herself to hope that despite all his denials, he was falling in love with her? Maybe dreams did come true. Maybe opposites did attract. If they did, she sure hoped absence made the heart grow fonder as well. If so, hopefully he'd be ready to consider a serious relationship when she returned.

After a long shower, she wrapped a towel around herself. She walked into her bedroom and stopped in the doorway. He sprawled naked across her bed. "I thought you'd left."

He shook his head. "I thought I'd offer you a ride to California."

She sat on the bed beside him. "I have a ticket."

"First class?"

"Coach."

"My pilot is standing by ready to fly you there first class."

"Alone?"

"If that's the way you want it."

It wasn't but perhaps it was time she started to play a little harder to get. "It is."

"Are you sure? Can I join you in a day or two?"

"No."

"Why not? Would your parents object to your dating me?"

"Not for the reason you're hinting at but they are old fashioned."

"Meaning?"

"Meaning when I was sixteen, they insisted on meeting and getting to know my dates. That stopped mid-way through college. These days, if I were to bring a man home, they'd expect him to be my future husband. If I took you home or even introduced you to them, Mom would be sizing you up to see what kind of husband and father you'd likely make while Dad would be grilling you as to your intentions and to see if you were financially able to take care of me and a family.

"You're not interested in any of that happening. Are you?"

She watched the muscles in his jaw clench before he spoke. "Fine. My pilot and the plane are at your disposal."

She leaned forward and kissed his cheek. "Thanks."

He slipped an arm around her. "Can I count on your not seeing him while you're in California?"

"Yes. You can but when I return, all bets are off. I'll be thirty-one soon and I'm not going to blow a chance with him on the off chance that you'll ever fall in love with me."

He stared at her. "Benai—"

She pressed a finger against his lips. "That's the way things are, Randall. I'd very much like you to fall for me but I'm not going to let that futile hope ruin my chances with other men who are more inclined to want to give me what I need from a relationship."

He leaned away from her fingers, his gaze narrowed.

"I need to get dressed. We can talk when I return."

"Okay." He rose. "I need to shower before I leave."

She nodded.

He bent to kiss her lips. "I'll miss you."

"I'll miss you too, Randall."

"Then don't go."

"Not only are my parents expecting me but I think we can both use the time apart to reassess what we want."

"I know what I want, Benai. You."

"I'll bear that in mind while I'm away."

"Are you sure I can't change your mind?"

"I'm positive."

Three hours later, she was aboard his private jet on her way to California.

* * * * *

Later that night Randall, along with all the Grayhawks, with the exception of Bancroft and Lelia met at Layton's mansion after dinner to discuss how to help Bancroft.

"How should we proceed, Lan?" Layton asked.

Declan, who they all acknowledged had what their mother had called a "healing touch," sighed. "That depends."

"On what?"

Randall, standing near the terrace doors in the rec room felt all eyes turned in his direction. He turned to glance at Declan before he responded to Layton's question. "I think he means it depends on me, Hawk."

Declan nodded. "How much are you willing to sacrifice to help him, Hawk?"

Randall swallowed and raked a hand through his hair. He knew what Declan was asking—what all of his brothers with the possible exception of Peyton wanted of him. "She's not interested in Bancroft. I made sure of that before I…" Aware of how defensive he sounded, he allowed his voice to trail off. He sounded as if he were trying to excuse the inexcusable.

"How do you feel about her, Randall?"

He looked at Layton. "How do I… I…like her."

A brief smile touched Layton's lips. "I think that much is obvious. The real question is how much do you like her?"

"A lot."

"Enough that this like might be mistaken for love?"

"That's a strong word."

"I know. Do you love her?"

"I...I'm not... I don't think I...do."

He heard Peyton's indrawn breath but he kept his gaze trained on Layton, who sat on a high back barstool. "Are you sure you don't love her?"

He hesitated and then nodded slowly, unable to voice the denial again.

Layton nodded and turned his attention to Declan. "Given that he's not in love with her, how should we proceed?"

Declan looked at Randall. "Since you don't love her, you'll need to stop seeing her."

And leave the way open for that damned Bill to move in and win her heart back? Hell no! He parted his lips.

"The hell he will!" Peyton, who had sprawled on one of the many recliners, exploded to his feet.

Randall crossed the room and put a hand on Peyton's shoulder. "It's all right."

Peyton shook his hand off. "No it's not all right! Be honest about your feelings, Randy, and no one will ask or expect you to stop seeing her."

He shook his head. "I said it's all right."

"Oh? Then you're prepared to stop seeing her and watch her start dating her former lover?"

Just the thought of Benai rekindling her relationship with Bill sent him into an emotional panic. But if he'd kept his word and not asked her out, Bancroft wouldn't be so close to the edge of despair. They were all fearful of what would happen if he didn't soon regain his sense of balance. "I wouldn't like it but I don't like what I've done to Bancroft either."

Peyton grabbed his arms and shook him, his eyes blazing. "You haven't done anything to Bancroft. It's not your fault that she isn't interested in him. She's never been interested in him. You want her. She wants you. There doesn't need to be a problem — if you'll only admit how you feel."

He pulled away from Peyton. "I knew Bancroft considered her his when I asked her out. I've been nothing but selfish and thoughtless since I met her. It's time I had to answer for that behavior, Peyton."

"What the hell are you talking about? You are the least selfish person in this family and the most giving and generous. If you pursued her knowing Bancroft considered her his, it's because of how deeply you feel for her. Admit it, damn it!"

He shrugged. "How I feel doesn't matter. Bancroft's in danger. I'm responsible for the depth of his despair. I have to help him, Peyton."

Peyton swung around to stare at the others. "You may all sit here and expect him to stop seeing Benai as if it's no big deal but you don't know what you're asking of him." Peyton stalked across the floor to stare down at Declan. "You know he's not being honest about his feelings for her, Lan. If you push this so called solution, instead of one brother in despair, we'll have two. Nothing we can say or do here is going to make Benai want Bancroft when she's in love with Randall."

Layton rose and crossed the room to place a hand on Peyton's shoulder. "We're not asking him to stop seeing her permanently. We're only asking him to stop seeing her until we can work things out with Bancroft."

Peyton shook Layton's hand off and faced him. "And what if she falls in love with someone else and he loses her? Then what? How are we going to atone for having asked him to sacrifice his chance for happiness?"

Layton narrowed his gaze. "He said he's not in love with her."

"If you believe that, I'll believe you're not in love with Tempest, Hawk."

Layton stared at Peyton. "Are you implying we don't have Randall's best interests at heart?"

Randall watched Peyton maintain Layton's cold gaze. "I know it's not intentional but asking him to stop seeing her is not in his best interests. I'm asking all of you to reconsider the facts. Remember that he's seeing her despite his promise not to. What does that tell you about how he really feels about her, Hawk?"

Brandon, Bancroft's twin, who had been silent, rose from one of the recliners. "I think Peyton's right. We can't interfere with Randall and Benai's relationship."

Randall sighed and stared at Brandon. He moistened his lips. "If you have a way to help Croft that would also allow me to continue seeing Benai, I'd be eternally grateful."

Brandon crossed the room to palm the back of his neck. "You need to listen to Peyton, Randall. If you feel half of what Peyton thinks you do for her, you don't want to risk losing her. Trust me, there's nothing worse than losing a love you can never regain."

He shook his head. "I...I know Peyton thinks I love her but—"

"You don't?"

With Brandon's probing palm still on the back of his neck, he averted his gaze and remained silent.

"Never mind." Brandon slapped the back of his neck.

Layton sighed. "Then what do you suggest we do, Brandon?"

"Right now Croft is filled with rage—all of it misdirected at Randall. I say we allow him to work some of it out."

"How?"

Brandon turned to look at Randall. "He'll have to work his aggression out with Randall."

Certain Peyton was about to object, Randall clasped a hand on to his twin's shoulder. "It's all right, Peyton. That's the lesser of two evils."

Peyton turned to face him. "But, Randy—"

Randall shook his head. "We have to help him. It's one or the other, Peyton. This is preferable to not seeing her."

Peyton sighed and slowly nodded.

Randall squeezed his shoulder before he turned his attention to Brandon. "I'm ready to do whatever is necessary to help him."

Layton placed a hand on his shoulder. "We never doubted that you would but there's something Brandon and I particularly want to make sure you understand, Randall. At no time did you behave in a less than honorable manner. You don't deserve this and I'm so sorry we have to ask this of you but at this point you're our only hope of helping him."

Randall nodded. "I understand."

* * * * *

"Can I join you, Benai?"

Seated on her parents' patio sipping green tea in the moonlight, Benai looked up. Her mother stood in the doorway leading into living room. The fireworks had ended several hours earlier. Her brother Reed and his family had returned to the hotel where they were staying while in California. Her father had gone to bed.

"Of course, Mom.

Her mother walked onto the patio and sat across the table from her. "Couldn't you sleep, dear?"

She shook her head. "No. What about you?"

"I heard you get up and then I heard the patio door slide open."

"I didn't mean to disturb you, Mom."

Her mother patted her hand. "Your father always teases me that the moment you or your brother arrive, I revert back to waking at the slightest sound as I did when you were both home."

She smiled. "We used to hate that we couldn't slip out of the house in the middle of the night because you had such sharp ears."

Her mother laughed. "All part of the mother hen routine."

"Do you want some tea? I can make you a cup."

"No." Her mother sighed. "Do you want to talk about him?"

"Who?"

"This man who's keeping you up at night."

"Oh. Him."

"Is he special?"

"I'm not sure." She hesitated and then told her mother about Randall and Bill.

To her surprise, her mother seemed to dismiss Bill and concentrated on Randall. "This Randall. He's one of Tempest's brothers-in-law?"

"Yes."

"Judging by the pictures you sent of the wedding party, the Grayhawks are all very attractive men."

She nodded. "Yes, they are."

"And this Randall is interested in you?"

"We've had a few dates."

"How do you feel about him?"

"I like him a lot."

"And Bill? Do you still like him as well?"

"He's... I don't really know him. It's been so long since I loved him and—I just don't know."

"Do you want to like Bill a lot?"

"I need to because lightning isn't going to strike twice. Layton fell in love with Temp but I don't think Randall is going to allow himself to fall in love with me."

"And yet he went through the expense of sending you here on his private jet."

She shrugged. "He's one of those internet multimillionaires who have more money than he could spend in several lifetimes."

"Even so, I doubt if he flies every woman he dates around on his jet."

"Probably not but I need to be realistic about him, Mom."

She nodded. "Yes, you do but that doesn't mean you should rule anything out. "Tell me about him."

She shrugged. "There's not much to tell."

"Where did you meet him?"

"I met him for the first time at the rehearsal dinner."

"Were you attracted to each other at first sight?"

"Hardly. He took one look at me and looked away."

"And?"

"He drove me home after the reception. He didn't call for seven weeks to ask me out."

"I can tell that you care for him. Does he care for you?"

"I'd like to think he does but he's been hurt and now he's determined not to fall in love again or get married."

"Does he know you want both?"

"Yes."

"And he still wants to see you?"

"Yes."

"Why, if he doesn't want either?"

"I don't know why."

"What does he want from you?"

She shook her head. "Nothing I'd want to admit to you or Dad."

"I see. Are you inclined to give him what he wants?"

"Yes. But I won't. At least I hope I won't. I want to get married to a man I can spend the rest of my life with." She smiled at her mother. "I want to love and trust him just as you do Dad."

"You'd like Randall to be that man?"

"Yes but that's not likely to happen because of how he feels about love. Forget marriage. He's totally against both of them."

"Which doesn't mean he won't succumb to both in due time with the right woman."

"He likes tiny, gorgeous blondes."

"Is your Randall dating anyone else?"

"No."

"So you two have an exclusive relationship?"

"Yes. He doesn't want to see other women. He just doesn't want to… He's afraid of being hurt again."

"Is he more afraid of that than he is of losing you?"

"I think he is."

"How are you going to handle that?"

"I'm not sure, Mom. Do you have any suggestions?"

"Do you think he's worth risking getting hurt again?"

"When I'm not with him I think he's not. When we're together, I think he is. But I'm not getting any younger and I don't know how much time I can afford to waste with him."

"Thirty-one is very young these days." Her mother squeezed her hand. "I think you can afford to give him and yourself a little time before you panic, dear."

"Thanks, Mom."

"Now tell me about him. Is he handsome? Tall? Dark?"

"He's absolutely gorgeous. He has a twin, Peyton. They're both tall and handsome. All the Grayhawks are but Randall and Peyton have blue-green eyes. Randall is charming and he makes me feel beautiful. He could have any woman he wants—"

"And he wants you? I have to say he has great taste in women."

Benai laughed. "You're just saying that because you're my mom."

"I'm saying it because it's true and apparently the handsome Randall agrees with me."

"Yes. He does."

"So he can't be all bad."

"No but I'd rather you didn't mention him to Dad."

"You can tell him yourself when you're ready. I think I'll go back to bed or your father will come looking for me." She smiled and rose. "He says he can't sleep unless I'm beside him."

Maybe Randall would feel like that about her one day. "Dad's a wise man." She rose and kissed her mother's cheek. "I think I'm going to go home early and see if I can't stir things up with Randall. Do you mind?"

"Of course your dad and I will be sorry to see you go home early but I understand. Good night."

"Good night, Mom."

* * * * *

Peyton met Benai at the airport when she returned to Philadelphia three days later. She smiled. "Peyton, hello."

He slipped an arm around her waist and kissed her cheek. "Hello, honey."

"I didn't expect to see you or am I being presumptuous assuming you're here because of me?"

"Of course I'm here because of you. I've come to offer you a lift home."

"How did you know my arrival time or even that I was coming home early?"

"I asked Tempest."

"Why?"

"Because we all wanted to know how much longer we'd have to put up with Randy's short temper. He's snapped at everyone at least twice—even Layton."

She feigned horror. "He dared to snap at older brother Layton?"

He laughed. "Shows you how badly he's missed you. Doesn't it? Did you miss him?"

"Yes."

"Good." He slipped an arm around her shoulders. "Let's go get your bags and you can tell me if you've decided to put him out of his misery."

"What do you mean?"

"I mean are you still intent on dating this old boyfriend of yours?"

"If he asks me out, I'll probably say yes."

"Why?"

"Because I'm not going to fall in love with Randall."

He stopped and lifted her chin. "Isn't it a little late to try to close that barn door, Benai?"

She blushed and walked away from him.

He followed her and caught her hand. "Benai—"

She jerked away from him. "I don't want to discuss my personal life with you, Peyton."

He nodded. "Understood." He extended a hand.

She moistened her lips and finally slipped her hand into his. "I don't want to talk about Bill or Randall."

"Okay." He squeezed her hand. "What would you like to talk about?"

"Nothing. I just want a ride home—in relative silence—*sans* the country music."

He laughed and gave her shoulders a squeeze. "I wouldn't discount country music if I were you. You can learn a lot from Randall by the songs he listens to in your presence."

"We weren't going to discuss him."

"We're not discussing him. I'm just passing on some personal information you might find useful. If I were you, I'd be very interested if he ever plays a song for you called "Love Out Loud". It's about a man who loves a woman but doesn't tell her. Afraid of losing her because he can't admit how he feels, he tells her love out loud doesn't come easy for him but inside, where it really counts, he loves her."

She swallowed slowly. "What are you trying to tell me, Peyton? Are you saying he's—"

"I'm suggesting that if he plays the song in your presence, you might want to take particular note of the words and know that he might or might not be trying to tell you something you may or may not be interested in knowing."

"Is he in love with me?"

He shrugged. "You didn't want to discuss him."

"I've changed my mind. I want to know if he's in love with me."

"He tells me he's not going to fall in love ever again."

She ground her teeth. "Damn, you are infuriating!"

He grinned and squeezed her hand. "It's one of my more endearing qualities."

She snatched her hand from his. "I'm glad you think so."

He recaptured her hand. "You could do a lot worse but no better than him."

"That's what Randall told me about Bancroft."

"And he was right. Please don't make the mistake of thinking just because Bancroft isn't himself at the moment that he's not a prize catch. He's an amazing man. But then so is Randall."

"He doesn't want to fall in love with me. Not after Pam."

He turned her to face him. "How do you know about Pam?"

"He told me about her."

"He did?"

She nodded. "Why do you sound so surprised?"

"He rarely discusses her with me and he and I have very few secrets from each other."

"Then I should be flattered?"

"In a word—yes."

"I'll take it under advisement."

"You do that."

"In the meantime, what does 'I love you' sound like in Cherokee?"

He caressed her cheek. "Trust me. You'll know it when you hear it."

"I will? How do I know I haven't already heard it? He lapses into Cherokee a lot when we're…" She moistened her lips.

He grinned. "Making love?"

Her cheeks burned but she maintained gaze. "Just give me a hint."

"If he's driven to say it, he'll say it with enough feeling that you'll know without understanding a single word of Cherokee that he's telling you he loves you."

"So you're saying I'm likely to hear it?"

"You'd be a better judge of that than I am. Only you know what lengths making love to you drive him."

"You're determined to be as unhelpful as possible. Aren't you?"

"Not intentionally." He kissed her cheek. "Now let me take you home."

"Thanks for coming to meet me, Peyton."

"My pleasure."

In his car, they listened to jazz in silence for the first twenty minutes of the drive before he turned down the sound. "Have you heard from Bancroft?"

She turned to study his profile. "No. Why should I?"

He shrugged. "I'm just making conversation."

She placed a hand on his arm. "You're not just making conversation. Be honest with me, Peyton."

He sighed. "We don't know where he is and we...I wondered if he'd contacted you."

"Why would he?"

"Because he still thinks of you as his. Given that fact, he's bound to contact you sooner or later."

"I'm not his."

"I understand that but he's not himself, Benai."

She tensed. "So you really do think he's likely to contact me?"

"Yes."

Great. "Am I going to need to be concerned if or when he does?"

He cast a brief look at her. "He might make what you'd consider a nuisance of himself but he'd never hurt you."

"You're sure of that?"

"Absolutely. We all are."

She relaxed. "Great. I'd hate to think I needed to be afraid of him."

"You don't."

She nodded.

He turned the stereo back up and they made the rest of the drive in silence.

Several vases of roses sat outside her apartment door.

She glanced at Peyton.

He grinned. "He heard you liked roses."

"Where is he?"

"Out trying to find Bancroft...along with the rest of our siblings."

"Is that why you came instead of him?"

"I'm not the one Croft has a problem with. Randy is."

"They're not likely to... They can work the problem between them out without—"

"A physical fight?"

"Yes."

He sighed. "Nothing like this has ever happened to us. We don't get into disputes over women."

She blushed.

He lifted her chin. "The misunderstanding between Randy and Croft isn't anyone's fault. It's certainly not yours."

"They're not likely to have a physical fight. Are they?"

"That's not something you need to worry about."

Her heart raced. "Please don't treat me like an idiot, Peyton. Are they likely to fight?"

"Croft is in a very dark place at the moment and all his negative energy is centered on Randall."

"Because of me."

"No. Not because of you. We're facing this problem because Croft extended himself helping Brandon. If not for that, none of this would be a problem."

"What can I do to help?"

"This is a very difficult time for Randall. You can help by being patient with him and firm with Croft when he contacts you. If you have any fears or concerns, you have my numbers. You can call me day or night and I'll be with you as quickly as possibly."

She stretched up to kiss his cheek. "Thank you, Peyton."

"You're very important to Randall. You do know that. Don't you?"

"I'd like to think I'm important to him."

"You are, which makes you very important to me. No thanks necessary."

"Can you stay awhile?"

He glanced at his watch. "I'd better not."

"Okay."

He carried her luggage and the vases inside, refused her offer of coffee and kissed her cheek. "When you see Randy again, be gentle and patient with him."

"I'll try."

"This thing with Croft is tearing him apart."

She nodded. "I know."

"He's torn between the two of you. Part of the problem with Croft would probably vanish—if Randy ended his relationship with you."

She sucked in a breath.

He squeezed her hand. "Don't worry, honey, that's not likely to happen."

She gripped his hand. "Are you sure?"

"I'm positive." He kissed her cheek. "I have to go but try not to worry."

Long after she was alone, she paced her living room, the words haunting her. *If he ended his relationship with you.* Should she call Randall? She longed to see him but a call from her would probably distract him or make things worse between him and Bancroft.

She unpacked and ran a bath. Stripping off her clothes, she took the cordless phone into the bathroom with her. It rang as she was about to place it on the floor by the tub.

She glanced at the caller ID screen. She smiled and slipped into the warm, scented water. "Hi Randall."

"How are you, Benai?"

"I'm fine. How are you?"

"Lonely and horny as hell."

"And a little on the short-tempered side…or so I've been told."

"Peyton talks too damned much."

"He's your biggest cheerleader."

"Did he kiss you?"

"Several times. On the cheek."

"Lucky for him. How was your vacation?"

"It was wonderful to see my parents and my brother and his family again. I couldn't believe how much the boys have grown. We visit at least once each year but I always start missing them the moment I get on a plane to head for home."

"So your parents were well? And your brother and his family?"

"Yes. Everyone was fine and we had a great time. We always do."

"Great. And did you date while you were there?"

"No, Randall, I didn't."

"Did you want to?"

"No."

"Did he call you?"

"No, he didn't but then neither did you."

"Did you want me to?"

"Yes and no."

"I wanted to but I wanted you to miss me."

"Mission accomplished."

"Good. I missed you too."

"Have you found Bancroft?"

He sighed. "Peyton's been talking again."

"Have you?"

"No."

"Are you all right with that, Randall?"

"How can I be? He thinks I betrayed him with you."

"I'm sorry. I know how you feel about him."

"He's never let me down. Benai. Never. Now he's somewhere alone thinking I stuck a knife in his back."

She sat up. "Please don't sound like that, Randall. You didn't betray him."

"Didn't I?"

"No!"

"I didn't have to... I should have stayed away from you."

She sighed, closing her eyes. "Damn it, Randall. You're going to have to piss or get off the damned pot. Lord knows Peyton has worked hard enough to impress upon me how upset you are. I understand that but I am not going to allow you to jerk me around. I know things are difficult for you. They're difficult for me as well. But you either want to see me or you don't."

"Think twice if you're about to issue an ultimatum, Benai. I'm not in a very good mood and you might not like my choice."

"Because I know you're upset, I'm going to overlook the inherent threat in your words, Randall."

"You do that."

She shook her head. Why the hell didn't she tell him to take a flying leap off the nearest high rise? "We should end this call before one of us says something the other will find difficult to forget or forgive."

"Shit. I'm sorry. It's just that—"

"Things are difficult I know. Let's talk tomorrow."

"No. I…I need to see you."

"Call me tomorrow and—"

"No. I need to see you tonight. Now."

"That wouldn't be a good idea, Randall."

"Probably not."

"I'm glad you agree we need some time apa—"

"We don't need any more damned time apart, Benai. What I need is to see you."

"That would be nice but—"

"We can spend the weekend together."

"I'm having a bath, Randall. When I get out—"

"I'll be there to drive you here to spend the weekend with me."

She shook her head. "No."

"I'm lonely, confused and I need to see you tonight. Don't make me beg."

The raw emotion in his tone both dismayed her and gave her hope. Surely he wouldn't expose so much of himself to her unless he cared about her. "Randall—"

"Why have you returned early if not to see me?"

"My world doesn't revolve around you, Randall."

"That's unfortunate because mine does revolve around you."

"No it doesn't."

"You have no idea how I feel, Benai."

"I would if you'd be honest about your feelings."

"No matter what you say, I know you know how I feel about you."

"Then say it!"

"Why should the words be so important when you know how I feel?"

"Randall—"

"I'll be there in thirty minutes, Benai."

She sighed. "Thirty minutes." She removed the phone from her ear and stared at it for several moments before she set it down on the floor beside the tub. She lay back against her inflatable pillow. Even as she told herself she was not going to spend the weekend with him, she tingled at the thought of another opportunity to test the bounds of his feelings for her as she washed.

Glancing at the clock over the bathroom door, she sat up. It was time to get dressed. She slipped into an expensive black silk dress she'd bought on vacation. The top was form fitting with a built-in bra that left her shoulders and back bare. The skirt hugged her hips and ended just above her knees. She stepped into a pair of black leather pumps. She slipped a matching bag over her shoulder that had cost more than the dress.

Studying her reflection, she smiled. Instead of the plain woman she'd have seen before, she saw a tall, statuesque one with a body and a luxuriant head of hair and an engaging smile and dark, sexy eyes capable of catching and keeping the attention of a handsome, successful man like Randall.

Since you're unable to resist him, you'd better manage to win his heart within a month, or you are going to end this relationship, even if it means you have to move out of state.

Her doorbell rang. She moved over to her intercom. "Randall?"

"Yes."

"You're ten minutes early."

"Let me in."

She released the lobby door and moved into the living room. Her apartment door rang several minutes later.

The moment she opened the door, he took her in his arms. He held her, rubbing his cheek against hers. "I missed you."

"I missed you too." She lifted her face, her lips parted, expecting and wanting to be kissed.

He hugged her but didn't kiss her.

She placed her hands on his shoulders. "What does a woman have to do to get a kiss around here? Beg?"

"If I start kissing you, we'll end up in bed."

She stroked her fingers through his hair. "And that would be a bad thing because of what?"

"Because I need you to believe I want and need more from you than sex."

She caressed his cheek. "You're a sweet, sexy man, Randall Grayhawk. No wonder I'm so nuts about you."

He laughed and kissed her cheek. He released her and stepped back to survey her outfit. "Damn, Benai. You take my breath away."

She shook her head. "Randall, you're going to my head."

He engulfed her in a warm embrace. "That's the plan, sweetheart."

She clung to him. "I wish I were your sweetheart."

"You are."

She lifted her head to meet his gaze. "That's the first time you've called me sweetheart when we weren't intimate."

"I've never said anything to you I didn't mean."

She frowned. God, she hoped that wasn't true or he'd never fall in love with her or want to marry her. She dismissed the thought and stroked her hands over his shoulders. "What have you been doing while I've been away?"

"Missing you." He released her and glanced at his watch. "We have reservations at Le-Bec Fin," he said, naming one of Philadelphia's premier restaurants. "Are you ready?"

"Yes. Just let me get my wrap."

He caught her arm as she started to turn away. "Do you have your overnight bag packed for the weekend?"

"Yes, Randall, I do."

"I'll come with you to get it."

She grinned at him. "Is that a flimsy excuse to get me alone in the bedroom?"

He slapped her ass. "Do I need an excuse to get you alone?"

"No."

He slipped an arm around her waist. "That's my woman."

She looked up at him. "I am your woman, Randall. Be very careful not to hurt me."

"I wouldn't willingly hurt you for several million dollars."

"God, help me, I'm starting to believe that."

He followed her into her bedroom. Instead of picking up her overnight bag, which sat beside the bed, he walked over to stand in front of the mirrors on her closet doors.

She smiled. "Admiring yourself?"

He lifted a long, gold jeweler's box from his right pocket and turned to look at her. "Actually I was wondering what this would look like around your neck."

"A gift for me?"

He nodded. "Come see if you like it."

She crossed the room. He handed her the box. She moistened her lips before she lifted the top off. Inside was an eighteen–karat white–gold diamond eternity necklace. The numerous diamonds were set in a classic three-prong setting that showed the fire in each stone.

When she stood staring down at it in silent wonder, he lifted the necklace from the box, moved behind her and fastened it around her neck.

She stared at her reflection. The beautiful necklace circled her skin like a ring of pale fire. She lifted her gaze to meet his in the mirror. "Oh, Randall."

"Do you like it or shall I return it and pick out something else?"

"Do I? I love it."

"But?"

She turned to face him. "It's exquisite and I love it but it must have cost more than some people make in a year."

He shrugged. "You're worth every penny. I spent several hours picking it out. Please don't tell me you can't or won't accept it."

"I shouldn't."

"But you're going to?"

"Yes."

He grinned. "Good and while you're doing that, here's something to go with it."

"Not another gift, Randall."

"It's just a little something to complement the necklace." He removed her earrings, handed them to her and lifted a small, rectangular box from his other pocket. He opened it to reveal a matching pair of diamond stud earrings.

She stood still as he put them on.

He then stepped back and met her gaze in the mirror. He stroked his fingers down either side of her neck. "Damn, you are so beautiful, Benai."

She turned and linked her arms around his neck. "Who wouldn't look attractive wearing this much ice?"

He shook his head. "Don't you know by now you'd be beautiful dressed in a sack? The necklace and earrings only showcase your natural, god-given beauty."

She stared at him. Her natural, god-given beauty? Damn, he must be in love. "I don't know what to say, Randall."

"You don't need to say anything—at least not now. There is something I'd love to hear you say later."

"What?"

"We can discuss it tonight." He glanced at the bed before he kissed her cheek. "We'd better go before we end up in bed."

She nodded. "Not that I'd object to that but I am hungry. So let's go."

Chapter Nine

ಬಂ

During dinner he alternated between being charming and inattentive. He seemed to have lost his appetite and several times she looked up to find him staring at her with an inscrutable look in his eyes.

She laid her fork down. "What's wrong, Randall?"

"I'm with you. What could possibly be wrong?"

She smiled briefly. "Nice try but of course there's something wrong. What is it?"

"Maybe I should have said nothing new was wrong. I'm just worried about Croft. We don't know where he is or what kind of shape he's in."

"Is there anything I can do to help?"

He gave her a wan smile. "I don't suppose you can give me some type of potion to help me get over this...thing I have for you?"

She shook her head. "Why would I want to do that?"

"My life would be so much easier if I didn't want you so much. If I didn't want you, my relationship with Croft wouldn't be shattered."

"Are you sorry we met?"

"Yes."

She sucked in a breath and fought to keep tears from stinging her eyes. "Oh, Randall."

"And no." He sighed. "Part of me is sorry because I'm afraid I might not be able to repair my relationship with Croft. I can't tell you how sad that makes me. But another, bigger part of me could never regret meeting you—no matter what."

"I'd like you to want me even more, not less, Randall." She touched his hand. "While I am sorry about Croft, I don't regret anything with you either."

He sighed. "It was just wishful thinking. Like the singer in one of Peyton's favorite songs, I'm past the point of rescue."

She liked that he feared he was past the point of rescue from his feelings for her. "Aren't you happy with me?"

"Yes."

He put so much feeling into the single syllable she knew he meant it. "Then why does that need to be such a bad thing?"

"It wouldn't be—if not for the situation with Croft."

"I'm sorry about that, Randall."

He nodded. "I know. Would you like anything else?"

"No. Thanks."

He glanced at his watch. "Would you like to go dancing?"

"Yes—at home."

"Home?"

She nodded, squeezing his hand. "Home."

"Yours or mine?"

"Yours but first I need to use the ladies' room."

He nodded and rose.

Several minutes later as she was brushing her hair, a beautiful blonde joined her at the mirror. Benai immediately recognized her as Juliet Warner, the woman Randall had introduced her to after they'd gone horseback riding.

Benai ignored her. Perhaps the woman wouldn't recognize her.

"That's an exquisite necklace."

Benai flashed a brief smile.

"A gift from Randall?"

"Yes, it is."

Juliet arched a brow. "Of course this isn't as impressive as the trinket he gave you but it's also presents from him." She lifted her left wrist.

Benai glanced down at a pretty tennis bracelet. "Nice," she said quietly and turned back to her reflection.

"I'm surprised you're still seeing Randall."

"Well I am. In fact I'm here with him."

"Amazing. You're not exactly his type. Are you?"

Benai decided she'd taken enough shit. She turned to face her. "Being his type hasn't exactly done you much good, now, has it, honey? Apparently he's decided he wants a real woman who weighs more than seventy pounds fully dressed."

Juliet narrowed her gaze. "Would you be so confident if I told you we've fucked several times since he introduced us?"

Benai shook her head. "Let me save us both some time. There's no way you're going to convince me that he's been with you or any other woman since he's been with me."

"You're that confident of him and yourself?"

"Yes." She leaned forward to stare into the other woman's eyes. "You might have had him in the past but he's mine now and I fully intend to keep him. So you should come to grips with the reality that the closest you're ever going to get to him again is in daydreams or fantasies."

"Okay. So maybe you're the flavor of the week but his underlying tastes haven't changed. He's just slumming with you. You know men in his position. They like to take a walk on the wild side and sample the forbidden every so often."

"So I'm a phase he's going through?"

"Yes. When he's tired of your meat and potatoes, he'll come back to me for filet mignon." She smiled, shaking her head so that her long, blonde curls cascaded around her slim shoulders. "I know how much he loves his filet mignon."

"If I were you, I'd face the facts. And fact one is that he doesn't want you or any other woman. Fact two is he's my man now and I'm keeping him."

"I wouldn't count on a man with his looks, money and power not to want a trophy wife on his arm when he's ready to settle down. At the risk of sounding like a bitch, that kind of leaves you out in the damned cold, girlfriend, doesn't it?"

Benai arched a brow. "Say what you like, I'm the one who'll be sharing his bed tonight."

"Don't let that go to your head. It won't last. When he wants a woman on his arm he can be proud of again, I'll be waiting to take him back into my arms, bed and pussy."

"Dream on, *girlfriend*. It'll be a damn cold day in hell before you get your paws on him again."

"We'll see about that."

"Yes we will. If you want to lose yourself in unrealistic fantasies, go right ahead. "

Juliet blushed and quickly left the ladies' room.

Benai stared after her. *Take that, you has been.* She turned back to her reflection, smiling. *He's yours now, Nai, and you're going to keep him so happy he won't even have time to recall that he used to like women like her.*

She was even more certain of that fact when she noted the light in his eyes at her return to the dining room. The intimacy in his smile assured her she had nothing to fear from the Juliet Warners of the world. He was hers.

Once seated in his car, she told him she'd encountered Juliet without mentioning what they'd discussed.

"Some women don't know how to let go when a relationship is over." He glanced at her. "No matter what she might have said I haven't seen or talked to her since you and I went riding."

She nodded. "I know."

"You do?"

193

"Yes, Randall, I do."

"Good." He started the car. "How about some music?"

She settled against her seat. "Great. Let's hear some good old-fashioned country music."

"Really? You're serious?"

"Yes. I'm serious."

He started the CD. The mellow voice of a man lamenting that he wasn't any good at expressing his feelings filled the interior of the car.

She turned to look at his profile. He had his gaze on the road ahead. "What's the name of this song?"

"'Love Out Loud'."

"What?"

"It's called 'Love Out Loud'. Do you like it?"

This must be a banner night for her. First, he told her he was beyond being rescued from his feelings for her and now he was playing the song Peyton had told her was important. "Do you?"

"Yes, Benai, I do."

She closed her eyes and listened as the singer begged his woman not·to take his silence as a reason to doubt his love. Randall played the song three times on the fifty-minute drive to his mansion. Was that his way of telling her he loved her without actually saying the words? If he was in love with her, did he love her enough to ask her to marry him? Or did he expect her to be satisfied with expensive gifts in lieu of marriage?

At his mansion, he ushered her into the family room.

She sank onto the loveseat.

"Would you like a drink?"

"A martini please."

He poured her drink and handed it to her. "Make yourself at home while I take your overnight bag upstairs." As he left the room, he pointed a remote at the stereo system and soft jazz filled the air.

She walked around the room, studying the various pictures of the Grayhawks adorning the walls. There were numerous pictures of Malita Grayhawk. She couldn't find a single picture of Randall's father. She frowned. What was his name? She couldn't recall ever hearing it.

She turned to smile at Randall when he returned to the family room. "There you are."

He crossed the room to take her in his arms. "Missed me?"

She slipped her arms around his neck. "Every second we're apart."

He hugged her, brushing his lips against her face. "You're making me crazy."

She leaned back to look at him. "Why don't we go to bed and you can tell me about it?"

"We were going to dance first."

She stroked her fingers through his hair. "Would you think me shameless if I admitted that the only dance I'm interested in is when your cock is dancing inside me?"

"Yes." He grinned, cupping her ass. "But that's how I like my women—shamelessly honest about their desire and need for me."

"Then you should be quite fond of me."

"I am quite fond of you." He hugged her. "Let's go upstairs and I'll show you just how fond of you I am."

She stroked her fingers through his hair. "Okay."

Upstairs in his bedroom, they slowly undressed each other. She lay in bed, watching as he placed several condoms, lube and a slender, ebony-colored vibrator on the nightstand before he joined her in bed.

She smiled as he slipped between her legs. "You're just where you belong, handsome."

"Yes," he agreed his voice brusque. "I belong in your arms because you're mine."

She caressed his shoulders and back. "I am yours, Randall."

He rolled her onto her back and kissed her slowly, rubbing his flaccid cock against her leg as he cajoled her lips apart.

She parted both her lips and her legs for him. "I'm yours, my Randall."

"Mine, sweetheart. All mine." He thumped his hips against her and whispered softly to her in Cherokee between warm, slow, honey-sweet kisses.

Lying under his big body, with her eyes closed and his lips, tongue and hands creating a magic world in which only the two of them existed, she quickly surrendered to her desire and need for him.

His cock lengthened and hardened against her thigh. He sucked her breasts while he fingered her slit, making her burn for him. With her pussy flooded and aching, she longed to have him inside her. "Love me," she whispered.

She moaned a soft protest when he eased out of her.

He urged her onto her stomach. She kept her eyes closed as he spread her nether cheeks and slipped a lubed finger into her rectum. He rubbed his face against her ass cheeks before he rained biting kisses against them. As he did, he slipped a second finger into her. He gently eased his fingers in and out of her rear.

Wonderful sensations seized her. "Oh…"

He licked her cheeks. "Get ready to have your lovely ass filled, sweetheart."

"I'm not quite ready to have your cock up there yet, Randall."

"I know. This is just the second step in the process. Get ready."

She felt the smooth, warm length of the vibrator pierce her rear and slide several inches up into her rectum. She sucked in a breath.

He paused. "Are you all right?"

She nodded. "I'm ready to have more of it inserted."

"Yeah?" He eased a little more into her. "Is that all right?"

She licked her lips. "Yes."

Keeping her on her side, he slipped his body close to hers. He lifted her chin. "Look at me."

She opened her eyes.

"Do you like my cock?"

"Oh, you know I do, Randall."

He smiled. "How much?"

She caressed her shoulders. "A lot."

"Right answer." He thrust deep into her.

She gasped and clung to him. "Lord, you feel so good."

"Is it only my cock you like so much?"

"No," she moaned. "I like you too."

"How much?"

"A lot."

He drew his hips back.

She moaned in protest as she felt his cock withdrawing from her. "Don't stop, Randall."

"Do you just like me, Benai?"

She closed her eyes. "I more than like you."

He dragged his tongue over her breasts before he lifted his head. "Open your eyes and tell me what I want to hear."

She shook her head.

"Open your eyes," he commanded in a soft but insistent voice.

She obeyed.

"Now tell me what I want to hear."

"Why?"

"You want to say it and I want to hear it. We're on the same page, sweetheart."

She moistened her lips. "I...you know how I feel."

"I think I do but I just want to hear you admit it."

"I...love...you. There. I've said it. Are you satisfied?"

"No."

She stiffened. "What?"

"Say it again...louder this time and try to sound more decisive, as if you mean it."

"You bastard. You know how I feel about you."

"Then sound like you mean it." He slapped her ass.

She gasped as his striking palm drove the last inch of the vibrator into her rear.

"I'm waiting, Benai."

She balled a hand into a fist and hit it against his shoulder. "I love you."

He sucked in a breath, a slow smile spreading across his face. "Again. I want to hear you say you love me again."

"Why? I know I'm not the first woman to say it."

"You're the only one who really matters. Say it again."

Delighted with his admission, she repeated it again and again. She chanted it until he silenced her with a slow, warm, lingering kiss. He savored her lips, tasting them as if he were sampling fine wine. His passion infused her with a delicious level of delight that overwhelmed her senses. "Fuck me," she pleaded.

"No fucking tonight," he groaned. "I'm going to make love to you until you melt in my arms and explode all around me."

"Please do."

He eased her onto her back. He rested his weight on his extended arms. "Are you okay on your back with that lucky vibrator in your ass?"

She wiggled her hips. "I've never been better."

"You're about to be." Lowering his weight onto her body, he made slow, sweet love to her. The touch of his fingers sent heat and chills along her sensitive nerve endings. He lingered over every caress. He made each kiss count. Tasting and nibbling at her lips. Sucking her tongue into his mouth until the muscles in her stomach clenched and her entire body pulsed with anticipation of the exquisite delight to come.

She clung to him, lost in a world where he was her reason for living. Her need for him grew and swelled until it rivaled her need to breathe.

He fed her need with each long, deep stroke into her body. His slick length sliding in and out of her sent her spiraling that much closer to the most luscious climax of her life.

When he tore his lips away from hers, he pressed his cheek against hers. He murmured to her in Cherokee, caressing her breasts as he continued the leisurely strokes in and out of her pussy. At some point he'd reached behind her to turn the vibrator on to a slow buzz.

With it buzzing in her rear, her climax built slowly, overshadowing everything else. She floated over a high cliff, hanging on by her nails, wanting to fall over into the warm, wet water below but afraid the fall would totally consume and destroy her, drown her in an ocean of need.

"Tell me you love me again," he demanded, rubbing his chest against her breasts.

"I do," she moaned. "I adore you. I need you. I love you so much I ache with it."

"Now I'm going to make you ache with pleasure," he warned.

"Randall... Oh, Randall."

He thrust into her—deep and hard, grinding his pubic hair against her clit as he bottomed out in her.

A jolt of pure pleasure, sweeter and more wonderful than any she'd ever experienced sliced through her in an endless succession of waves. He whispered to her, filling her ears with soft endearments. The exotic words combined with the exquisite friction of his cock pounding in her pussy and the vibrator buzzing in her ass overwhelmed her.

She lost her grip on reality, sobbed his name and tumbled into the welcoming water below. She was dragged under where she happily drowned in a sea of ultimate pleasure, where, happy and sated, she lay until she drifted to sleep.

* * * * *

Long after Benai fell asleep, Randall lay awake with his body curled against her back. He was tired and longed to sleep but the enormity of the mess he'd managed to get himself into held sleep at bay. He'd never felt more helpless to control his life and future.

Nor had he ever felt more selfish. After his disastrous relationship with Pam, he'd taken care to ensure he remained in control of all his romantic entanglements. He'd always ended each relationship long before he found himself in any danger of feeling anything more than desire.

And he'd never allowed himself to develop an interest in any woman on whom one of his brothers had staked a claim— until he looked across the room at Layton and Tempest's wedding rehearsal dinner and saw Benai for the first time. Looking into her dark, seductive gaze, his entire carefully crafted world had collapsed around him, imperiling not only his sense of honor but Bancroft's mental stability.

He'd clearly lost his mind along with his sense of balance. Betraying Bancroft's trust for a woman so far removed from his ideal one was beyond insane. It defied belief. Yet when Declan had suggested he stop seeing her, he'd felt as if Declan had attempted to rip out his heart.

Not even for Pam's love would he have considered betraying one of his brothers. He stroked a hand over Benai's large, warm breasts. What was it about her that captivated him and robbed him of his sense of honor? Why hadn't sleeping with her abated the need for her that overrode his concern for everything he held dear? He knew Peyton would insist he was in love. But hell would freeze over before he gave his heart to another woman.

Nevertheless, hearing her say she loved him and knowing she meant it had touched a part of his emotions he'd jealously guarded for years.

She murmured in her sleep, rubbing her ass against his groin.

The desire to lift her upper leg and thrust his bare cock deep into her pussy left him aching. He stroked his hand down her body to palm her. Slipping a finger inside her, he closed his eyes, imaging how her tight, hot channel would feel flooded with his seed. The thought excited his passions.

He would only need to push inside her and make love to her. She'd probably be angry at first but wouldn't a woman in love welcome sex without barriers, even without the benefit of marriage?

There was only one way to find out. It would only take a few seconds to slide inside her. He was confident that once that happened, her protest would die under the weight of their shared desire.

She murmured his name.

Should he view her soft sound as a signal for him to thrust into her? He lifted her top leg and maneuvered his body so that his cock was poised at her entrance. He fingered her slit. She was wet and in position to be impaled on his cock. One swift movement and he'd be buried balls deep inside her.

Just one thrust. She loved him. She'd forgive him and if he was lucky they'd welcome their baby in less than a year. He'd love their baby. But the child would have a father who put his own selfish needs ahead of his honor...much like Randall's father had done most of his life. Hell would freeze before he stooped to his father's level—uncaring how much he hurt those who loved him.

He groaned, lowered her leg and jerked his hips backward.

She made a small sound of protest.

He waited a moment and then eased his body away from hers. Seated on the side of the bed, he glanced at the bedside clock—twelve ten a.m.

It was going to be a long night. He rose from the bed and padded across the carpet to his walk-in closet. He slipped a pair of jeans over his bare body before he left the bedroom. Crossing the hall to one of the guest bedrooms, he picked up the phone.

With his finger on the keypad, he shook his head and laid the phone down. There was no need to disturb Peyton just because he was too guilt ridden to sleep. He stretched out on his back on the bed and lay staring up at the ceiling until he drifted into an uneasy sleep, which quickly turned into a nightmare.

Randall bolted into a sitting position in bed, his heart racing. Sweat rolled down his bare chest. He stared around the moonlit room, taking slow deep breaths. He closed his eyes quickly and then took another deep breath, afraid he'd actually see Bancroft's lifeless body.

It had been a nightmare. Thank god. He groaned and fell back across the bed only to sit up again when the bedroom door opened.

Benai stood in the doorway. The light from the hallway behind her revealed her long, bare legs. She wore the shirt he'd discarded the night before. With her long hair falling around her shoulders in a dark cloud, she was absolutely stunning. He couldn't imagine a single woman, blonde or otherwise, who could compare favorably to her.

"Randall?"

He glanced at the bedside clock—three forty a.m. "Benai? What's wrong?"

She stepped inside. She quickly crossed the room to sit on the side of the bed. "I heard you shout."

"I'm sorry. I had a nightmare."

"Do you want to talk about it?"

There was no point in subjecting her to his guilt-driven nightmare. He shook his head. "Thanks but it's over."

"Are you all right?"

"I...ah...yes."

She brushed a hand against his cheek. "You're sweating. Are you sure you're all right?"

He nodded. "Yes."

She stroked his hair. "What are you doing in here, Randall?"

He decided to be honest with her. "I needed to get away from the temptation you presented."

"What temptation?"

"To make love to you without a condom."

Her fingers stilled in his hair. She leaned away from him. "While I was asleep?"

Hearing the censure in her voice, he nodded slowly. "Yes."

She frowned. "How could you even consider doing that? I told you I don't have unprotected sex."

"There's no need to sound so damned holier than thou, Benai. It's not like you woke up and had to fight me off. I was tempted but I resisted the temptation. I didn't do it."

"But you were tempted to?"

"Clearly or I wouldn't be in here."

She shook her head and then stroked her hand down his chest. "No one's perfect, Randall. It doesn't matter that you were tempted. What matters is that you resisted the temptation." She kissed his cheek. "Now come back to bed."

He leaned his forehead against hers. "I don't think you can trust me."

She linked her arms around his neck. "I can and do trust you. I know you won't let me down, Randall."

"I'm not so sure your faith is well founded, Benai. Croft trusted me too and look how well that turned out for him."

She pressed a finger against his lips. "Oh, Randall, please. You have to stop beating up on yourself. There's nothing you can say that's going to make me question your trustworthiness."

He closed his eyes, reliving the horror of his nightmare.

"Randall?"

He sighed and opened his eyes. "I'm not nearly as worthy of your trust as you seem to think I am."

She hugged him, rubbing her cheek against his. "Let's go back to bed."

"If you're sure."

"I'm very sure. I know you always try to do the right thing, even when you don't want to."

"Try telling that to Croft."

"No." She drew away from him. "I don't want to hear that you think you've betrayed him. You haven't and if he's half the man I know he is, he knows that too. Just wait for him to get better so he can tell you himself. Now let's go back to bed. I want to hold you."

He'd never wanted to be held more. He nodded. "Okay."

Back in his bedroom, he expected to lie sleepless. But Benai drew him into her arms. "Go to sleep, Randall."

He burrowed against her.

She held him, whispering to him softly. She stroked his back and peppered him with gentle kisses until he relaxed and finally fell asleep.

* * * * *

The ringing phone woke Randall. He groaned and rolled over onto his side. Benai lay on her side, still asleep. He glanced at his bedside clock. It showed eight oh five. Hadn't he just closed his eyes? He snatched the cordless phone from his nightstand before it woke Benai. "Hello," he said, closing his eyes.

"What are you doing still at home, Hawk?" his sister demanded. "You were supposed to be standing outside my door five minutes ago."

He sat up, swearing softly. He raked a hand through his hair. "Oh, hell. I forgot about the charity breakfast. Can you drive yourself there and make my apologies for being late? I'll be there as soon as possible."

"Benai's with you, isn't she?"

"Never mind who I'm with, Lelia."

"Looks like I'm going to have to get to work on another batch of lover's balm."

Aware of Benai stirring beside him, he lowered his voice. "Just please do as I ask."

"Okay, Hawk. Peyton and I will be there in less than twenty minutes."

"Peyton's with you?"

"Yes. He showed up at my door twenty minutes ago and told me he'd take your place."

"I'll be there in time for dessert." He hung up and found Benai sitting up watching him.

She still wore his shirt. He smiled. "I'm going to need you to amuse yourself for a few hours. I have a charity breakfast I forgot about."

"Should I go home?"

"No." He kissed her cheek. "Please stay. I'll be back as soon as I can."

"Okay."

"Go back to sleep." He kissed her lips and went into the bathroom to shower. When he emerged from the bathroom, she'd fallen asleep. He bent and kissed her cheek before he left the bedroom.

* * * * *

Benai woke again just after ten. Feeling hungry, she showered and dressed. When she left the bedroom, she found a small, wheeled table outside the door. It contained several warming trays.

She wheeled the tray inside the bedroom and closed the door. She removed her blouse, replaced it with Randall's shirt and ate a leisurely breakfast on the balcony outside his bedroom.

After breakfast, she stretched out on one of the chaise lounges and dozed.

Randall kissed her awake later. "Wake up, sleeping beauty."

She smiled and opened her eyes. Randall sat on the side of her lounger. She caressed his cheek. "How did your charity affair go?"

"Peyton and Lelia tell me it went just fine. I arrived in time to write a check."

"I'll bet you're very generous."

"I have my moments."

She yawned. "What time is it?"

"One thirty. Are you hungry?"

"No."

"Good. Then get dressed so we can go riding."

She stiffened. "Riding? You mean on that creature of yours?"

"His name is Gray and he'd love to carry you anywhere you'd like to go."

"Oh, he would, would he?"

"Count on it. He's almost as devoted to you as I am." He caressed her cheek. "Come riding with me and Gray?"

She linked her arms around his neck. "I'm such a pushover for you."

He kissed her. "That's what happens when you fall in love."

"One of these days, Randall, I'm going to want to hear that I'm not in love alone."

He sighed. "You know how I feel about love."

"And you know how I feel about it. One of us is going to have to bend a little."

He nodded. "I know but can we leave it for now? I'm really not feeling at my best, Benai. I just want to shut out the rest of the world and spend some time with you."

Hearing the tension in his voice, she nodded. "Okay. Today it'll be just me and you."

"And Gray," he said, smiling.

She laughed. "You, me and a horse named Gray. We'll shut the rest of the world out."

"That's the spirit. Once you get to know Gray, you'll love him as I do."

She grimaced. "I'll probably come to...tolerate him. Eventually I might even like him."

He grinned. "That's my girl."

Later, sitting on the big stallion in front of Randall, she felt relaxed enough to glance around and enjoy the beautiful scenery of the Wissahickon Valley Park.

Randall showed no inclination to kiss or caress her during their second horseback ride together. He seemed preoccupied. They made most of the ride in silence.

After the ride, they returned to his mansion to shower and change. When they left the mansion, there was a luxury car parked in the oval.

"Wow. That's beautiful."

He slipped a hand into his pants pocket and dropped a set of keys in her palm. "Would you like to drive?"

"Are you kidding?"

"Nope." He held the driver's door open for her.

"This must have cost at least sixty grand."

He shrugged. "What's sixty grand between a man and his woman?"

She smiled and slipped inside.

She drove to an exclusive restaurant on the outskirts of the city.

He picked at his food and didn't seem inclined to talk.

She glanced at her watch after coffee. "It's getting late. Take me home?"

He looked up, frowning. "Home? You're spending the night with me."

"I'd like to but I really don't think you're in the mood for company."

He reached across the table to hold her hand. "I am tired and a little preoccupied but not so tired that I don't want to fall asleep with you. And I'm not too tired to dance."

She tilted her head. "Are you sure?"

"Positive. I'll never be too tired to hold you in my arms."

She smiled. "You are a sweet man, Randall Grayhawk."

He grinned. "Is that why you love me?"

She shrugged. "That and your bank balance."

He arched a brow. "You know what? Even if that were true, I'd still need you with a desperation I can almost taste."

"Oh Randall. Let's go dance."

They danced for half an hour on the hotel terrace under the stars before returning to his mansion.

After undressing each other, they slipped into the hot tub on his balcony. Within minutes, he fell asleep. She let him sleep for a half an hour before she woke him.

"Let's get you to bed."

"I'm sorry."

She pressed a finger against his lips. "Don't apologize for being tired."

They went to bed where he quickly fell back asleep.

Chapter Ten

೮ා

Benai woke alone in bed the next morning. After a quick shower, she had a long soak in the whirlpool bath. Then she left the bedroom in search of Randall. She heard voices coming from the family room. She quickened her pace.

The sound of feminine laughter drifted into the hallway from the open door of the family room.

Still smiling, she stepped inside. Her smile quickly vanished.

Randall wasn't alone. A beautiful woman with short blonde hair shared the loveseat with him. She had a hand on his arm and her eyes trained on his face. Everything about the woman's attitude indicated she was totally attracted to Randall. And she was exactly the type of woman to hold more than a passing attraction for Randall.

As if he felt her gaze on him, Randall looked up. He smiled and rose. "There you are." He crossed the room to her.

She stared up at him, her lips pressed into a tight line.

He narrowed his gaze and spoke softly. "So. It's still like that, is it?"

"What?"

He leaned close so that his lips nearly touched her ear. "You said you trusted me but that trust didn't extend to finding me talking to women. Does it?"

Blood rushed to her cheeks. "I never said that."

"But the look in your eyes tells me you don't."

"Don't put words in my mouth."

"She's my assistant, not my woman." He straightened, cupping a hand under her elbow. "Come meet Bali."

She nodded and walked across the room with him.

The woman turned a pair of cool green eyes that shot daggers at Benai even as she flashed a fake smile in her direction.

"Benai, this is my executive assistant and right hand, Bali Jordon. Bali, this is Benai Peters."

Benai smiled and extended her hand. "Nice to meet you."

Bali touched her hand briefly and widened her fake smile. "Likewise." She turned to look at Randall. "Can you spare me a few more minutes, Randall?"

Benai suspected Bali wanted more than a few minutes with him. Was Randall interested? If he was, there was nothing she could do about it. "I'll leave you two alone."

Bali nodded. "Would you? I won't keep him much longer."

Benai started to turn.

Randall stopped her with a hand on her arm. "No. Don't leave, Benai." He turned to look at Bali. "Benai and I are going to spend the rest of the day together. I'm sure the rest can wait until tomorrow, Bali."

"Oh. Okay." She picked up a briefcase from the floor. "Then I'll see you tomorrow?"

"Yes — in the office." He flashed her a brief smile. "Thanks for coming by. Enjoy the rest of your weekend and close the door on you way out, will you?"

She nodded, cast a cool look at Benai and left the room with obvious reluctance.

Benai stared after her. The idea of Randall working so closely with a woman who so clearly had the hots for him unsettled her.

Randall turned her to face him. "What are you thinking?"

She spoke quickly before she changed her mind. "Are all your staff and employees tiny, gorgeous blondes?"

He arched a brow. "I told you I liked petite blondes."

He could say that after practically devouring her the previous night? "Yes. You did. Are they?"

"All of them? No. You've seen several of the staff here." He shrugged. "Are some of them blonde? Yes but I can't see why you'd allow that to become a problem between us when you know you're the only woman I'm interested in."

Would he feel the same way if she surrounded herself with Denzel Washington lookalikes? She doubted it. She glanced at her watch. "It's after ten. Can you have your driver take me home?"

He caught her hand and turned her back to face him. "I hoped we could spend the day together here."

After she'd displayed a jealous streak she had no business feeling? She knew in her heart there was no basis to be jealous of any woman. She'd withstood Juliet Warner's attempts to make her jealous. Why had she freaked with this Bali?

She shook her head. "I need a ride home."

He slid his hand down her arm to link his fingers through hers. "Why? Because my assistant is a blonde? Don't you think you're overreacting?"

His stating the obvious annoyed her. She pulled her hand away from his. "Am I going to need to call a cab, Randall?"

He stared at her.

"Fine. I'll call a cab." She crossed the room to the door.

He followed her and placed his palm on the door panel.

When she reluctantly turned, he bent his head and kissed her. "Stay with me, Benai."

She shivered but pressed her hands against his shoulders. "We both wanted this weekend but it's time to get back to reality, Randall."

He slipped his arms around her waist and hugged her. "Isn't this real?"

"How can it be when you surround yourself with tiny blondes and I couldn't be less like your ideal woman?"

He brushed his lips against her cheek. "Did you think I wanted to be with anyone but you for a single minute of the last two days?"

Recalling the pleasure they'd shared, she knew she'd been the only object of his desire. She curled her hands into fists against his chest to keep from linking them around his neck. "No but—"

He lifted his head and looked down at her. He pressed her against the door and held her there with the weight of his body. "Do you think I'd rather be with anyone else now?"

She could feel his cock stirring. "No but—"

"But what? What is your problem, Benai? When you thought I might bow to Croft's wishes and not see you, you weren't happy. Now that I've defied him, you're still not happy. This is not a good time for me. I don't need any more grief—especially not from you. Tell me what you want from me and I'll do my best to give it to you but don't expect me to be able to read your damned mind."

She stared at him, a chill spreading through her. "Who says I want anything more than the last nights?"

He released her and stepped back. "So you wanted a one-night stand?"

She shrugged. "People have them all the time."

"Do you?"

"No," she admitted.

"Are you asking to go home because you're not sure of me?"

"I am sure of what you want. You want to continue to avoid any real commitment and marriage with a succession of tiny, green-eyed blondes."

"Where does that leave you?"

In trouble since she'd been foolish enough to admit her love for him. "I think we both know where that leaves me, Randall. Waiting for my personal Mr. Right to come along."

"Hasn't he already come along in the form of your Bill?"

She balled her hands into fists. "I haven't seen or heard from him since the party but since I'm not likely to find my Mr. Right here, will you please ask your driver to take me home?"

He leaned against the door, looking at her. "Would it make any difference if I tell you I've lost my taste for tiny blondes?"

"No."

"No? Damn you know how to bust a man's balls, don't you?"

She sighed. "I'm not trying to bust your balls, Randall. I'm just trying to be realistic."

"Then why are you having such a problem accepting the obvious?"

"When we're together, I believe you want only me."

"Then what's the problem?"

"I wouldn't have one if you gave me reason to hope."

"Hope what?"

"That you'll be able to give me what I need and want most."

She watched his jaw clench. "I thought we weren't going to talk about love and marriage."

She sighed and shook her head. "We don't have to talk about anything, Randall. Will you please just arrange a ride home for me?"

"Fine." He straightened. "I'll take you home."

"Thanks but if you don't mind, I'd rather go with your driver."

"What?"

"Is your driver available?"

"Why the hell would you rather he take you home? You've never even met him."

"I don't think our seeing each other when we're both so at odds with each other is helpful."

"I need you to stay, Benai."

"You want me to stay but I can't see you needing me, Randall."

"Then why the hell would I want you to stay?"

She caressed his cheek. "Because you're used to having your way."

He took a deep breath before he spoke. "Will you do something for me, Benai?"

"Yes, if I can."

"Go to hell." He smiled, pulled the door open and stalked out of the room.

She sucked in a breath, blinking back tears. She waited until she could no longer hear his footsteps in the hall. Then she crossed the room and picked up the phone on one of the end tables.

"Ms. Peters?"

Startled, she dropped the phone and whirled around.

A man in his fifties with kind eyes and a nice tan stood in the doorway. He had her purse and overnight bag in his hand. "I didn't mean to startle you. I'm Jackson, Randall's driver. He asked me to take you home. Are you ready?"

"Yes. Thanks." She crossed the room and walked into the hallway. There was no sign of Randall.

Jackson held the front door open.

She hesitated. "Where is Randall?"

"He left."

He was probably on his way to see one of the tiny blondes he expected her to believe he no longer preferred. "Thanks." She walked through the open door.

She sat in the back of an expensive luxury car listening to soft jazz on the way home. What the hell had possessed her to walk away from him before she had to? If he wanted more than one night, how did she know he might not want lots of nights—all her nights—at least for a while?

The moment the car pulled to a stop in her apartment parking lot, while the driver was still inside, the back passenger door opened.

She glanced up.

Randall reached in and took her hand. "Hi."

She slipped out of the car and stood staring up at him. "You told me to go to hell."

He shrugged. "Your rejection stung like hell and I overreacted."

"I didn't reject you, Randall. I'm just trying to protect myself." She sighed. "When your driver told me you'd left the house, I thought you were on your way to see one of your blonde bimbos."

"One of my blonde…oh, Benai, it's time for you to give that shit a rest!"

She blinked. "Shit?"

"Yes, shit! How many times do I have to tell you that you have my complete attention? Why would I want to spend the day with anyone but you?"

"Randall—"

He leaned down and kissed her lips. "I apologize."

She slipped her arm through his and smiled up at him. "So do I."

"For what?"

"You're not the only one who overreacted. You haven't given me a single reason to be jealous. I'm sorry."

He smiled. "It's okay."

"No, it's not. A part of me knows I don't have to worry about you wanting other women."

"But?"

"Another part of me can't believe my good luck."

He cupped a palm over her face. "You're not the only one who feels lucky. I've never met anyone who moves me as you do and knowing that your ex-lover is waiting just drives me insane."

"It was fun spending the night talking and dancing with him at the Girls' Night Out, Randall, but you're the man of my dreams."

He sighed. "Great. Then let's go into your apartment so you can pack a fresh overnight bag and then you can come back home with me."

"Randall—"

"Is that a yes?"

"Give me a rain check."

"Let's spend the day and night together."

"I'm such a wuss when it comes to you."

"That's what happens when you're in love."

She cast her gaze skyward. "God spare me from overconfident men."

He laughed and hugged her. "Thanks, Jackson. Take the rest of the day and tomorrow off."

"Good night, Randall. Ms. Peters."

She lifted her head and smiled at Jackson. "Thanks."

She waited until he drove off before looking up at Randall. "Let's go inside. I want to cook dinner for you and then spend the night in my own bed."

"Alone?"

"Of course not."

They talked about books as she grilled steaks, baked potatoes and made a salad. He drank a beer with his meal while she sipped a chilled glass of wine. They cleaned the kitchen together and then cuddled on her loveseat and watched her favorite martial arts movie.

"I can't believe you like action movies," he told her during the closing credits.

She shrugged and used her remote to turn off the television. "I used to watch them with my father and brother— much to my mother's dismay."

He kissed her cheek. "You are the sweetest woman in the world."

She grinned. "Let's go to bed."

"Do you want to make love?"

She did but could see he was tired. She shook her head. "Let's just go to sleep in each other's arms."

"Sounds like a plan."

They undressed and slipped into bed.

She quickly fell asleep.

* * * * *

Bancroft floundered in a choppy ocean while Randall lay on the deck of a nearby yacht—making love to Benai and ignoring his downing brother. He wanted to help Bancroft, but the temptation Benai presented was impossible to resist. He lay naked on his side behind Benai. Her warm, bare ass rested against his groin.

He held her top leg in the air with his left hand. His right palm spread across her breasts. He kissed the back of her neck as he slowly eased his erect cock into Benai's incredibly tight ass. The amazing sensations radiating out from his cock quickly engulfed him. It permeated his mind while infusing his emotions with a sense of warmth and belonging he'd never felt.

Lost in feelings that overwhelmed him, he slid in and out of her ass, enjoying each slow descent. This was the first time she'd been able to take his entire shaft inside her and he wanted it to last for as long as possible.

He pinched her nipples and struggled to hold off his impending climax. She made that impossible by thrusting her cheeks back against his groin and tightening her anal muscles around him.

Each thrust felt like coming home to a loving, forever faithful woman after a long, treacherous journey.

She moaned, pressing his hand against her breasts.

He greedily sucked at the side of her neck, longing to erupt deep inside her rear.

"Come for me, my handsome Randall. Don't hold back. Come."

He groaned and lost the battle to prolong making anal love to her. Gripping her waist, he held her still and rutted into her with a passion he could no longer control. Within seconds, the world around him exploded and he shuddered to an intense but brief orgasm.

As he called out her name, Bancroft disappeared under the water for the final time. Instead of attempting a rescue, Randall continued to hold Benai tightly and enjoyed the last blissful seconds of his release.

It was only when he recovered from his climax that he realized Bancroft had drowned – while he'd lain just yards away fucking.

"No! No!" He shouted, pulled out of Benai, ran across the boat and dived into the water – only to find that he'd forgotten how to swim. He quickly sank. With his lungs bursting, he struggled to propel himself upward.

He broke the surface, gasping for air. Hoping that Bancroft had somehow managed to survive, he glanced around and –

"Randall? Honey, it's all right. It's all right."

He blinked. His eyes focused and he looked into Benai's anxious gaze. He sucked in a relieved breath. It had just been another nightmare.

She cupped her hands over his cheeks. "Randall? Let's talk about why you're having nightmares."

He shook his head. "I don't want to talk. I just want you to hold me. Please."

"Of course." She kissed his cheek and slipped her arm around his shoulders, drawing him back down to her bed.

He pressed into her arms, struggling to control his need to shake off the nightmare.

She whispered softly to him. Her voice soothed him.

"I love you," she said softly. "Only you, Randall."

Comforted by her voice and words, he drifted to sleep in her arms.

Long after Randall fell asleep, Benai lay awake too agitated to sleep. Randall's nightmares and his refusal to discuss them troubled her. Surely the fact that he didn't trust her enough to reveal the subject of his nightmares did not bode well for their future.

She stroked his back. "I love you," she whispered softly. "Please trust me enough to share your pain with me. Please."

He burrowed closer, his breathing deep and even.

She lay under him, staring up at the dark ceiling. *Please God, don't let me lose him. Please.*

She eventually drifted into an exhausted sleep. In the morning, she was disappointed to discover he'd left while she slept. And he hadn't bothered to leave a note.

Before she left for work, an elaborate bouquet of flowers arrived. The card bore no message—just his initials. Nevertheless, the flowers brightened her day. He wasn't ready to entrust his nightmares to her but she was still in his thoughts. That had to count for something.

* * * * *

Three nights later, Randall lay sleepless in bed, staring up at the ceiling as his heartbeat slowly returned to normal. He turned onto his side to look at his bedside clock. It showed one thirty-nine am. Although exhausted after two previous nights of nightmares, he was afraid to go back to sleep. He sat up, hesitated and reached for his cordless phone.

He'd dialed half of Benai's home number before he shook his head. There was no point waking her up and forcing her to share in his guilt. He called Peyton instead. Forty minutes later, he and Peyton faced each other in the family room.

"You have to release your guilt, Randy. It's not your fault."

"Why the hell isn't it my fault I'm having nightmares about abandoning him?"

"You didn't abandon him nor did you leave him to die. When Croft has regained his center of balance he'll know you can't always help who you fall in love with." Peyton sighed and raked a hand through his hair. "I think the nightmares and guilt would vanish if you'd just admit how you feel about her. If you did, it would make forgiving yourself easier."

"He's somewhere drowning and you want me to admit something that's not true?"

Peyton stared at him. "For the love of God, Randy, what is it going to take to make you admit you love her?"

"Maybe if I actually fall in love with her I'll admit it. Until that happens, I don't need any shit from you. I just need…"

"What?" Peyton shook his head, a bleak look in his eyes. "Just tell me what you need and want from me and I'm there for you, as I've always been and always will be."

Randall closed his eyes. "I know. I do. I just need you to be here. I don't want or need you to preach to me, Peyton. Just…sit with me."

Peyton glanced at his watch. "Fine. Let's go upstairs and I'll stay with you until you fall asleep."

Randall swallowed slowly. "You'll stay with me until I fall asleep? You make me sound like a little boy afraid of the dark."

Peyton crossed the room to place a hand on his shoulder. "I have news for you, Randy. When a man falls in love, he's as vulnerable as a little boy afraid of the dark. There's no shame in that. Now let's go upstairs. We could both use some sleep. I'll spend as many nights here as you want me to."

Randall stared silently up at him.

Peyton smiled down at him. "When or if you wake up again, I'll be here to share the pain and the fear, Randy."

He swallowed. "You are the best part of me, Peyton. I don't know what I'd do without your support."

"You'll never have to find out because I'm here for the duration and beyond, Randy. We're brothers of the flesh and spirit to death and beyond."

He nodded. "To death and beyond."

* * * * *

Two days later, Benai and Tempest had dinner at Tempest's mansion. "Have you decided if you're going to celebrate your birthday with your parents or are staying here?" Tempest asked.

Benai sipped from her glass of wine. "I'm conflicted. Part of me wants to go home. Another part of me wants to stay in town to see what Randall's next move is going to be."

"When did you last see him or hear from him?"

"Early Sunday morning. He spent the night but left before I woke on Monday. Other than the flowers he sent later that day, I haven't heard from him since then."

Tempest leaned forward. "I have a suggestion. Instead of waiting and hoping he'll call you and help you decide if you're staying in town for your birthday, why don't you call him then we can make plans for your birthday?"

Benai parted her lips. About to say she couldn't, she had a vivid memory of a conversation she'd had with Tempest months earlier. When Tempest had sat waiting for Layton to call her, Benai had insisted there was nothing wrong with her calling Layton.

"I know I should feel comfortable enough to call him."

Tempest nodded. "But?"

"But I don't."

"Why not? Do you think he wants to be with anyone else?"

"No...oh, Temp, now I understand how you felt with Layton. When we're together, I know I'm the only woman he's interested in. When we're apart, the doubts creep in."

"I don't think you have any reason to doubt him, Nai."

"I think he doubts us."

"Why?"

She sipped from her glass again. "He's having nightmares."

"What kind of nightmares?"

She shrugged. "He won't discuss them but I think they have something to do with his feeling guilty about seeing me."

"You might be right. Layton is worried about both Croft and Randall."

"Where is Bancroft?"

"I don't know but I didn't think you wanted to see him."

"I didn't but now I do."

"Why?"

"I need to see him so I can make it crystal clear to him that there's nothing between us. There never was and there never will be."

Tempest sighed. "I understand but when you see him, please remember he's not himself and be as gentle with him as possible."

She frowned. "This is going to make me sound unfeeling but when I think of the grief Randall's going through...that might not be so easy."

Tempest squeezed her hand. "Randall's in pain but, Nai, Bancroft is sick. He has to be handled delicately."

Benai drew her hand away. "At Randall's expense?"

"I know it doesn't seem fair and it might not be, but do you think Randall would have it any other way?"

"No, but that doesn't make it right."

"I know but they have a bond and closeness that's been forged over years of always knowing they could fully trust each other."

"And?"

"And now that Randall's…"

Benai stiffened. "Now that Randall's what? Please don't tell me you were about to blame him. If you were, you were right to stop because he's not responsible and I'm not going to sit here and listen to you pretending he is."

Tempest shook her head. "I'm sorry, Nai. I guess the Grayhawks are starting to rub off on me more than I thought."

"You're saying the others blame Randall?"

"I didn't say that."

"You implied it. Is that what they think? Don't start keeping secrets from me now, Temp."

Tempest moistened her lips. "It's because of the special bond they have. Knowing how Bancroft felt…unless Randall was in love with you, he…shouldn't have asked you out."

Benai shook her head. "Oh, God, how can you buy into that? There was never anything between me and Bancroft. You know that. Why should Bancroft's misguided beliefs dictate who Randall sees?"

"Because of their bond. I know Bancroft had no legitimate claim on you but as long as he thought he did and as long as Randall wasn't in love with you, he should have waited until things were straightened out in Bancroft's mind before seeing you. That's all I'm saying. If he loved you, none of his siblings would have asked or expected him to not see you."

"They wanted him to stop seeing me?"

Tempest sighed. "Nai—"

"Never mind. That's what you implied." Benai held up her hands. "I think I've had enough of the Grayhawks for a while."

"Does that include me, Nai?"

"You think he should have stayed away from me too. Don't you?"

"Nai—"

"It's okay. I can see the truth in your eyes."

"Only because Bancroft is so sick."

"Then why don't they get him some help? They can certainly afford it."

"He would never see a shrink and they've already decided how to resolve things between Randall and Bancroft."

Benai swallowed slowly. "And how is that?"

Tempest shrugged. "I don't know. Layton wouldn't tell me the details. He said he didn't want to worry me."

"Why do I get the feeling that whatever they've decided is going to involve Randall getting the short end of the deal?"

"Probably because it does."

"Oh, they are a very charming bunch."

"Don't judge them too harshly, Nai. They're just so afraid for Bancroft."

"And don't mind shafting Randall."

"Randall is strong—"

"So it's okay to dump all over him?" She bolted to her feet. "He's having nightmares, Temp. Maybe he's not as strong as they think he is. Maybe they need to give him a little more consideration."

"They love him too." Tempest rose. She extended a hand, a pleading look in her eyes. "Please don't let this come between us, Nai."

Benai sighed, shook her head and then clutched Tempest's hand. "Don't be silly. We've been through too much together to let anything come between us."

"Yes we have. What about you, Nai? Are you all right?"

"Yes."

"You're sure?"

"Yes."

She glanced at her watch. "Then I'd better go to the ladies' room before Layton arrives."

Benai nodded.

"Nai, please try not to think badly of Layton. This is a difficult time for him. He loves them both but — "

"But Bancroft's sick and Randall's not."

"Yes."

"I know you love him and he's my biggest client but just don't expect me to be too thrilled to see him tonight, Temp."

"I understand."

"But I'm not going to cause any problems between the two of you. He won't be any the wiser that I'd like to slap him into next week."

Tempest laughed and hugged her. "Understood. If it was Layton in Randall's place, I'd feel the same way about Randall as you do Layton."

* * * * *

Benai called Randall when she returned home. Peyton answered his cell phone in a low voice. "Hey, honey."

"Hi, Peyton? Is Randall there?"

"Yes but he's asleep. Normally I would wake him in a heartbeat but he hasn't really been sleeping well lately and — "

"He's still having nightmares?"

"Yes."

"They're about Bancroft and me. Aren't they?"

"Have you talked to Randall about them?"

"I tried to twice but he wouldn't cooperate."

"Then there's not much I can tell you."

"Has he... I haven't seen or heard from him for nearly a week. What should I read into that, Peyton?"

He spoke after an extended silence. "That he's very conflicted and in need of a great deal of patience from you. And that he cares more for you than he's prepared to admit."

"It would be nice to hear that from him."

"Trust me, honey, he pursued you in spite of Croft's objection. His high regard for Croft should provide some insight into how he feels about you."

"Will you tell him I called?"

"Yes. How are you?"

"Honestly, I'm not sure. Like Randall, I'm conflicted."

"Is there anything I can do to help?"

"Just stand by him—as I know you will and don't let the others dump all over him."

"They love him, Benai, but—"

"But he's not sick and Bancroft is."

"Yes."

The reluctance she heard in his voice endeared him to her. "I'd better go. Good night."

"Good night, honey."

* * * * *

The phone rang as Benai returned to her apartment from the supermarket late Saturday morning. Placing her bags on the hall table, she picked up the cordless phone. Randall's cell phone flashed on her caller ID screen. She leaned against the table. "Hi."

"Hi, Benai. How are you?"

"Okay. How are you?"

"I'm… I've been better but I'll survive. Peyton told me you'd called."

"Yes. I wanted to know how you were."

"That's sweet of you."

"And I wanted to see you."

The ensuing silence unnerved her. "Randall?"

"I'd like to see you too."

"I hear a but in your voice."

He sighed. "I'm just not very good company these days."

"They've convinced you to allow them to toss you under the bus. Haven't they?"

"You don't understand, Benai."

"No, I don't but—"

"Then don't misjudge my brothers."

"So you're shutting me out?"

"I didn't say that."

"But you're not coming to see me? Are you, Randall?"

"We need to talk. So actually, I am coming to see you."

The lack of enthusiasm in his voice chilled her. Why was he coming? To tell her it was over between them? "When are you coming?"

"I'll pick you up in two hours. We can have dinner in town and talk."

"Okay."

"I'm looking forward to seeing you again. I've missed you."

"You only had to call, Randall, and—"

"I…ah…can you bear with me for a little while longer, Benai?"

"I'll do my best."

He sighed in relief. "Thanks. That'll make the coming weeks easier. I'll see you in a few hours."

The warmer tone of his voice eased some of her apprehension. "I'll be waiting, Randall—eagerly."

She spent an hour soaking in the bath thinking about the coming evening with Randall. Certain they would be spending the night together, she was dressed and waiting impatiently in her living room when her intercom buzzed. She crossed the room and spoke into it. "Randall?"

"Yes."

"You're early," she said and pressed the button to release the lobby door.

Five minutes later, her apartment bell rang.

Smiling, she opened he door and tossed herself into Randall's arms.

He dropped the overnight bag he carried so he could wrap his arms around her and lifted her off her feet. "It's good to see you."

She linked her arms around his neck and gazed up at him when he sat her on her feet. He looked tired. "How are you?"

"I've been better."

"Does it help any to know I love you?"

"How could it not help?"

She smiled, leaning against him. "I have a great idea. Why don't we skip dinner and go right to dessert?"

"Are you sure?"

She stroked his hair. "I'm very sure."

He picked her up. "Then let's go get physical."

"Gladly."

Chapter Eleven
ಬ

Randall stripped quickly before he slowly peeled off her clothes. Then he stood staring at her in silence.

She tossed her head so her hair fell around her shoulders. Placing her hands on her hips, she smiled, rotating her hips slowly. "Are you just going to stare or are you actually going to remind me that I'm yours?"

"You are so beautiful." He cast a brief glance behind her to her bedroom balcony. "There's a full moon tonight. Do you want to take advantage of it?"

She nodded. "I have several spare blankets and pillows in the linen closet."

He caressed her ass. "Lead the way."

A thrill of anticipation surged through her. She took his hand and they went to the linen closet. Before going to the balcony, he removed a small black kit from his overnight case.

She felt sexy and wanton arranging the thick blankets and pillows in the moonlight on her balcony while they were both naked. Satisfied the balcony was as cushioned as possible she knelt on her hands and knees with her back to him.

He knelt behind her, stroking her rear cheeks. "Does this mean what I think it does?" he asked.

"Yes. I'm ready. Just be gentle."

He kissed her neck. "I'll be very gentle." He urged her onto her back. "Bend your knees and part your legs for me."

She obeyed.

He palmed her, then eased a finger inside her. "You're already wet."

"I get wet the moment I see you," she told him and watched a slow smile spread across his face.

"You are the most amazing and sexy woman I've ever met. I don't know what I did to deserve you but I'm thankful you're mine."

"It would take an act of God to make me anyone else's, Randall."

He whispered in Cherokee before he leaned over to kiss her.

"English, Randall."

He brushed his mouth over her cheek to her ear. "Don't give up on me."

"I don't think I could if I wanted to. Now make love to me."

Randall sat on his haunches and opened his traveling kit. After slipping on a condom, he laid a tube of lube on the pillow protruding from beneath her hips. Then he pressed a quick kiss against her lips.

Before she could fully respond, he trailed his lips down her body. Pausing at her breasts, he twirled his tongue around each nipple. When both nipples had hardened, he nibbled his way over her belly.

He dipped his tongue into her belly button.

She moaned, stroking her hands over his shoulders.

He continued his path down her body until she felt his lips sliding down her slit. At the bottom, he swept his tongue inside.

"Oh…"

He eased his hands under her rear. Lifting her hips, he slipped his tongue in and out of her, slowly at first and then more rapidly as she reached down and curled her fingers in his hair.

Shivers of pleasure shot through her. She moaned. Wanting his tongue as deep as possible, she pushed herself against his face. She gasped in dismay when he withdrew his tongue and sat back.

She opened her eyes. "Don't stop, Randall."

"Just for a few moments," he assured her.

She watched as he applied lube to his index and middle fingers and then lifted her hips.

He eased his index finger into her. He slipped it in and out several times before he added his middle finger.

"Hmm." She pushed her hips, driving his fingers as far up her as he could get them. "I like that."

"Good," he murmured and lowered his lips to her slit.

She closed her eyes on a soft sigh as he dragged his tongue along her slit several times before he kissed her and licked and slipped his tongue inside her. Nice. It was so nice to have his long fingers stroking in her as he teased her clit with his warm lips and tongue. A spiral of heat ignited in her belly and quickly engulfed her in a hot flame. Minutes later, while she writhed with pleasure, he withdrew his finger and tongue.

He leaned down and kissed her lips. "Are you ready for me?"

Her stomach muscles clenched and her heart raced but the thought of anal sex with him totally excited her. "Yes," she whispered.

"Are you sure?"

She opened her eyes. "I'm very sure."

He spread lube over the condom before he positioned himself between her thighs. "Which position do you prefer?"

"Doggie so you have access to my breasts, pussy and neck."

"You want it all?"

She caressed his thigh. "I want you to make love to every part of me."

She saw a flicker of emotion in his eyes. He parted his lips.

She tensed, half expecting, half hoping he'd say he loved every part of her.

"That's the way I want it too." He sat back.

Swallowing disappointment, she sat up and kneeled with her back to him.

As if aware of her disappointment, he cupped his hands over her breasts and gently touched his lips to her ear. "You're the only woman in the world for me."

It wasn't the admission she longed to hear but it sufficed for the moment.

She arched her back. "Love me, Randall."

He settled behind her, caressing her cheeks. "Are you sure you want this?"

"Yes."

"Show me how much you want it," he urged.

Benai frowned. It took several moments for her to realize what he wanted. She placed her hands on her ass and then slowly parted her cheeks. "Is this what you want?"

"Yes." He spoke in a low, hoarse voice.

She released one cheek and reached back and grasped his shaft, pressing it against her rear. "Make anal love to me, Randall."

He eased his hips forward, applying slow, steady pressure. The big head pushed its way into her tight opening.

She caught her breath and reached for his shaft.

He paused and leaned over to kiss the back of her neck. "Are you okay?"

She nodded. "Yes…I just…"

"Are you sure?"

"Yes. It's just been so long since I've had anal sex but I want it with you. Don't stop. Just be gentle."

"I will." He cupped his hands over her breasts. Raining warm, biting kisses against her neck and shoulders, he rolled her nipples between his fingers. "You're so beautiful...so sexy and sweet. I wouldn't trade a moment with you for a million with any other woman I've ever met or known."

Tears welled in her eyes at the sincerity in his voice. "I'm yours, Randall. Take me."

He pushed his hips forward.

Several inches of his cock slid up into her tight, anal channel. She caught her breath again and then bit her lip as he continued to slide into her. Feeling herself stretched around his width, she put a hand back to push against his stomach. "Randall..."

He paused. "Are you all right?"

"I...that's as much as I can take this time," she murmured.

"I'm sorry. I don't want to hurt you."

She shook her head. "It's not exactly painful. I just feel so full and stretched but I don't want you to stop."

He didn't. Massaging her breasts and pressing hot, moist kisses against her neck, he gently eased in and out of her ass, never thrusting or attempting to get more than half his cock into her ass.

"Oh...Randall...oh...yes."

She felt the tension in his body as he neared his climax. He whispered to her in Cherokee.

Although she didn't understand his words, they buffeted her like an exotic, wonderful series of caresses that combined with his rhythmic strokes left her on the edge of an orgasm.

He slipped a hand down her belly to her slit. With his cock in her rear and his fingers delighting her clit and pussy, she shuddered.

He sucked her neck, pinched a nipple and flicked his thumb against her clit. She arched her back and curled her toes. She then moaned softly as he surged forward into her, pushing more of his cock in her ass.

He groaned her name and then laid his body against her back as he shuddered to his own climax.

He didn't linger in her. Moments after he'd come, he held her hips still and eased out of her.

She turned onto her side.

He removed his condom before he drew her into his arms. "Are you all right?"

"Yes." She rubbed her cheek against his shoulder. "Oh, Randall, I knew anal sex with you would be good."

They snuggled under one of the blankets and drifted to sleep, holding each other. She woke later to find a condom over his fully aroused shaft, which he rubbed against her thigh.

She rolled onto her back and spread her legs.

He lay on top of her. As he kissed her, he finger fucked her until she was wet. Then with a desperation that surprised her, he plunged into her pussy and fucked her hard and fast with a fury that had them both crying out and climaxing within minutes.

Afterwards, they struggled to their feet and went inside to fall asleep in her bedroom.

Sunlight shone into room when he kissed her awake. "I have another charity breakfast this morning. Would you like to come?"

"When is it?" she asked sleepily.

"In an hour."

"I'd love to come but I don't think I can move for several more hours."

He kissed her again. "Then I'll be back to take you out to dinner later."

She linked her arms around his neck. "I'll be waiting, handsome."

He stroked the hair away from her face. "I made eggs, bacon and coffee for you."

She inhaled and turned her head. A covered tray and a coffee carafe sat on her nightstand. "Hmm. Handsome, hunky, considerate and generous. Layton is generous with his wealth as well. Is that a family trait, Randall?"

He shrugged. "My mother believed while there was nothing wrong with striving for greater financial means than we had growing up, that once we had that wealth, it was incumbent upon us to share it with those less fortunate than ourselves. We all try to live up to the ideals and beliefs she held dear."

She stroked her fingers through his hair. "I'm sure she would have been very proud of you all, Randall."

He sighed. "I'm not so sure she wouldn't be a little disappoint—"

She pressed her fingers against his lips. "You're a good, kind, generous man. Of course she wouldn't be disappointed in you."

He pressed his cheek against hers. "I hope so because if I were a better man than I am…less selfish…Bancroft—"

She drew away from him and cupped his face between her palms. "Randall, please! I didn't know her but I have a mother I consider just as amazing as I know you considered yours. And my mother wouldn't want or expect me to sacrifice my happiness for my brother's. I doubt your mother would expect any more of you than mine would expect of me. Don't think I'll allow you to dump on yourself in my presence because I won't." She kissed his lips. "I'll be waiting for you when you get back, Randall."

He nodded.

She yawned and sat up. The cover fell away, revealing her breasts.

He groaned, pressed a quick kiss against each nipple and rose. "I have to go. I'll see you at four for an early dinner?"

She nodded. "Yes."

Later that afternoon as she sat on her sofa waiting for Randall to arrive, her phone buzzed. It was only three ten.

She moved across the room to her intercom. Yes?"

"Benai."

Her name, spoken in that deep voice she adored warmed her. "You're early." Smiling, she released the lobby entrance door. Five minutes later, she opened the door and froze. "Bancroft!"

He arched a brow. "Surprised to see me, Benai?"

"I…well, yes. How are you?"

"How can I be—given the circumstances?"

She looked up into his dark, angry gaze and swallowed the impulsive words of rebuke for the hell he'd put Randall through. Not only would Randall not want that but she could see the pain and darkness in Bancroft's gaze. She could feel the difference in him since they'd met, as well as the lack of guile. He really thought he had a claim on her emotions.

"Given the circumstances…I'm not sure why you're here."

"You're not? I've come to see you. Are you going to keep me standing in the hall?"

She hesitated a moment before moving away from the door. "Of course not."

He stepped inside, leaning his weight against the closed door. "You're more stunning each time I see you." He sighed. "No wonder you enchanted Randall as well."

The sincerity in his voice unnerved her. Normally she welcomed having a handsome man think she was beautiful. But not him. She flashed him a brief smile. "Thank you. Can I get you anything?"

He shook his head, his gaze locked on her exposed cleavage. "You have a date?"

"Yes."

"With Randall?"

She bit her lip. There was no point in denying the obvious. Besides, Randall would probably arrive before she could get him out of her apartment. "Yes."

His lips tightened. "He's very charming for a backstabber. Isn't he?"

Treating him as gently as Randall would want wouldn't be easy. In fact, with her knowledge of Randall's anguish, the urge to slap Bancroft for his hurtful, angry words was difficult to resist. "You wouldn't say that if you knew how much he loves and admires you. He's never had anything bad to say about you."

"If he admires me so much, why the hell is he seeing you behind my back?"

She blinked, uncertain how to respond without losing her temper and her desire to be kind. Because of his unfounded obsession, he'd put Randall through hell. She sucked in a breath and reminded herself that Bancroft had probably been through hell as well. Just as Randall had insisted from the beginning of their relationship, Bancroft clearly believed he had a prior claim on her. How could she dissuade him without being unkind or making things more difficult for Randall? "It's not behind your back, Bancroft. It's never been behind your back. You must know Randall wouldn't stoop so low."

"Wouldn't he? You think I don't know how many times he's slept with you, breaking the bond of trust between us?"

She thought of the effects of hearing such angry, bitter words on the already emotionally wounded Randall. Her eyes welled with tears. The words would rip into Randall, tearing him apart. She balled her right hand into a fist, pressing it against her thigh. "Please don't say such things. If you only knew how bad he feels—"

"He should feel bad! We're brothers and he knew you were mine and yet he—"

"Yours?" She shook her head. "Bancroft, please. You never even called me or asked me out. How could you possibly think I was yours?"

"I told you how I felt the night we met."

"You were very charming and complimentary when we met—months ago. We didn't see each other again until the rehearsal dinner where you behaved as if I were invisible." She compressed her lips. "And I think we both remember how you behaved at the reception."

He sighed. "I can explain that."

"There's no need. I knew then you weren't really interested in me and I was fine with that, Bancroft."

"You have no idea how wrong you were. Are. I was just as attracted to you as I'd been the night we met."

"That's not what your behavior indicated."

"At the reception, I was having a hard time. I felt angry, lost and even among the siblings I love so much, I felt alone. Dancing with you aroused me so much I…it was a relief when Randall asked to cut in."

Her belief in his words didn't change how she felt. She sighed. "I didn't know… I thought you weren't interested."

"And then Randall moved in and started undercutting me."

"No! He never did any such thing."

"Then why did you sleep with him?"

Her cheeks burned but she maintained his gaze. "I was attracted to him the moment I saw him."

"I thought that described your reaction to meeting me."

"It did but…"

"But what?"

"You didn't follow up and then I met—"

"I'm following up now."

She sighed. "That's sweet and I'm flattered."

"But?"

"Now is too late, Bancroft."

"No it's not. Call Randall and tell him not to come."

She felt certain he presented no danger to her personally but the level of anger she sensed in him directed at Randall frightened her. "No."

"Your not calling him isn't going to change what's going to happen between us, Benai. He has to answer for breaking the trust between us."

"He didn't."

"I told all my brothers about you after we met. Only Randall betrayed me. Even he must know we have issues that have to be resolved."

"Bancroft...you should know that I'm in love with him."

"That's not going to change anything between us either. Call him and we can get this over sooner rather than later."

"Fine. If you'll excuse me, I'll go call him."

He nodded. "I'll be right here."

That's what she feared. "The living room is to your left. Please make yourself comfortable."

He nodded again.

In her bedroom, she sat on her bed and called Randall.

He answered on the second ring. "Hi. I'll be there in about twenty—"

"Don't come."

"What? I'm on my way. What's wrong? Did I do or say something I shouldn't have?"

"No but he's here, Randall."

"Who's there?"

"Bancroft's here."

There was a tense silence. "What? What do you mean he's there?"

"I mean he's in my living room. When he arrived I thought you'd arrived early and…he's here, Randall, and he's in a scary mood."

"Damn." He took a deep breath. "You don't need to be concerned, Benai. He won't hurt you."

"I know."

"You sound afraid."

"It's fear for you, Randall."

"You have no need to fear for me either, Benai. He's my older brother."

"He's dark and angry, Randall, and blaming you."

"I'll be there in ten minutes."

"I'm not afraid of him. Don't drive recklessly, Randall."

"I'll drive carefully."

"Randall…"

"Yes?"

"I think I made things worse by telling him I was in love with you."

"I'm sure that didn't go over well with him but—"

"It didn't. I'm sorry."

"You don't have anything to be sorry for. I'll be there soon."

She hung up the phone and returned to the living room. Bancroft stood near the balcony doors. "Did you tell him not to come?"

"Yes but he's still coming."

He shrugged. "So be it."

"Would you do me a favor?"

"Not if you're going to ask me to leave."

"Okay. I'm not asking you to leave. I'm telling you to leave."

He shook his head. "It's time he answered for his betrayal."

Don't panic, girl. He's big but Randall is bigger and more muscular. He was a boxer. He can handle himself. "I'm going to call Layton and—"

"That's not going to change the fact that it's time for a showdown between me and Randall."

"If you hurt him—"

"Trust me. A backstabber like him can take perfect care of himself."

"He hasn't stabbed you anywhere. There's nothing between you and me, Bancroft."

"How can there be when he's been undercutting me for weeks?"

She tossed up her hands. "All I'm going to say is you'd better not hurt him."

He didn't respond.

They stood staring at each other in silence until the lobby entrance door buzzer sounded ten minutes later. She moved across the room to the intercom. "Yes?"

"It's Randall."

She closed her eyes, fearful of what would happen when they were both inside her apartment.

"Benai? Buzz me in."

"I think you should call Layton first."

"I'm here now. Buzz me in."

"Randall, I—"

Bancroft leaned over her and deliberately pushed the button to release the lobby entrance door. She swung around to face him, angry tears filling her eyes. She had to clench her right hand into a fist to keep from slapping him. "Why are you doing this? You know there's nothing between us. There never has been."

"Hell will freeze over before I allow that ungrateful backstabber to get away with betraying me."

She swung away from him. The rapid tapping on her apartment door startled, then frightened her. While she still believed she had nothing to fear from Bancroft, she feared the same could not be said of his intentions toward Randall.

"Let him in, Benai."

She wiped at her cheeks and opened the door. "Randall."

He hugged her briefly before stepping inside. He closed the door. "Leave us alone, Benai."

She shook her head. "No."

"This isn't going to be pretty."

"I'm not leaving."

He turned to face Bancroft. "How are you, Hawk?"

"How the hell do you expect me to be with your knife stuck so firmly in my back?"

"I know you think I've betrayed you and I'd do almost anything to change that, Hawk, but—"

"Then leave my woman the hell alone, Randall."

Noting the distressed look on Randall's face, Benai lost what was left of her patience with Bancroft. "I'm not your woman, Bancroft. I never have been and I never will. If you can't understand that—"

Randall turned her to face him. "What do you think you're doing?"

"What do *you* think I'm doing? I'm doing what someone should have done weeks ago, set him straight."

"Stay out of this, Benai. Please."

"You're in my apartment arguing over who I belong to and you tell me to stay out of it? I'm not one of your subordinates, Randall. I don't take orders from you."

"I'm not asking you to take orders. I'm just asking you to realize that this is between me and Hawk."

Bancroft grabbed Randall's arm and swung him around to face him. "Are you satisfied? You've slept with her and turned her against me."

Randall shook his head. "Hawk, please let me explain. I–"

"There's only one way you can atone for what you've done."

Randall tensed as Bancroft's right fist swung out.

To Benai's horror, Randall made no effort to avoid Bancroft's fist. It connected with his jaw with a sickening sound, knocking him off his feet.

As he sprawled on his back, Bancroft leaned down and grabbed Randall's jacket, his fist still clenched. Still Randall made no effort to protect himself.

"No!" Benai grabbed Bancroft's fist. "Take your hands off him now or I'll brain you."

He abruptly released Randall's jacket. He leveled a finger at Randall, still sprawled on the floor. "Your little lover won't be around to protect you the next time," he warned before he abruptly stormed out of the room. Moments later, she heard her apartment door open and then slam shut.

She knelt next to Randall, wiping the blood from his mouth with the back of her hand. "Are you all right?"

To her surprise, he pushed her hand away and bolted to his feet. He wiped the back of his hand across his mouth and reached for the entrance doorknob.

She ran after him. "Randall."

He shook his head and pulled the apartment door open.

She pushed it closed.

He slowly turned to face her.

She tugged at his arm until he took several steps away from the door. Then she pressed her back against it.

He turned to face her.

"Where are you going, Randall? We have a date. Remember?"

"I'll have to take a rain check."

"I'm not offering one."

"I have to go after him."

"Why? So you can let him knock you down again? I know you could have stopped him. Why didn't you?"

"He needed to do that."

"He needed... Are you saying he needs to beat on you and you're going to follow him so he can?" She pushed against his shoulder. "No."

"You don't understand. He has to have a way to work out his anger and pain."

She stared up at him. "By using you as his punching bag?"

"I'm a big boy. I made it to the semi-finals in the Olympics as a light heavyweight. I can take a few punches."

She gripped his arm. "Randall, no."

"What do you expect me to do. Benai? Pretend this isn't my damn fault for wanting you when I had no right to want you?"

The cool look in his eyes sent a shiver of fear through her. "I don't belong to him. Wanting me wasn't wrong. What happened to him was not your fault."

"The hell it isn't. I pursued you knowing how he felt...knowing he considered you his...knowing I didn't..."

"Knowing what? That you don't love me?"

She watched the muscles in his jaw clench. "You were right when you wanted to end our relationship. I'm sorry I didn't listen then. I will now."

Her lips parted and she gasped, feeling as if a band constricted her ability to breathe. "What are you saying, Randall?"

He swallowed several times and sighed before he met her gaze. "I have to follow him and make sure he's all right."

"What about me, Randall?"

He shook his head. "Don't ask me to choose."

"I'm not asking you to choose between us. I'm asking you what about me? Was I a fool to believe you meant any of the things you said and implied about how you felt about me?"

"No. I never lied to you but I have made a big mess of everything. I can only see one way to make things right with him."

"How?"

"I'm sorry."

"Randall…don't…please."

"He's my brother and I hurt him."

"You're hurting me too." She caressed his face. "Don't go. Please. I'm not asking you to leave him to fend for himself. Call Layton or Brandon. Let one of them follow him."

"Benai, you don't understand the dynamics of our family structure. I'm the one who hurt him. I'm the one who has to atone. Not Brandon or Hawk."

She curled her fingers in his jacket, staring up at him. "Randall—"

He peeled her fingers away from his jacket. "I never meant to hurt you."

She fought hard not to cry. "Is this my dear Jane speech?"

He spread his hands, shaking his head. "I don't have time for this conversation. I have to go."

"And you don't care what condition you leave me in?"

"You must know that's not true. Benai, please…try to understand why I have to be the one to follow him."

On a familial level she did understand but on the primal level of a woman in love, she felt as if he were gutting her. She moved away from the door. "So go."

He hesitated. "Benai…" He touched her shoulder.

She shook his hand off her arm. "Okay. Go. Just go do what you have to do, Randall."

He turned her to face him. "Benai, I'll come back as soon as I make things right with him."

"And how are you going to do that? By ending our relationship? You think I want you to come back and explain that to me? Don't bother."

"Benai, I need you to give me a break now more than ever."

She slapped his hand away, tears spilling down her cheeks. "Go do what you have to do, Randall."

"Will you be here when I return?"

She wanted to tell him she'd wait through an ice age for him. But the honest admission of her feelings hadn't exactly earned her any rewards or a single *I love you too*. She shrugged. "I don't know."

"I know this isn't easy for you but please don't give up on me now."

"We can use the time apart to reevaluate our feelings."

"I don't need time to reevaluate anything about our relationship."

"Well maybe I do. You'd better go before Bancroft gets away from you."

"I have to go."

"So go." She turned and walked away from him.

When she heard the entrance door open and close, she sank down to her knees and sobbed. She lay there with tears streaming down her cheeks half an hour later when the entrance door buzzed.

Hopeful that Randall had returned, she rose and went to the intercom. "Yes?"

"Honey, it's Peyton."

A wave of disappointment overwhelmed her. "Go away."

"I know you're hurt and upset but I'm not going away. Buzz me in, Benai, or I'll ring every bell in this building until someone buzzes me in. Then I'll pound on your apartment door until you either let me in or call the police. Even if they haul me away, when they release me I'll be back to start the process all over again."

"Go away and leave me alone, Peyton. I don't think I want to see any of you damned Grayhawks ever again."

"Buzz me in, honey, and you can tell me that to my face."

"I hate him and I hate you."

"I know. Let me in."

"What are you doing here?"

"Randy asked me to come. He hated leaving you when you were so upset but—"

"I've heard the last of his buts I want to hear and I don't want to see you either."

"I'm not going away until I make sure you're all right. I'm getting in one way or another. Let's do this the easy way, honey. As soon as I'm satisfied you're all right, I'll leave and won't ever darken your door again. Buzz me in."

She sucked in a gulping breath and released the entrance door. She wiped her face and returned to the hallway to open the door when he rang her doorbell.

When she would have turned away, he took her in his arms.

She burrowed against him, pressing her cheek against his shoulder. This was probably as close as she'd ever get to being in Randall's arms again. She shivered.

Keeping one arm linked around her waist, he tipped up her chin.

She kept her eyes closed, not wanting him to see the hurt in her eyes.

"Open your eyes."

"No."

He caressed her cheek. "You can trust me. Open your eyes."

She obeyed, fighting to keep tears at bay.

He sighed. "I know things look bleak now but Randy's feelings for you run deep. Just give him time to work things out with Croft."

"Isn't that going to require he end our relationship?"

"That's not something I can see him doing."

"Even if he decides it's the only way to salvage his relationship with Bancroft?"

She watched his long lashes sweep down, concealing his expression. "He greatly values that relationship but he also values his relationship with you."

She pressed her clenched fists against his shoulders. "I'm not sure there's any relationship left to value."

He tightened his arm around her waist. "I can see you're about to write him off."

She opened her hands and pushed against his shoulders. "I have to protect myself so there's no use in your thinking you're going to sweet talk me into anything."

"Talk? Who said anything about talking?" He bent his head. "Sometimes a man has to do more than talk to get his point across."

His lips, warm and insistent, brushed against hers.

She shivered, pulling her lips away from his. "What do you think you're doing?"

He curled the fingers of one hand in her hair. "Whatever's necessary to make sure you give Randy the breathing room and understanding he needs." He brushed his lips against her cheek and neck.

She jerked out of his arms, taking several steps away from him. "You're not the one I want, Peyton."

"I'm the one who's here and if you close your eyes, you can pretend I'm Randy."

She backed away.

He followed her until she felt the wall at her back. Then he placed his hands on her waist. He rubbed his cheek against hers. "You don't ever need to be afraid of me, honey. I'd rather walk through the hottest hell imaginable than do anything to hurt Randy and doing anything to make you unhappy or afraid would hurt him."

She relaxed, closed her eyes and leaned against him. "Hold me," she whispered.

He wrapped his arms around her. "It's going to be all right, honey."

She clung to him. He was right. With her eyes closed, she could pretend she was in Randall's arms. When he lifted her off her feet, she linked her arms around his neck. She didn't protest when he carried her to the living room and sank down onto the loveseat with her across his lap.

* * * * *

Naked and aroused, Benai lay on her side on the carpet in Randall's living room. She faced the balcony where she could see Peyton and Bancroft looking in at them. Randall lay behind her. Knowing two of his brothers watched as Randall's erect cock probed her entrance from the rear, sent a delicious shudder down her spine. Eager to impale herself on Randall's naked length, she lifted her top leg. He gripped it and held it in the air, whispering softly to her in Cherokee.

Pushing her hips backward, she looked at Peyton. She maintained Peyton's gaze while savoring the delight of Randall's big cock sliding into her pussy. With him buried as deep as possible inside her, she cupped a hand over his big, firm balls. She massaged them and ground her ass against his groin.

He eased out of her until only the head remained within her wet slit, then he quickly thrust back into her. He pinched her nipples with his free hand while he fucked her with short, hard movements. She suspected taking her without protection while his brothers looked on got him even hotter – as it did her.

Feeling wanton, she licked her lips and smiled at Peyton. Noting a flicker of desire in his blue-green gaze, she beckoned to him.

He remained where he was, his gaze sliding down the length of her body like an illicit caress.

She moved her hand from Randall's balls to his thigh, giving Peyton an unfettered view of her pussy full of hard, hot, thrusting cock.

As Randall fucked her, she watched the clear outline of Peyton's cock hardening along the side of his right leg. It looked as thick and inviting as the one sliding in and out of her pussy, driving her to a quick, explosive climax.

Randall groaned and gripped her hip, pumping her with a satisfying swiftness that set her pussy on fire. She dug her nails in his thigh as she came.

Without warning, Randall pulled out of her pussy and eased his still-erect, bare cock into her ass.

She gasped and shuddered. "Oh…God!" She closed her eyes, her lips parted. "Oh…oh…"

She heard the balcony door glide open. Moments later something hard and thick pressed against her slit.

Her eyes flew open just as Peyton, plunged his big, bare cock into her flooded pussy with one swift plunge.

With half of Randall's cock buried in her ass and Peyton's stretching her pussy, it only took a few strokes before, sandwiched between the two handsome twins, she had her most incredible orgasm ever. When both came within moments of her, she linked her arms around Peyton's neck and offered him her parted lips.

He sucked her tongue between his lips, pulling it into his mouth. They devoured each other's lips. While she and Peyton continued to kiss, Randall nibbled at her neck and caressed her breasts. Within moments, Peyton and Randall were moving in and out of her body with a sweet harmony, as if they were used to sharing their women.

251

As Randall drew his hips backward, Peyton thrust his cock back into her with enough force to drive Randall's hard shaft deeper up into her ass than any cock had ever been. She exploded again — happily lost in the sheer ecstasy of being fucked by the two most handsome men she'd ever known.

She ground her hips against Peyton's. Beyond delicious…delectable.

Peyton lifted her chin. "Did you enjoy having us fuck you together?"

"Is the sky blue?"

"Is it?"

She realized she was still impaled on Peyton's bare cock. Peyton's. Not Randall's. She gasped and bolted into a sitting position. "No. No."

"No. No. No."

Benai opened her eyes as Peyton sat up in the bed beside her.

"Hey. Hey, it's okay. It's okay."

She stared at him in horror until she realized they were both fully dressed.

He drew her into his arms.

She collapsed against him, sobbing in relief and shame at her dream.

"It's okay, honey. Whatever nightmare you had is ended." He kissed her hair. "You're okay."

She pressed her cheek against his. "No. I'm not. I'm confused and afraid. I don't know what Randall is going to say to me when he returns and that scares the hell out of me."

He stroked her hair. "Just because he has difficulty telling you he loves you doesn't mean he doesn't."

She pulled away from him. "Well how am I supposed to know how he feels if he doesn't tell me?"

He caressed her cheek. "He can show you."

"How?"

"Go home without telling him. He doesn't run after women. He doesn't need to because there are always a plethora of other women ready to take a departing one's place in his bed. If he comes after you, you can safely deduce that he loves you — even if he finds it difficult to admit."

"He doesn't know where my parents live."

"Trust me, honey, he'll find them and you and put all your doubts about his feelings for you to rest. Go home."

She nodded. "Okay. I'll see if I can get a flight to —"

"You can use his jet."

"Without his permission?"

He grinned at her. "With the exception of you, what's his is mine. I have the keys to the jet and I have a pilot's license. How about I take you home and meet your parents so they'll recognize Randall when he comes to claim you?"

She gripped his hand. "Do you think he'll come?"

"Of course he will."

He sounded so certain, she nodded. "Okay. Take me home."

* * * * *

Randall bolted up in the dark bedroom, his body drenched with sweat. It only took a few moments for him to realize his heart raced with excitement rather than fear. As his gaze acclimated to the darkness he saw his mother. She stood near the window, exuding an aura of warmth and love.

He started to rise.

She shook her head. "Don't get up, little one."

Her voice was as soft and reassuring as he remembered. He sat with his back against the headboard, staring at her.

She moved across the dark room to sit on the side of his bed. She caressed his cheek with a cool hand.

He winced. Although her touch was gentle, the bruises on his face were tender.

She sighed. "Oh, my precious little one, you've taken a beating you never deserved."

He swallowed and leaned away from her hand. "He's still hurting. It might take a few more…encounters before he's ready to start healing. It's not pleasant but I can take it and it's a small price to pay to help him regain his sense of balance."

"No. No more, Randall." She shook her head. "I will allow no more."

"He still has a lot of rage. I have to atone—"

"You have nothing you need atone for. Bancroft has lost his sense of balance. You've done as much as I will allow you to."

"If I stop now, we'll lose him. He'll—"

"No, Randy, you and your brothers will not lose him. I won't allow it. You've already done more than your share to atone for a sin you never committed. Croft knows this, my little one. He's always known this."

"I shouldn't have pursued her. I knew how he felt. I knew—"

She pressed a finger against his lips. "You followed your heart, Randall. I will make sure Croft understands that. Right now he's feeling alone and afraid but when I talk to him, I'll make sure he understands.

"For now, I want you to leave Croft to me. I will accompany him as he follows the path back to his personal center of balance." She traced the bruises on his face. "Will you do something for me?"

"Yes. Anything."

He saw the gleam of her teeth as she smiled. "You were ever the most giving and unselfish of your siblings, my little one. You've always been so willing to put yourself out for them—even when it made things more difficult for you personally. Just this once, put yourself first. Go to your *sheenea*, Randall before you lose her."

He lifted a hand and gestured toward his face. "Like this? Even without my face being... I think it's too late. I think I've already lost her."

"Not if you go to her and tell her how you feel."

"After the things I've said about love and marriage? She won't believe me."

"A woman in love is always willing to give the object of her heart the benefit of the doubt. Go to her."

He moistened his lips. "Not with my face like this. She doesn't understand our ways and if she sees me like this, it will only make her bitter toward Croft."

"She loves you, little one and she has a great capacity for forgiving. A few bruises aren't going to scare her off and you'll find a way to make her understand our values. But I understand a man wanting to look his best when he pours his heart out to his *sheenea*. Give yourself a few days and have Declan prepare some of his healing balm and then go claim her. Will you do this for me, little one?"

He nodded.

She placed her hands on his shoulders, urging him onto his back. "Leave Croft to me. You sleep now and when you've used Declan's balm, go claim your *sheenea*."

He stretched out on his back, reaching for her hand. "Don't leave me, Mother."

Soft cool lips brushed against his forehead. "I'll stay for as long as I can. Sleep now, Randall."

He closed his eyes and for the first time in weeks, his sleep was undisturbed by nightmares. When he woke, the sun shone into the room and he was alone. There was no sign that anyone else had been in his bedroom during the night. But he felt rested and hopeful for the first time in weeks. He knew his mother's presence was responsible for that and for giving him hope that Benai would forgive him for leaving her when she was afraid and confused. Hopefully she wouldn't harbor any bitterness toward Bancroft.

He turned onto his stomach and drifted back to sleep.

When he woke again, Bancroft stood by the window in his bedroom. Even before Bancroft turned to face him, the lack of tension and anger emanating from him gave Randall hope he was firmly on the path to regaining his spiritual balance.

He sat up. "How are you, Hawk?"

Bancroft crossed the room to sit on the side of his bed. He cupped a hand over his cheek. "Thanks to your unselfishness and a visit from Mom, I can see my way back to regaining my spiritual balance."

"Can you forgive me, Hawk?"

"Can I forgive you? There's nothing to forgive, Randall. I'm the one who needs your forgiveness. I never had any claim on Benai. I'm not sure how I got so confused and off balance that I made things nearly impossible for you and actually..." He swallowed before he touched Randall's bruised face. "I'm sorry, Randall, that I could get so spiritually lost that hitting you was not only acceptable but—"

"It wouldn't have come to that if I had been more understanding. I tried for weeks to stay away from her before I... I couldn't."

Bancroft nodded. "I know. I'm sorry you couldn't enjoy the wonder of finding your *sheenea* as you should have."

"So you no longer consider her yours?"

"No. While I readily admit you have a very attractive *sheenea*, there was never anything between us. There's a reason why I never called her until I lost my balance—because part of me always knew she was not my *sheenea*. She's yours and I know the two of you will be very happy together."

Randall sighed in relief and then put a hand over his face.

Bancroft put an arm around his shoulder and they embraced. Randall felt most of the anguish and tension he'd lived with since he met Benai melt away. Now the main obstacle to his claiming her was gone. Bancroft was once again spiritually grounded and Benai was his.

Chapter Twelve

৪০

Five days later, just two days before her birthday, Benai returned from shopping to find her parents entertaining Randall.

He rose at her entrance.

Her heart ached at the signs of the bruises remaining on his face. Damn Bancroft for hurting him. "Randall...this is...an unexpected surprise."

"I hope it's a welcome one."

That depended on why he'd come. Had he come to deliver a dear Jane note in person or had Peyton been right and he'd come to...to what? It was crazy to think he might have come to tell her what she desperately wanted to hear from him. Granted Peyton probably knew him better than anyone else.

With his expression shielded by his lowered lids, she was afraid to read too much into his smile.

She shrugged. "It depends why you're here."

He crossed the room and bent to kiss her cheek. "You know why I'm here."

"Do I?"

"I've come to take you home."

"My parents are here. I am home."

"Home is with me. Isn't it?"

She pressed her lips together, then nodded.

"Good."

She lifted her face and touched his cheek. "He hurt you."

He took her hand in his and kissed her palm. "I'm fine or I'm hoping to be after we talk." He glanced around. "Can we go somewhere private to talk?"

Then it was bad news. He wanted to give her the dear Benai letter in private. She swallowed hard and then moistened her lips. She eased her hand from his. "How is Bancroft?"

He smiled. "He's much better."

"Now that he's battered you almost beyond recognition."

He shook his head. "Please don't hold this against him, Benai."

"How can I not when he hurt you like this?" She traced the various healing bruises on his face.

He grinned. "Does that mean you only loved me for my looks?"

"Why are you here?"

"I already told you I came to take you home. Before I do that we probably need to talk."

"So talk. I'm listening."

"What I have to say isn't easy for me. Can't we talk in private?"

"Here will do just fine."

He sighed. "You want me to pour my heart out with an audience?"

Her mother and father rose. "We can leave you two alone to talk, Benai."

She shook her head. "Stay, Mom."

"You're sure?"

She nodded. When her parents resumed their seats, she turned her attention back to Randall. "Why did you come?"

"That's the third time you asked me that. The answer might get longer but the basic substance isn't going to change. I've come to take you home with me." He raked a hand through his hair, glanced at her parents and then took her hand in his. "I've also come to talk to your parents."

She smiled. Peyton had been right after all. There could be only one reason he wanted to talk to her parents.

"I've come to tell your parents that I come from a long line of love." He turned to face her parents. "Mrs. Peters, I wanted to promise you that I will cherish and adore Benai as long as I live. Mr. Peters, I wanted to assure you that I have the financial means to ensure Benai will never have to work another day — unless she wants to. I'll take very good care of her and I'll never stray."

Her father nodded and her mother's eyes gleamed with an I-told-you-so look.

Benai blinked, shaking her head. "Randall? What are you saying? I don't understand."

"Don't you? Then let me make it clear." He went down on one knee. "I'm asking you to marry me. Will you?"

She stared down at him through a sudden mist of tears. "Marry you? You're asking me to marry you?"

"Yes. Will you?"

"Why?"

He squeezed her hand. "For the usual reason."

Oh God! What was he implying he loved her? "And what's that?"

He shrugged. "You know what I mean, Benai."

She nodded. "I think I do but I need to hear you say the words, Randall."

He glanced over his shoulder at her parents who were staring at them before looking up at her.

She tugged on his hand. "If you really feel it, you shouldn't be ashamed to say it in front of my parents."

"That won't be necessary, Benai."

She glanced over his shoulder to see her parents rise. "Dad?"

"A man shouldn't have to propose in front of an audience, Benai," her father said. "Your mother and I will have dinner out so you and your young man can talk in private." He took her mother's hand in his and led her from the room.

She looked down at Randall. "What's the usual reason?"

"I'm not much good at love out loud, Benai. You know that. Doesn't my presence here tell you anything?"

"Yes but I need to hear you say it, Randall."

"Love."

She'd never heard anything more welcome than that one tense word. She dropped down on her knees in front of him. "Love?"

He nodded. "Yes, Benai. Love. I'd never propose for any other reason."

Her heart beat so quickly she feared she'd hyperventilate. "You love me or you're in love with me?"

"Both." He caressed her cheek. "Will you marry me?"

The tears spilled down her cheeks. "Say it."

He wiped her cheeks. "Say what?"

"The actual words. I feel as if I've spent years waiting to hear them."

He stared into her eyes. "I love you."

Oh, God, thank you. "Since when?"

He shrugged. "Probably since the moment I saw you."

"How can that be?"

"You're my *sheenea*…the one person in the whole world who completes me, Benai. There's a part of me that knew that the moment I saw you. That's why I couldn't stay away from you — even when I believed you belonged to Bancroft."

Tears spilled down her cheeks. "I never belonged to him but I was yours for the taking the moment our gazes met and locked. You know I love you."

"I know and I love you too." He lifted her in his arms and carried her across the room to sit on the sofa. He brushed the back of his hand along her wet cheeks. "Can you stop sobbing long enough to put me out of my misery?" He bent his head and kissed her lips. "Will you marry me?"

She nodded. "Yes. You know I will."

"Yes?" He laughed and wrapped his arms around her. "I was so afraid I'd lost you."

He trembled against her, taking deep, shuddering breaths.

She pulled back and caressed his face. "Lost me? Get real, Randall. There's no way you could lose me so easily."

"You ran away."

"I didn't run away, Randall. I was afraid of what Bancroft was doing to you and I was hurt, angry, scared and confused. I had all these pent-up emotions I couldn't handle alone. I needed to be in a place where I felt safe and grounded and that's always been with my parents."

She linked her arms around his neck and smiled. "And now I'll have two places where I'll feel safe and grounded — with them and with you."

He squeezed her, pressing his face against her breasts. "I'm sorry I made you unhappy. I would have protected you from that scene with Bancroft if I could have."

"I know that, Randall." She kissed his hair. "And I know you only did what you thought you had to do. I'm still a little angry that he beat on you but I understand why you felt you had to allow it."

He lifted his head and met her gaze. "You do? Peyton found a way to explain it so you'd understand?"

"No. I had a visit from a very special person. The last person I ever expected to meet."

He frowned. "Who?"

"You're going to think I'm nuts, Randall but...your mother came to me."

"My mother's been dead—"

"I know she's dead and I know it's hard to believe but it wasn't a dream. I was wide awake when it happened. She came to me and when she took my hand...I felt this incredible infusion of... I understood why you felt the need to allow Bancroft an avenue to work off his aggression when you could so easily have protected yourself from him."

She stroked her fingers through his hair. "She is so proud of you."

"She was a remarkable woman and an incredible mother."

"And she had a remarkable and selfless son."

"I didn't do anything for Croft he or any of the others wouldn't have done for me."

She nodded. "I know but forgive me if I want to think of you as totally wonderful and head and shoulders above every other man I've ever met—including all your amazing siblings."

He grinned. "I think I can live with that flaw in your character."

She smiled. "So you've finally told me you love me. Now I want you to take me somewhere and show me."

He brushed his lips against her ear. "We have two family suites in one of the finer hotels out here."

"Two?"

"There are a lot of us and one is suitable for Lelia to stay in with her friends. The other is suitable for the rest of us with or without a significant other. Would your parents think badly of me if I asked you to spend the night there with me?"

"They'd probably prefer not to think about our making love but they know you love me and they sure know I love you. Speaking of unmentionable things, I have a confession to make."

"I'm listening."

"It's about Peyton."

"What about him?

"I had this rather…disturbing…fantasy—"

"Fantasy? You're fantasizing about Peyton?"

"No. I meant dream."

"And?"

"It's embarrassing and…" she paused, uncertain how best to tell him of her dream without having him think she harbored romantic or sexual interest in Peyton.

He tipped up her chin. "A fantasy dream about Peyton making love to you?"

Her cheeks burned. "I'm not sexually interested in him, Randall. I don't know why… I don't want you to think—"

To her surprise, he laughed. "There's no need to work so hard to explain it, Benai. We're identical twins. Many people who know us both have difficulty telling us apart. So your dreaming of Peyton in a sexual context isn't that surprising or upsetting."

She studied his face. Noting no tightening of his lips or clenching of his jaw, she sighed in relief. "I was afraid you'd be upset or…"

"Or jealous?" He shrugged. "Peyton is a much better man than I am."

"He is not."

He nodded. "Yes, Benai. Trust me. He really is a better man than I am. So maybe I am a little envious of him. You're not the first woman to daydream about him. All my siblings are amazing but Peyton is…anything in me that you think is good or kind or generous is a result of his influence. He's the best part of who I am and is beyond amazing. He's extraordinary."

"He is but the dream didn't… I was with you both in the dream. At the same time. You were both…inside me."

He arched a brow.

She hesitated and then told him Bancroft had also been in the dream but hadn't been involved in making love to her.

"That's quite a fantasy you have there, sweetheart."

"It was a silly dream. Not a fantasy. You're the object of all my fantasies, Randall. Not Peyton and not Bancroft."

His lips twitched. "Poor Peyton and Bancroft."

"You find this amusing?"

He caressed her cheek. "It was a dream, Benai. They don't always make sense."

"No they don't. Do you want to tell me about yours?"

"About my dreams?"

"Not about your dreams. About your nightmares."

He tensed. "My nightmares? What—"

She pressed her fingers against his lips. "Please don't tell me you didn't have any because I know you did."

He sighed. "Okay. Like everyone else, I've had my share of nightmares."

"Are you going to tell me about them?"

"I'd rather not."

"Are we going to start off keeping secrets from each other?"

"No. We're not."

"But?"

He sighed. "But those nightmares were very unpleasant and I don't want to burden you with something that my guilt triggered. There's no need for you to share something so ugly."

"I love you. Sharing something that worries you is not a burden, Randall. It's part of loving you."

"The nightmares weren't just unpleasant. They were…shameful."

She linked her arms around his neck. "You can share anything with me…no matter how shameful."

He drew away from her.

"Randall?"

He walked over to the patio doors. Staring out to the patio, he spoke of his nightmares in a low, barely audible voice.

She crossed the room to him. She slipped her arms around him, pressing her cheek against his back. "They were nightmares, Randall. Nothing you need to be ashamed of."

"They felt real."

"But they weren't real."

He pulled away from her and stared down at her. "But they were almost real."

"How could they be?"

"When I left you to follow Croft…I felt… I've never felt as I felt then. When he hit me again and told me you were his, I nearly lost it. The thought of him touching you made me crazy and I felt a darkness of my own that almost rivaled his. I bolted to my feet, grabbed him and…"

"And what?"

"I nearly… I wanted to beat him to a pulp and toss him into the nearest body of water."

"But you didn't."

"Only because he stumbled and fell backward. If he hadn't…"

She shook her head. "You're not going to convince me you would have hurt him."

"Hurt him? I wanted to knock his block off to keep him away from you."

"But you wouldn't have." She smiled. "He's far too amazing to damage. Right?"

He laughed, his shoulders relaxing. "Right."

"Right."

"Let's stop talking about him and go do something that not only makes sense but also feels very good. Okay?"

She nodded. "I'll leave a note for my parents and then I'm all yours to have your wicked way with me."

* * * * *

Benai stood in the shower in the luxury hotel suite. Her long hair was pulled back into a ponytail. Through the clear glass door, Randall could see water glistening on her dark, smooth skin.

Standing nude in the doorway watching her, Randall applied a condom and then picked up the small traveler's kit from the counter in the bathroom before he slid back the shower door and stepped inside. He placed the open kit on one of the shower shelves.

She shut the water off and turned to smile at him. "There you are and I see you come bearing goodies."

He grinned. "That I do."

She removed a medium sized butt plug from the kit, covered it with lube and handed it to him.

Taking it, he slipped one arm around her waist, easing the plug between her cheeks and into her rear. "Is that comfortable?"

"Yes." She lifted her chin, linking arms around his neck.

He tightened his arm around her waist and bent his head to taste her lips. As he did, he stroked his fingers inside her. "Hmm. You're already wet," he murmured.

"I think I already told you how easily you arouse me, handsome." She reached between their bodies. "You're nice and hard—just the way I like you. Let's do something about that."

He nibbled at her neck. "Like what?"

"Like fuck."

He laughed. "I like the way you think but I want to taste you first."

She shivered and stepped out of his arms. "Taste away."

He eased her against the wall, forcing the plug all the way into her rear.

She licked her lips, enjoying the fullness in her ass.

He extended his tongue, licking his way down from her neck to her breasts. Holding her by the waist, he flicked his tongue against each nipple. When they were both hardened pebbles, he continued kissing and nibbling his way down her body to her midsection.

He twirled his tongue in her bellybutton.

"Hmm."

He pressed a kiss against it before he knelt in front of her.

She glanced down at him. "If you're waiting for an invitation, dive in already."

He sighed and glanced up at her. "Have I ever told you what a pretty pussy you have?"

She smiled. "I don't know that you have."

"I love everything about it. Its size, color, tightness—everything."

She thrust her labia forward. "Show me."

He pulled her hips forward and dragged his tongue along her slit.

She closed her eyes. "Hmm."

He pressed his tongue against her clit.

She sucked in a breath and pressed herself against his face.

Slipping his hands around her body to cup her ass, he thrust his tongue into her.

"Yes," she whispered. She curled her fingers in his hair as he ate her with a slow, sweet torture. Her stomach muscles clenched, her back arched as her passion started to rush toward her climax.

He pressed her cheeks together around the plug, sucking at her clit.

Randall's pleasing assault on her clit while he pinched and massaged her ass sent an involuntarily shudder through her. It spread down to her slit. He sucked her clit again and she exploded against his lips.

While she was still in the midst of her climax, he rose and thrust his cock into her.

She linked her arms around his neck and moaned against his lips as he kissed her. Tasting herself on his mouth, she arched into him. He wrapped his arms around her waist. He fucked her with quick, powerful strokes.

She clung to him meeting him thrust for thrust.

He devoured her lips and lifted one of her legs off the floor. Keeping her lifted leg draped over his, he plunged his cock in and out of her wet slit with a rapid pace that that drove him into a sexual fury. He fucked her hard, fast and deep. Within minutes of her orgasm, he groaned, clutched an ass cheek in each hand and detonated inside her.

She held him as he shuddered and groaned through his climax. He pressed against her, laying his head against her shoulder.

She kissed his hair. "Oh, Randall. I love you."

He murmured to her in Cherokee before he lifted his head to stare down at her. "Let's go to bed. After we make love we can discover your birthday present."

She nodded.

They took a quick shower before they dried off and went to cuddle in the bedroom.

"Am I going to like my present?"

Lying behind her with his arms around her waste, he nodded. "At least I hope you will."

"Give me a hint."

"It will go well with Gray."

"Is it a new saddle or a set of reins?"

"Yes."

"Which one?"

"Both."

"Both?" She glanced over her shoulder at him. "Why both? Does Gray need new ones?"

"No, the mare I bought you will need them."

She turned in his arms, her heart racing. "A mare? You've bought me a horse?"

"That's one of the presents. There's another at home I hope you'll like."

"What more could a woman want other than a mare?"

He shrugged. "I hear some women insist on wanting jewelry."

"Imagine that," she teased.

"You can have anything you want that my money can buy."

"I already have the one thing I could never be happy without—your love."

"Right answer," he whispered.

She kissed his lips and cuddled with him. She fell asleep in his arms.

* * * * *

Forty-eight hours later, back in her apartment in Philly, she paced her living room nervously. Randall stood by the balcony doors watching her. "Just keep reminding yourself how amazing he is."

She laughed and turned to look at him. "I guess I'm so nervous because I wasn't very kind or considerate of him when he needed both the most."

"I think you're going to find that he doesn't agree with you. We all know this has been a very difficult time for you, Benai."

"It was an even worse one for him but I was so afraid of losing you that I kept losing sight of that fact."

"If you'd rather not do this, you only have to say so and I'll talk to him."

She shook her head. "No. Let's do it."

"Yes?"

"Yes."

He extended his hand.

She crossed the room and sighed when he embraced her. "I love you so much."

He kissed her hair. "And I love you too."

When her apartment bell rang, Benai took a deep breath.

"My staying would make this more awkward for Croft but if you want me to stay, I will."

"I agreed to meet with Bancroft because you said he needed to apologize to me as part of his continuing healing process. I think I need to apologize to him as well."

"Do you want me to stay?"

She smiled. "Thanks but I'm sure we'll be fine alone."

He studied her in silence. "You're sure?"

She nodded. "Yes."

He kissed her lips and crossed the room to the entrance door. When he opened the door, he and Bancroft embraced briefly before he left.

Bancroft stepped into the living room and leaned against the closed door.

"Hello, Bancroft. How are you?"

"Me? I'm…" He sighed and spread his hands. "I know you're angry and upset about what happened between me and Randall. I understand that. I don't know what to say to you to increase the chances of your one day forgiving me."

She saw a look of regret and pain in his dark eyes. Any remaining resentment she'd been harboring vanished. His love for and his selfless efforts to help Brandon had led to his spiritual imbalance, which in turn had led to his becoming fixated on her. Like Randall, he'd put the needs of his brother ahead of his own. Like Randall, he was a good man. Despite the battering he'd taken, Randall still loved and admired Bancroft. Anyone capable of inspiring that kind of devotion had to be worth forgiving.

"Randall loves and admires you more than ever. He tells me you are a devoted, loving brother and a remarkable man." Bancroft had been the first of the Grayhawk brothers to make her feel capable of attracting the attention of handsome, successful men. She smiled and held out a hand. "I'm inclined to agree with him."

He stared at her in silence for several moments. "You… You're… You can forgive me for hurting him? I really never meant to… I was just out of my mind and…"

"I know." She tilted her head. "Are you going to leave me here holding my hand out like this?"

He pushed himself away from the door. Closing the distance between them, he took her hand between both of his. He kissed the back of it and then held it against his chest. "Randall is a very lucky man and you couldn't possibly have fallen in love with anyone who will love, cherish and adore you more than he does."

She smiled. "I kind of think most of the luck is on my side. He's handsome, charming and everything a woman could want in a lover. That he should want me is—"

"Is perfectly understandable." He caressed her cheek. "You mustn't sell yourself short. You are an attractive woman. The two of you will complement each other perfectly and help continue the Grayhawk long line of love."

Her smile wavered. "You... You're not still... I mean..."

He arched a brow, a slow smile spreading across his face. "If you're trying to find a delicate way of asking if I'm still obsessed with you, the answer is no." He lifted her hand to his lips again. "I will always think you are one of the most stunning women I've ever met but you're Randall's *sheenea*. Had my center of balance not been off, I would have realized you were not my *sheenea* and I wouldn't have caused everyone so much grief."

"And now?"

"I've regained my spiritual balance and my heart is up for grabs—just as it's always been. I'm sorry I frightened you and made what should have been a happy and exciting time for you and Randall a painful and difficult one instead. That you can even consider forgiving me is a testament to yo—"

"It's a testament to your worth, Bancroft." She placed a palm on the back of his neck and tugged at it. When he bent his head, she placed her free hand on his chest and kissed his cheek. "I'm sorry I wasn't more understanding. I made things more difficult for Randall than I should have because I forgot that it takes two to make a relationship work and when he really needed my understanding, I—"

He placed a finger against her lips. "We Grayhawks love deeply and devotedly but we aren't always easy to love or understand. You gave Randall something he thought he'd lost forever—the ability to fall completely and helplessly in love with a woman who loves him the same way. That's priceless. I'm sure he'll do a better job of helping you to understand our values and beliefs now that he doesn't have to look over his shoulder for me."

"I'm sure he will. Now. He tells me you're going to be his best man."

He shook his head. "Randall asked me to be his best man as a way of assuring me he held no grudges. I was tempted to accept but the position of Randall's best man is one which rightly belongs to Peyton."

She nodded. "No one could be any more loyal or deserving than Peyton."

"You're right and I'll be damned if I'll shortchange another of my little brothers."

"Like you, Peyton will be a great best man."

"Yes he will. Are we okay, Benai?"

"When we first met, you were charming and sweet and made me feel attractive and as sexy as hell."

"That's probably because you're both those things."

She smiled. "You Grayhawks have a wonderful ability to make a woman feel beautiful. Are we all right? Yes. I just wish I'd been more understanding but I was just so…confused and so uncertain of Randall…and honestly I was afraid he'd stop seeing me because of you and I'm ashamed to say I let that fear interfere with my showing compassion for you."

"Please don't apologize, Benai. You were a woman afraid of losing the man you love. I don't blame you for being annoyed or angry with me. I'm annoyed and angry that I could hurt him. That's not something I'd ever have thought myself capable of.

"So why don't we both try to forgive ourselves for feelings and angst neither of us was capable of controlling at the time?"

She released a deep breath. "Randall was so right about you. You are a remarkable man, Bancroft."

"If I am, it's because of my remarkable, loving and forgiving siblings. They'd bring out the best in anyone."

"They all happen to think you're pretty remarkable—especially Randall."

He smiled. "I think he's the most unselfish of us all. I'm very happy that he has you."

"Thank you. So how are you, Bancroft? I mean really?"

"I'm fine. Really."

"Is there someone special in your life?"

"A woman?" He shook his head. "But unlike Layton and Randall, I'm not quite ready to settle down." He tilted his head. "When I meet someone who makes me so wild that I lapse into Cherokee when we make love, I'll snap her up and settle down with her."

Her cheeks burned. "Who told you that?"

He shrugged. "We're a close-knit family. We have very few secrets from each other."

Lord she hoped Randall hadn't mentioned her dream. "Oh."

He arched a brow. "Until then I intend to fully enjoy all the benefits of being heart-whole and unmarried in a world full of lonely, single women."

She smiled. "Sounds like Mr. smooth, handsome, ultra charming Grayhawk is back."

He grinned. "There's a lovely lady waiting for me who seems to agree with you."

"I'll bet."

"So we're okay, Benai?

"Yes. We are."

"Great." He engulfed her in a brief bear hug. "There are a lot of single women waiting to be charmed and Lelia wants a quick word with you, so I'll be on my way."

"Lelia?"

He nodded. "She probably wants to talk to you to find out how long she has to make lover's balm."

"You think so?"

"Yes."

Emotion overwhelmed Benai. She knew from Tempest the recipe for lover's balm had been passed down through generations of Grayhawk women. Lelia had spent weeks mixing the special combination of herbs, spices and roots for Tempest. The Grayhawks believed use of it on the wedding night strengthened the long line of love.

After Bancroft left, Benai looked out her living room window. As Bancroft crossed the parking lot, the passenger door of a luxury car opened and a beautiful brunette got out and rushed into his arms.

Benai smiled. He really was okay. She turned away at the tap on her door. She crossed the room to the entrance door. "Yes?"

"It's Lelia."

Benai opened the door and a smiling Lelia entered and hugged her. "This is such an exciting time for me. When I saw Randall watching you at the reception, I had a feeling I would be gaining a new sister soon."

"I'm looking forward to that, Lelia."

Lelia released her. "I won't stay long. I just wanted you to know I've started to make lover's balm for your wedding night."

Benai's eyes welled with tears. "I know it takes a long time to make it so I'm very touched that you want to expend the effort to make it for me."

"I'm making it for you and Randall so your wedding night will be even more special." She kissed Benai's cheek. "I'll call you in a few days and we can do lunch or dinner?"

"I'd love that."

"Can you can stand one more visitor?"

Although she longed to be left alone with Randall, she nodded. "Sure."

Lelia kissed her cheek. "Good." She opened the door.

Peyton kissed Lelia's cheek and closed the door after she left. He smiled at Benai. "Hi, honey."

"Peyton!" She tossed her arms around his neck, pressing her cheek against his shoulder.

He kissed her hair. "So? Was he worth the effort?"

She lifted her head to gaze up into the blue-green eyes so like Randall's. "Yes. Yes he was." She caressed his cheek. "I hope you won't take this the wrong way but I'm very afraid that I love you, Peyton."

His arms tightened around her waist. "Just between you and me, the feeling is mutual, honey."

"I mean like another brother, Peyton."

He nodded. "I know and that's what I meant as well, honey. There's no question of romantic or sexual love or attraction between us. You belong to Randy and I... My heart already belongs to another." He sighed. "One of these days I'll get lucky and find her again."

"Yes. I think you will and when you do she'll be a very lucky woman."

He grinned. "When I do I'll be as lucky as Randy is to have you. Until then, I'm content to find sensual albeit temporary pleasure with the occasional willing woman. So don't worry about me. I know I'll find her again."

"When you do, I'll be waiting to tell her just how wonderful you are."

"I'll count on that, honey." He kissed her cheek and left.

Half an hour after Peyton left, Benai and Randall lay naked in her bed.

"Bancroft looks happy and balanced, Randall."

"He's going to be fine. He has a harem of women only too happy to help keep him grounded and sexually sated." He caressed her bare breasts. "Now talking of being sexually sated, have I ever told you how much you mean to me?"

She rolled over to lie on top of him. "Tell me more."

"Do you remember when I told you how the earth had moved under my feet only once in my life when I met a woman?"

She nodded, a slow smile spreading across her face.

He tipped up her chin.

She met his intense blue-green gaze.

"That happened when we met. I looked into your beautiful dark eyes and my world was turned upside down. I've felt as if I were walking a few inches off the ground since then."

She rubbed her breasts against his chest. "A few inches off the ground? Hmm. That sounds a little dangerous."

He eased her onto her back. "Falling in love with a beautiful woman almost every other man will want is always a little dangerous."

"But danger can be exciting too." She parted her legs and rubbed her slit. "Come here and let me show you what I mean."

He slid between her legs. He entered her slowly and then lay still, staring down into her eyes, resting his weight on his extended arms.

She slipped her hands into his hair. "What's wrong?"

"Nothing...it's just hard to believe that nearly everything's right in my world again. You'll soon be my wife, as well as the love of my life, Croft is well again and we'll be welcoming a new Grayhawk into the family in a few months."

She stroked a hand down to his tight ass. "Then what's not quite right?"

He sighed. "Peyton has yet to find a woman who'll make him half as happy and content as you make me."

"Don't you handsome Native American hunks believe that there's a *sheenea* for everyone? He's an amazing man with a lot to give to some lucky woman. Don't worry, Randall. He'll find his *sheenea* and be as happy as we're going to be."

He nodded and lowered his head until she could feel his breath on her lips. "Yes. He will."

"Or…if you like, since he's so charming, he can sleep with me when you're away on business," she teased, draping her legs over his.

"Oh yeah?"

She nodded, her lips twitching. "It would be a chore but I'm sure I could manage it — for the good of the family."

"I'll share you with him as soon as hell freezes over," he told her.

"Right answer, my handsome Randall. You're the only man I'll ever want or need."

"Just as well because you belong to me." He lowered his chest onto her breasts and shoved his hips downward, driving his cock into her pussy. "Only mine."

She slid her hands down his body to clutch his ass. "Yours forever. Only yours," she promised. "Now love me like you mean it."

"Oh, I mean it. I have from the moment I saw you."

"I love you, Randall. You can tell me how much you love me when we're in Egypt."

"Are we going to Egypt?"

"Oh, yes. You never shared your pictures with me so now you'll just have to take me there — for our honeymoon."

"Sounds like a plan." He kissed her.

She would have liked him to tell her again that he loved her but realistically she knew it would take time before those three precious words came as easily to his lips as they did to hers. Until then, she would be content knowing that even if he wasn't good at saying the actual words, he was an expert at making her feel loved and adored.

She closed her eyes and held him, her body moving in time with his. Once they were married, she'd have a lifetime of hearing him say "I love you". During their time together, she'd also explore the wonders and benefits of living with and loving a man who believed she was the one woman in the world who completed him—just as she believed he was the one man—the only man who could fully complete her.

Also by Marilyn Lee

இ

About the Author

෨

Marilyn Lee lives, works, and writes on the East Coast. In addition to thoroughly enjoying writing erotic romances, she enjoys roller-skating, spending time with her large, extended family, and rooting for all her hometown sports teams. Her other interests include collecting Doc Savage pulp novels from the thirties and forties and collecting Marvel comics from the seventies and eighties (particularly Thor and The Avengers). Her favorite TV shows are forensic shows, westerns (Gunsmoke and Have Gun, Will Travel are particular favors), mysteries (love the old Charlie Chan mysteries. All time favorite mystery movie is probably Dead, Again), and nearly every vampire movie or television show ever made (Forever Knight and Count Yorga, Vampire are favors). She thoroughly enjoys hearing from readers.

Marilyn welcomes comments from readers. You can find her website and email address on her author bio page at www.ellorascave.com.

Tell Us What You Think
We appreciate hearing reader opinions about our books. You can email us at Comments@EllorasCave.com.

Why an electronic book?

We live in the Information Age—an exciting time in the history of human civilization, in which technology rules supreme and continues to progress in leaps and bounds every minute of every day. For a multitude of reasons, more and more avid literary fans are opting to purchase e-books instead of paper books. The question from those not yet initiated into the world of electronic reading is simply: *Why?*

1. *Price.* An electronic title at Ellora's Cave Publishing and Cerridwen Press runs anywhere from 40% to 75% less than the cover price of the exact same title in paperback format. Why? Basic mathematics and cost. It is less expensive to publish an e-book (no paper and printing, no warehousing and shipping) than it is to publish a paperback, so the savings are passed along to the consumer.

2. *Space.* Running out of room in your house for your books? That is one worry you will never have with electronic books. For a low one-time cost, you can purchase a handheld device specifically designed for e-reading. Many e-readers have large, convenient screens for viewing. Better yet, hundreds of titles can be stored within your new library—on a single microchip. There are a variety of e-readers from different manufacturers. You can also read e-books on your PC or laptop computer. (Please note that Ellora's Cave does not endorse any specific brands.

You can check our websites at www.ellorascave.com or www.cerridwenpress.com for information we make available to new consumers.)

3. *Mobility.* Because your new e-library consists of only a microchip within a small, easily transportable e-reader, your entire cache of books can be taken with you wherever you go.

4. *Personal Viewing Preferences.* Are the words you are currently reading too small? Too large? Too… ANNOYING? Paperback books cannot be modified according to personal preferences, but e-books can.

5. *Instant Gratification.* Is it the middle of the night and all the bookstores near you are closed? Are you tired of waiting days, sometimes weeks, for bookstores to ship the novels you bought? Ellora's Cave Publishing sells instantaneous downloads twenty-four hours a day, seven days a week, every day of the year. Our webstore is never closed. Our e-book delivery system is 100% automated, meaning your order is filled as soon as you pay for it.

Those are a few of the top reasons why electronic books are replacing paperbacks for many avid readers.

As always, Ellora's Cave and Cerridwen Press welcome your questions and comments. We invite you to email us at Comments@ellorascave.com or write to us directly at Ellora's Cave Publishing Inc., 1056 Home Avenue, Akron, OH 44310-3502.

erridwen, the Celtic Goddess of wisdom, was the muse who brought inspiration to storytellers and those in the creative arts. Cerridwen Press encompasses the best and most innovative stories in all genres of today's fiction. Visit our site and discover the newest titles by talented authors who still get inspired - much like the ancient storytellers did, once upon a time.

Cerridwen Press

www.cerridwenpress.com

Discover for yourself why readers can't get enough of the multiple award-winning publisher Ellora's Cave.

Whether you prefer e-books or paperbacks,

be sure to visit EC on the web at www.ellorascave.com

for an erotic reading experience that will leave you breathless.

2153570

Made in the USA